PETE KALU

ACT NORMAL

JOY AND DESPAIR IN POST COLONIAL BRITAIN
A MEMOIR

HopeRoad Publishing
17 Kings Avenue
Leeds LS6 1QS
www.hoperoadpublishing.com

A CIP catalogue record for this book is available from
the British Library

ISBN: 978-1-913109-44-8
e-ISBN: 978-1-913109-50-9

EU GPSR Authorised Representative
LOGOS EUROPE, 9 rue Nicolas Poussin, 17000,
LA ROCHELLE, France

10 9 8 7 6 5 4 3 2 1

ACT NORMAL

250 errant mini-essays

Dandruff-nibbling monkeys

The monkeys were our friends and me and my brother were always visiting them. One blue sky afternoon, soon as the home-time bell rang, we pelted out from primary school to where the man who kept the monkeys lived. You had to be quick, and it was never certain, but this day he had them out in his front garden, and we were first. We sat on the wall and the monkeys climbed onto our shoulders and started picking through our hair, inspecting strands, nibbling our dandruff. Later, other kids showed, and the fickle monkeys climbed off our shoulders onto theirs, and we went home. My brother shot up to our room, but Mum cornered me and said she needed to wash my hair. I wriggled free, saying there was no need, I was off out to play football, and anyway the monkeys had already cleaned my hair. Mum shouted up to my older brother, 'What's he on about, monkeys cleaned his hair?' and my brother came down and said, 'You know our kid, always off with the fairies. I'm off out too.' And we went out and played football.

Pram

I remember toddling by my Danish mother's side when I was four in the mid-60's. She's unhappy, her jaw clenched, pushing my sister in the pram. We're on the high street of NormalVille, South Manchester, and we've been in and out of some shops. She bought sausages and lard from the butcher's, and we reach a public bench by a junction near the hospital road. Three old women wearing scarves are sitting there and ask to stroke the beautiful curls of my hair. Mum lets them and they say, 'So beautiful, so beautiful' as they stroke

1

my hair and my mum bursts into tears. Now – meaning decades later – with my memory's windscreen wipers on high, I think, of course, my mother probably had racist stereotypes knocking around her thoughts when she started dating my dad. But when your child is born, the shock-love that this engenders – the devotion to this particular living wonder you've given birth to – eclipses stereotype: you want your child to grow freely and fully, unconstrained by the reduction that is racism. Yet, pushing that pram along NormalVille high street, the whispers, the cold, the faces slipping into momentary disgust, would have brought on confusion then anger in my mum. Because society was saying, "Your children can never be normal because they are black and therefore unfit for full acceptance. Walk among us by all means, but walk with shame." And we reach the three old ladies on the bench again. And yes, to stroke a Black child's hair and marvel at it, is 'othering'. But, back then, it was everything my mother needed. My four-year-old self just knew it made her happy. Now, looking back, I can see she wanted to swing down the high street proud of her brood, saying, look what we did, look what wonders we brought into the world! Instead, she walked with tears, hunched shoulders. And afterwards, back inside the house, a Danish swear word, delivered to the walls, before turning to the pile of clothes in the wash tub.

White strutting

Strutting takes a toll on your back. All these white people wrapped up in white supremacy strutting around need lower-back massages. This is why the doctors' surgeries are overflowing on lower back day. The white people have all got lower back pain, carrying that imaginary white man's burden. The GPs can't cope, especially as all the migrants who used to work for the NHS have quit, gone back home to a less hostile environment. The back pain tribe end up at the high street acupuncture clinic in an upstairs room with torn net curtains having needles stuck in them by a Chinese devil with firm hands and a card reader. They wonder where all the normal acupuncture people are, you know, the white ones – why is it always immigrants pummelling me, sticking needles in my back? As fast as the acupuncturist needles those lower back muscles loose, they tense up again. No amount of needles helps. The acupuncturist gets them off the bench. Try walking normally, they say, instead of strutting. Like me. Normal. Watch. The client cusses and struts off.

Autophagy

Art, like play, normalises Black self-destruction. In my tarmac childhood, we ran around playing Cowboys and Indians in which tragic Indians attacked hero cowboys and we hero cowboys shot the tragic, ungrateful Indians dead. We played this, not realising that we were the Indians, that we were shooting ourselves dead. A significant subset of West Coast rap lyrics of the 00s invited us to eat our own souls in the name of success as represented by flash cars, jewellery and bought black bodies. We rapped along not realising that we were the bought black bodies, that we were being invited to consume ourselves. White-framed culture constantly generates reductive stereotypes for Black consumption. The semiotic signs are all over inviting us to: eat. We eat ourselves. This is our normality.

We all wake up and consider which part of ourselves we should eat today.

Amen to the fallen:
Requiem for the vanguard, for the conk-haired,
& for the soft-shoe shufflers

The conk-haired built the houses that we now live in. They fitted in and got on with holding down stuff – jobs and families. While the Afro-picked vanguard was marching around with placards and loudhailers and protesting, the conk-haired were changing the nappies, holding down the 9-to-5s, and paying the rent money – or charming the landlord in lieu of rent. We should not underestimate their sacrifices. They too served the cause. They became masters of placating whites, so that the next generation could avoid having to do the same. God bless the conk-haired. Let them relax in peace.

Let's hear it, too, for The Vanguard. Most Vanguardists did not become so out of political ambition. As kids, they wanted to be champion roller-skaters or bike racers or pianists. It was just a matter of integrity, and one thing led to another and they ended up in the police station having their fingers broken in a back room in the days before CCTV and body cams and duty solicitors. They left the police station with their fingers at angles so they could no longer hit the keys of a piano with their fingers, so their voices became their instrument instead and they spoke truth to power. Their integrity meant they were pitch perfect when they spoke, their tone pure. And the people heard. So we thank them for giving us voice. All hail the Vanguard. Their fingers were broken but their hands stayed clean.

Now let's tap-a-tap a short while for the soft shoe shufflers. Soft-shoe shuffling aint easy. It aint easy to minstrel. It aint easy to sell out. You can only sell out so many times till you got nothing left to sell and they'll discard you, and everyone knows ex-Minstrels go direct to Hell and Do Not Pass Go. Black people can't tap dance no more; it just don't look right. The Minstrellers have seen to that. This is a requiem not a condemnation. Raise your hand those of us who have never minstrelled. I see no hands raised. We all got a face we fix on for white people. We all got our soft-shoe shuffle ways of getting past them, entertaining them while we ease our way past. Amen. Let me hear it. Amen. Amen to the suit-and-tie soft shoe shufflers. Amen to the respectably combed hair soft-shoe shufflers. Amen to grey-socks soft-shoe shufflers. Amen to the skin whitener soft-shoe shufflers. Amen to the nylon hair soft-shoe shufflers. Amen to the these-rings-will-make-me-look-younger-and-whiter soft shoe shufflers. God bless the soft shoe hustlers whatever their hustle. God bless the conk-haired who held things down. God bless the Vanguardists and their broke fingers. God bless us all. Let the choir stand and play us out.

*Soft-shoe shufflers: minstrels in black face. Con men. Tap dancers in soft bottomed shoes.

Art & the white body

Art is in love with the white body. There are no lengths art will not go to celebrate it. I was flicking through reams and reams of art pages at a university's History of Art Library because I was bored with my law books. They showcased white bodies, from the heavily garbed Elizabeth I Armada portrait of 1581, onwards to 2020, the white body becoming more and more unclothed and in a dizzying array of poses. Be specific, I'm often urged. OK. Here's specific. They tended to be stretching out to adjust curtains in the morning. Or pouring their hair into bowls. Or posed elegantly in country house gardens. Then there was Courbet's *L'Origine du Monde*. I had thought we – meaning all of us in the human species – traced back to Africa. But Courbet's painting has the vagina of a white woman at the centre of its canvas. The woman whose anatomy is featured is clearly white. I must have got that history lesson wrong. Whatever. Now, though, with ever rising fuel bills, that process may finally go into reverse. If so, it will start with socks, the models insisting on a decent pair since by now painters can't afford to heat their studios. Then gloves, because it is always the extremities that suffer frostbite first. Then a pair of leggings, to eliminate the goosebumps. Also, a snug top. Maybe a hat. As the heating bills soar and the studios freeze, more and more layers will be going on. Until the models are as stuffed, petticoated and lagged as Elizabeth I in her 1581 Armada portrait. We arrive back where we began.

Line-ups: a sideboard memory

Police approached me, they were looking for someone to make up an ID parade. Yes or no? Umm. What if I am chosen by the victim? All Black men look alike through white eyes. If picked, I could be fitted up by the cops. In the line-up, I consider the line-ups of my childhood. Who stole the biscuits from the biscuit tin? It wasn't me. Five times the question is asked. Five times a child's head shakes. Mum is exasperated and has us all sit on the sideboard: 'Stay there till one of you confesses.' Time goes by. Reels and reels of time. No one cracks. Mum is flummoxed. I notice that the other four siblings are acting normal, faces a picture of innocence. I also know that, since I did not nab the biscuits on this occasion, one of the other four did, but I also realise there is no way of objectively knowing this. The truth is not something that exists in the world to be found like a lost sock. Only evidence. Probability. Calculations. Or a confession. Mum looks. We are all crumb-free. Five inscrutable faces gaze back at her. Reels and reels more time. 'Me!' says my brother finally, shuffling off the sideboard, head low. 'I ate the biscuits.' Doubt immediately slides into my mind because I know my brother and while I can't tell from his silence or his not-speaking face where the truth is with him, I can tell from how he speaks, and his voice is saying that he didn't do it, despite his confession, that he's just bored with sitting on the sideboard and wants it to end. 'I ate the biscuits. There.' Mum had him sweep the stairs. The guilty – one of my three sisters – got off scot-free.

In the police line-up, I am not chosen.

Death run

The block of flats where the hunchback made tepees in the summer round the back was surrounded by tarmac. It was our Stade Velodrome. We spent shirtless summer days pedalling round furiously on cool bikes that we traded, stole, found, fixed, borrowed or were gifted for favours. When we got bored whirling round the flats there, we went to a piste behind another high-rise block near where the owner of Grand National champion, Red Rum lived. It had a dead-end road that slid down to a concrete ledge where garages were going to be built as soon as the planning permission came through. It was our Death Run. First to the end was the winner. First to the end was also first to smash into the fencing poles guaranteeing blood as well as victory. I went back recently on a whim. The Stade Velodrome tarmac was a donut of land, big enough for five cars to park on, max. The death run was a gentle slope. Never return.

Bang bang, you're dead

Everybody I've shot, I've liked. I shot my brother so many times. My sisters were riddled with bullets every summer. Bang, bang, you're dead. I shot Johnny in the arse, then the heart and he died an excellent death, tumbling off the wall and into the rose bed, a flower in his hand. I shot Tommy in the head, haha, but he kept running and said I'd missed, but everyone knew he was a cheater. I shot Michael out of a tree, but he was too chicken to fall out of it. I bulls-eyed Rosalind behind the old piano, but she said she wasn't playing anymore, silly, so it didn't count. I told her, you're dead anyway. It was felt necessary to tell the person you shot that they were dead. Otherwise, they'd do that rolling-around-in-agony-and-moaning-and-gurgling-blood-before-suddenly-pulling-the-bullet-out-of-themselves-wedging-a-finger-in-the-hole-and-running-off-to-recover-and be-back-in-the-game-ten-seconds-later routine. Or you shot them, and they'd leap up and play on as a zombie (unless there was a 'no zombies' rule agreed before the game began). Tommy won most of the Bang Bang games. We didn't play them if our dad was around because of Biafra.

Apples

The genius city planners planted crab apple trees in the grass strip between two sides of a dual carriageway to attract us kids and lower the local under-10 population thereby. And it worked. We weaved through lanes to get to that central reservation and its crab apples – little shrub trees that grew only up to our chests and had apples the size of a baby's fist. We ate them three at a time to see who spat out first because their taste was bitter as piss. Later, Laura got run over on that dual carriageway.

Time waxed. I drove along that dual carriageway and looked at the central reservation. The crab apple trees are gone.

Headless dog

As we watched the twitches of her mottled knees, Mrs Bevan read the story about the woodcutter in the forest with his dog that barked when it heard the wolves coming to eat them, and the dog's reward was to lose all four legs which were, one-by-one, chopped off by the woodcutter who wanted to sleep for Heaven's Sake – all this barking – he kept getting woken by the infernal barking. Until finally, on the fifth night, there were no legs left to cut off, and he chopped off the dog's head, and the woodcutter finally slept, and the wolves finally got to the woodcutter and ate him. It was my favourite story as a four-year-old, but in my new class, Miss Jones refused to read it. From this, I learned teachers were all different and I began marking their cards. Later, Mr Ellis was the best and he wasn't even a teacher. In the upper hall at the reading table, he'd found and let me read him the story of the wolves and the woodcutter. He was Polish, his accent close to that of my Danish mother, and he was rumoured to have flown Spitfire planes in The War. He hardly interrupted – a corrected pronunciation here, a chuckle there, and asking me to slow down when I got to the best bit – where the wolves finally got to eat the woodcutter. He and the blind piano tuner I got along with fine at primary school.

Black boys diptych

This is a boy waiting with other boys for their friend to show up.

This is a large youth gathering with others for the purpose of threatening the peace.

This is a boy in a shop undecided between Tango Orange Burst and Irn Bru.

This is a shoplifter waiting for the coast to be clear before attempting the theft of items from a fridge.

This is a boy leaning on a wall saying hi to a friend on his phone.

This is a gang member giving a secret sign to his accomplice as to the whereabouts of a person they are conspiring to kill, which will be their joint enterprise that evening.

This is a boy.

This is a boy leaving New Century Hall, Manchester, 1978, after the Under 16's disco has ended without him sneaking so much as a kiss off of Christine because her dad had whisked her away fast. This boy is walking along Market Street heading to the bus terminal to catch his bus home. He is dreaming of becoming John Travolta. This is the boy in court charged with criminal damage to five plate-glass windows along Market Steet in Manchester city centre and the assault of five young citizens who were merely going about their lawful business in the city centre that night, according to the identical notebooks of the arresting officers, and had not at all jumped the defendant – the five good citizens' National Front tattoos were of no relevance. This was England, 1978. This was me. This was my normal.

The Gora punkah wallah

Money isn't everything. The reparations argument requires a little creativity. How about this? In colonial times, the tender, colonising Brits in India got very hot building their Empire by day, and found it hard to sleep at night, what with the humidity and all. So, they introduced punkah wallahs whose job it was to keep a fan wafting in the tender white person's bedroom, so they were cool enough to sleep, bless them. Of course, any wallah whose job this was, would have been exhausted by the morning with the constant fanning through the night, but nobody bothered about that. Until now. How about once a year – as a form of combined Post-Colonial Reparations and National Service – all young white men (and even the old ones if they fancy it) be invited to walk alongside a member of the Black population of Britain, carrying a large frond-like fan to fan the Black person as and when required, for the length of a Post-Colonial National Service Reparations Day? This service would of course be 99% symbolic given the absence of humidity in these parts. It could join other national once-a-year actual and possible ceremonies – like the burning of Guy Fawkes, Royal British Legion Poppy Day, and the Drown the Migrants in the Channel Day. Post-Colonial National Service Reparations Day. It could become part and parcel of normal British life. Please sign the petition.

Bathing and aromas

Other species must look upon us with pity. We are mostly hairless and have no auto-clean function. Some humans have bathing routines that resemble shrine rituals, their bathrooms filled with reliquaries holding holy fluids and infusions. Occasionally, I visit such a shrine. Cocoa butter still sends my head into a spin. Come carnival, the aromas are heavenly, folk all buttered up. I drift among the sweet/chemical geri-curl wafts of the 80s. Then further back, into the 70s. Here I pause. As kids, we had a bath once a week. Did we reek? Those old black and white photos – ought they to stink?

No honour among Empire thieves

'The sun never sets on the British Empire' is a saying dripping with irony, not only because of its obvious inaccuracy – the said sun having long ago set on the said empire, but also because the saying was stolen from the Spanish who back in their colonial boom times (boom times which preceded the Brits') would boast of their *imperio donde nunca se pone el sol*. Before these two ocean-surfing bandits, the Egyptians, Mesopotamians, Persians and Romans had similar sayings. The take-away here?

The sun sets on all empires.

Black octopus

Octopuses get through small gaps by shapeshifting – becoming whatever shape they need to be to survive. So too with humans. In an otherwise all-white environment, the Black person becomes the person they need to be to survive. Complications arise when another Black person enters this environment. Whether they become allies or enemies depends on the concordat they reach for dealing with white people. One may want an easy life. The other may want to confront issues head on. One may focus on promotion. The other may believe in principles. Cue the office Christmas party test.

At Christmas, there is always one white person at the office party who finds a stray braid that has dropped out of some Black person's head, bless them, and begins to circulate the party with that evil-innocent energy and a fake sincere face asking all the Black folk loud enough to make it a spectacle (but soft enough for it to be defended as innocent), 'Whose braid is this?' This poses dilemmas for the Black folk at the party. Do we play along, swallow the collective embarrassment? Do we bite down the temptation to answer back, 'If it is my braid, what am I meant to do with it?' Or do we (and this becomes a more and more tempting option as the evening of braid-calling stretches on) punch them, get sacked, but not care anyway?

Three hustles

I was wandering along the docks of Old Calabar, Nigeria, when I saw a distant rusting hulk and was seized by its beauty. A man wandering nearby asked if I would like to get closer to it. I said sure, fine. We walked fifty steps closer. He asked for money. I smiled. The hustle is real. Walking fifty metres with me is not a transaction, I said to him with a shake of my head. He disagreed and began remonstrating. Seeking to duck out of the situation, I whistled to a motorbike taxi – an okada. The man puo-puo'd the taxi and the okada driver obeyed him and went away. My self-described guide said he was an important person in this place, and I should pay him the money. He kept up the volume. A small crowd became a large crowd. Debate was aired about whether money was due, and if so, how much. It had a village square feel to it, everyone having an opinion and being listened to. A woman took my side, saying 'Let him go'. She whispered to me in English, it is better to pay him off some small sum than argue, not that you are wrong. I gave him the naira equivalent of a couple of dollars. He took his money and disappeared. The crowd melted. The okada re-appeared. The hustle is real.

The hustle is real. At a duck pond park in England, a man sat with a chess set and a spare chair. By the legs of the chess table hung a sign with a hand-written explanation of his predicament, which ended with: 'I need money – play chess with me and if you lose you give me £5, if you win, you've had some entertainment from me. Good day.' I took up his challenge. A small crowd gathered. I was losing badly and about to resign when a homeless person shuffled onto the scene, pushing his possessions in a shopping trolley. He pulled up and people gave him space. He took in the game in all of ten seconds, then said, 'Don't give up,' and pointed out a move to me that would shore up my collapsing forces. I looked closer. He was right. I went on to win the game. By the time I won, the homeless guy had disappeared, as had the thin crowd. 'Who was that guy?' I asked the park chess player. 'Don't know and happy never to see him again!' came the reply. We both laughed. I gave him his £5, as, in fairness, he'd had me beat. 'Don't give up'. The words of the homeless guy reverberated in me.

The hustle is real. I was homeless in San Francisco. There is safety in numbers. I joined the bums lounging on the sidewalk before a white-stoned town-hall-like building. Every so often, the San Francisco motor police weaved their motorbikes among us, just for plain old harassment's sake. Gino, our leader, told us not to react. They just did this for kicks, they wanted a reaction. Late afternoon, a guy drove up, got out of his truck and approached me, said he was fresh out of prison, and wanted to eat, would I like to eat with him? A free meal is a free meal. We ate tacos at a Taco Bell then went our ways. Night fell and he returned, approached again. I could sleep in his truck if I wanted. Gino looked over, shook his head to me. I declined. I slept in bushes and woke up next day still alive.

The girl who sang at the youth club

When I was thirteen and my ears were sharp as a hummingbird's, I walked into my youth club's singing night and this ghostly white girl in a check dress was on the mic, singing. Like, she really sang. Looking back, I wonder if she was one of a musical family, or if she'd had singing lessons, or was going to one of those stage schools that did singing as part of their activities. Yet I recall her body was stiff, and she held the mic up to her face nervously – very un-stage school. It was a moment in my life of something momentarily wonderous. She sang and then was gone into the sea of other youth club faces. What happened to her? Where is she now? These two thoughts spring up immediately when her image bubbles up now, and her voice once more takes flight in my mind. Did she make it as a singer or was it a passing phase? We crave stories to be complete. I saw her beginning but not her middle or end. How weird it is that this moment she sang should stick with me all these years, that I should carry the beauty of that girl's voice with me all this time, and that maybe for her it is a day she has long forgotten. And for sure, she would never remember me. Is that who we all are: a scattering of moments in the blurred, pocked, long-term memories of others? And from this, a mathematics of fame: is fame being this kind of memory in the minds of many?

The Hollywood kiss

Hollywood had hungry lips. Thespians of the silver screen were always only a short scene away from kissing. The one exception – if you were an actor with pigmentation. Back then, Black and brown actors didn't need to pack their lip gloss when travelling to the set. "Box office doesn't like a Black kiss" was a mantra that ran through every level of the Hollywood machine. Script writers, editors, directors, producers all got the memo. Ashy-lipped Black actors didn't need sweat: their lips would see no lip-on-lip action. They were locked into the no-lips-needed roles of effervescent best friend of the (melanin-free) face-sucking star. Or they were the strong shoulder-to-lean-on of the star white smoocher. Public kissing by Black people is still frowned upon. The danger of wanton black lips is a thing that tippety-toes down the corridors of history from the first lynchings of the antebellum all the way up to Emmett Till. But white folk are free to kiss away. Lord Nelson's was the first big white kiss in English history: Now kiss me, Hardy.

Grandma & the job market

I eavesdropped on a conversation between my friend and her grandma and heard only the grandma's words. "I need to look at you," said the grandma. "You going for that job, right? So you need to fix your hair. You can't go into the interview with your hair all nappy and Afro'd like that… I know, I know it's natural and I know Black is beautiful and women's feminism and Angela Davis and all that, chile, but you got responsibilities now. You're a mom and that no-good-rotten-good-for-nothing eejit, left you with... yes, two children off of him and on your own, so now you got to think and move smart. To feed the children, you got to get the job. To get the job, you got to please the white folk. To please the white folk, you got to look a bit like them. To look a bit like them, you got to fix you hair. To fix you hair, you can't have it looking so nappy – to Live in the House that Jack Built! You understand, chile? Cho!"

The staircase kids

Sometimes, events wind you. You carry on, acting normal, but you're reeling. Aged nine, I had a gardening round and rich customers, and occasionally I got to play with their children. This one occasion, I'd finished weeding some crazy paving and I was playing with the kids of a professor on the grand staircase of his big house. We were probably going to play hide & seek and needed to decide who was 'it'. And, as kids do to settle such matters, the professor's kids started on a playground rhyme to decide. They sang: "Eenie meenie minee mo, catch a nigger by his toe." And I'm looking at them like, are you real? While at the same time, swallowing it, trying to act normal, lip-synching. I have no memory of what happened after. Only a memory of up to that moment when I'm on the staircase, lip-synching.

Act normal: the Huckleberry version

'Go jump in a lake' is good advice for someone whose arse is on fire. Our arses were often on fire in those long summer holidays of our teens, and we'd go to a flooded quarry behind the municipal tip and jump in. There, you saw that all the white kids could swim like fish. And we the Black kids would plough and churn and half-drown. We'd retreat out of the water and into the defence of higher bone density making our skeletons heavier, hence we couldn't swim like white folk, but we were better divers. It was generally agreed that this was the case, and thus our honour was preserved. Then along came Alfonso. He was part boy, part dolphin. He peeled off his clothes and his glistening brown body dipped in and out of that water to the manner born. It was Socrates (named after the footballer not the philosopher) who saved the day. 'For every rule, there is an exception,' Socrates opined, 'and Alfonso is the exception that proves the rule.' We nodded sagely, our honour restored.

White Hypnosis

I bought a bottle of aftershave from a high street Pound Shop. Its name was White Hypnosis. The packaging said: *Made in the People's Republic of China*. I splashed it on and went out to see if it had any effect. I was confident: the Chinese know a thing or two about white people and mind-altering substances since they had to endure the Opium Wars – that period when the British got the Chinese hooked on opium and fought gunship battles to keep them hooked. I imagined the pissed-off Chinese back then saying among themselves, "These gweilo are the devil's spawn. The only way to stop them is to hypnotise them." In 1977, a perfume called Opium was launched by the European company, Yves Saint Laurent. Its scent was 'sultry, provocative, enthralling'. There were protests when it was launched. It was alleged to be 'insensitive to Chinese history.' I love understatement. I imagine the two perfume bottles in a battle. Opium!

versus White Hypnosis! Western Orientalism! versus Eastern Mystic Smarts! As I'm imagining this, I'm walking along the pavement in my cloud of White Hypnosis. The pavement has narrowed, and a white man is walking towards me. There is only room for one of us. I shrug. Ha, my internal voice says to me, a Raskolnikov moment – I must have dropped into the Dostoyevsky novel. At the last second, the white man steps off the path and into the road and I continue my walk on the pavement unimpeded. White Hypnosis, I think, marvelling. This shit actually works.

Drama school

"Excellent! And now everyone walk about the stage, acting normal!" I was seized with this thought: what does the drama coach mean by act normal? Does she mean normal as in how Black folk act when white folk are among them? Or normal as in when it's only Black folk in a room? Or is it normal as in I'm meant to become a shuffling, loose-panted celluloid cliché of Black youth? Or is there a hereditary or cultural 'Black Essential' which is the normal? In which case I'm actually an inauthentic Black person because, having been brought up mostly by a white mother, I may not have been given the full code for Black Normal? Do I need to study other Black people to learn this normal and then fake it till I'm convincing – test out my Black normal in Black bars and clubs and church and such? Umm. If I copy the only other Black actor in the room, will she notice I'm copying her? Maybe she in turn is copying someone else. Uumm. Maybe she's copying me? In which case, we could devise a composite Black normal between us and agree to use it whenever the coach calls out "Act normal!" We could form The Society of Young Black Normal Thespians. "OK, end of normal. And now you are a fridge!" she calls. What does a fridge even mean? I'm on the wrong course. Maybe accountancy.

Bank robbers

My rich family tree includes bank robbers. This is a fable for them.

In a small town that doesn't exist, there was a bank that was robbed on average twice a year. This was felt a reprehensible but inevitable consequence of modernity and after a number of years in subcommittee discussions, the town board agreed to formalize the role and assign it to every adult citizen in town in turn – so that there would be a fair and equal distribution of bank-robbing roles among the population, free entirely of prejudice and guaranteeing that every citizen, if they were on the town's electoral role and lived long enough, would have their turn to rob the town's one and only bank. It was further agreed that the clothing and the language used during such robberies – including body language – would be standardised so as to be able to distinguish the official, designated town bank robber from any rogue, out-of-town bank robber. Accordingly, a set of sartorial and elocutional standards were drawn up for officially-appointed town-bank robbers to adhere to. These standards became itemised as the Citizen Bank Robber Protocols and were passed into the town's bye-laws under Ordinance Section 312: Normalization of Small Town Fiduciary Extractive Roles.

The bus stop thespians

There were three of us Black boys doing the school play (*Happy End* by Bertolt Brecht, music by Kurt Weill) and after evening rehearsals we'd stroll to our bus stop and hang there for the 109 bus that never showed. These were dreamy evenings, shooting the acting breeze, convinced we were destined to be catapulted from wheezing Wythenshawe to Glitzy Hollywood. We prepared for fame by trying out the latest acting styles and accents. Paul Newman. Robert Redford. Laurence Olivier. James Cagney, James Dean. Marlon Brando. Richard Burton. They were all white actors. We acted them out and thought nothing of it. All Hollywood had shown us blackness-wise was Sidney Poitier, and he was in a suit whereas we wanted to be gun-toting, hip-swinging, swaggering mavericks – which teenager doesn't? Feeling lucky, punk? Clint Eastwood. We saw all his films. John Travolta? Nobody could throw off a school blazer and spin, twist our necks and stare with upturned upper lip better than us. At the drop of a hat, or spin of a gun, we could leap off an imaginary cliff (read wall or bus shelter roof) *à la* Newman and Redford in *Butch Cassidy and the Sundance Kid*.

And, is this hindsight, or were there lags in our bus stop conversations, pauses at the edge of our acting out, when we absorbed how white our street theatre was, when we were puzzled, unable to figure out how we had arrived here, in a white landscape, acting white? Then on we went. Filling the wait for the bus with doing the High Noon Walk, switching into the cool drawly voices of Westerns. The bus never came. We didn't mind. Hollywood would never come for any of us, either. But we didn't know that then. We were living our dreams, and in that sacred realm of teenage imagination was more joy than the real Hollywood could probably ever deliver. We were in love with our dreams. Yet, for all our fantasies, none of us was anything more than a side character in the school play, *Happy End*. A white kid played the lead role, as they always did.

Doorways

In my late teens, when travelling on a Euro rail ticket across Europe, the doorways of the French were the most congenial – paysans would feed me when I woke and give me lifts in Citroen 2CVs (a car I love even to this day). The *je ne sais quoi* of rattling along French boulevards, my backpack loaded in the front boot, the 2CV top rolled back, my Afro blowing in the wind, aviator sunglasses, a baguette and a chunk of salami in my face! To be young and free and rolling in a 2CV was to live forever. The doorways got bleaker as time moved on.

Jump two years and I backpacked across the USA on my way to Barb, the girl who lived in Peoria, Illinois and who I'd met in Jim's Hostel in Amsterdam where she'd been ill, and I'd fed her soup as she lay in her shivering bunk bed. On the way back, I hunkered down in a doorway on the approach road to La Guardia N.Y. airport and a cop car, a wide-bodied, black-and-white saloon with square flood headlights picked me out. They liked my accent, but I couldn't sleep there, so I slept in the bushes like all the other homeless of New York. In the daytime, I talked my way into a job selling hot dogs from a push-cart – though they kept my passport as insurance against me stealing the cart.

Now I'm rich enough to own my own doorway and full-size blanket and bed. Yet I find myself thinking, will I one day be shivering in a doorway again?

Bed geometrics

There is more than one way to sleep in a relationship. Different sides of the bed offer themselves to each member of a couple at different times. The geometrics of settling in a bed together can have its own beauty as hip and arm and leg and shoulder find angles and rotate in a Rubik's cube of configurations across a night, a week, a month, years. In this breathing kaleidoscope, occasionally, I've found myself spreadeagled in the centre of the bed. Other times, I've found myself on the rim of the mattress. Nothing in sleep is accidental. The edge of a bed can be the loneliest place in a relationship.

Hollywood speeches I prepared just in case: No. 1

Academy Award Greats, I'm just a normal British bloke. I want to thank all the people at the Crown and Anchor pub – drinks are on me when I get back, lads. I want to thank also, the folks at Bet Fred Bookies on Oldham Street. Thanks for all those tips, fellas – they kept me broke, haha. Enjoy your condominium, Fred. Also, my work coach at Universal Credit. Thanks for having no faith at all in my scriptwriting. I get it now. You were using Reverse psychology. Thanks.

So, Biyi Bandele, who I've just pipped at the post for this Award. Biyi, your *Half of a Yellow Sun* was mighty fine. But your sequel, *Quarter of a Golden Moon* came second, Biyi, and it was a bit formulaic. If you'd used Super 8 wet film, splicing it together old-school style like I'd suggested at the bar that time we met, you might have done better. That's what a film maker is. They've got to innovate. Learn from me, Biyi. OK. And to the Small Axe team, good try. But cut the loooo-ng establishing shots and go straight to the action, nuh? Thank me later. It's heavy this Award isn't it? Pure gold. This is dedicated above all to my mother, who sadly, is not around to see this, the pinnacle of my achievements so far. You told me I'd never make it, Ma, but look at me now. Your boy done good, right?

The blind piano tuner

The blind piano tuner came to school once a year. He was led by the elbow across the polished parquet of the upper floor, his eyes behind sunglasses, his gait stiff, his mouth partially open. He wore blue woolly jumpers and black trousers with creases. He stopped at the edge of the piano and felt for the keyboard corner, lifted the lid, then spread a hand across and shuffled, found the stool, pulled it to him and sat. Some words were exchanged with the person who had guided him, and she guided his hand to where she had placed his white stick, leaning on the side of the piano, then she walked off and he began his work. The stiffness left his face, and his fingers ran across the keys, riffing arpeggios. Then one note, again, again, again. Whang. A teacher tapped the back of my head with a ruler. 'Concentrate, Peter. You are meant to be calculating the area of that circle, not daydreaming.'

Head on fire

Chasing around the playground with your head on fire is only possible for a short while. Having whistled some beauties past Fatty the Goalkeeper, I settled against the cool of a brick wall and looked into the cause of the fire. It was a circus of nits, awakened from my scalp by the heat and sweat of my chasing around. I resolved to play my football in a slower style so as not to disturb them. In a parallel universe, I went on to become an international footballer with the slow but silky skills of Lionel Messi. In the actual world, I morphed from a fast and inaccurate football player to a slow and inaccurate football player. Fatty, meanwhile, went on to keep goal for a major football team.

Vote! Vote! Vote!

Elections were a good earner for me and Rico. Our main scam was canvassing leaflets. Whichever party, we'd take their leaflets and, for cash in hand, promise to post them through the letterboxes of local houses. Once the party officials had seen us dutifully work a couple of streets, they'd disappear, bored. Then we'd dump the leaflets in bins and hedges. By the threat of violence to other kids, we quickly cornered the market in political child labour and foot-soldiering, and the Labour and Conservative parties soon bid for our services (the Liberals were too broke to bid). Rico worked for Labour; I worked for the Conservatives. The Labour campaign HQ was a townhouse mansion, and the daughter of the Labour candidate rode ponies up and down the streets around it. The Conservative candidate (who usually won) was an oily estate agent. Their HQ was a tiny café and ladies with pearls around their necks ran their canvassing team. They treated me to cream cakes if I found the right line in flattery and forelock tugging. On Voting Day, me and Rico stood outside polling stations with rosettes in our shirts – mine blue for Conservatives, his red for Labour – and collected polling cards from voters so the campaign teams could figure out who had voted, who hadn't, and how the vote was going. Looking back, it was radical of the Conservative party to appoint this scrawny Black kid with holes in his shoes to their canvassing team. Or maybe they just got a kick out if it – behold the class traitor, working for us! Party-wise, I was an agnostic. Whichever candidate got in, nothing changed, so I filled my pockets without allegiance. Spin fifty years, and Rico is now a property developer while I follow ponies, collecting their manure for my allotment.

Waving

She liked to lean out of her upstairs bedroom window and wave to us as we played out. She was a solid woman, like a block of pink carbolic soap, her head square and a lion's mane for hair. When I saw her, I always waved back. She lived in my world only as a head and shoulders, waving, but in my mum's world there must have been more, including conversation, because Mum told me she was sixty-something and about to retire, hooray. Next week, Mum was crying. When I asked why, she said the waving woman had died; she had only just retired and now she's dead and that was so unfair. We sat on our step and cried for the waving woman.

The Jewish folk singer

Never look back. Research kills things. Top among school visitors I loved was the itinerant Jewish folk singer who called once a year with his guitar and did a concert for the older primary school kids. His best song began: 'Kosher Bailey had an engine. That was always needing mendin'. And according to the power, it could go four miles an hour!' I loved that a Jewish singer visited us, especially with 'Jew' being a racial epithet very close to 'nigger' in the playground. I joined in his singing with gusto. Later, researching for this book, I discover that the name of the character in the song is spelt Cosher not Kosher, and that the story is Welsh, and therefore the singer visiting our school was probably not Jewish. This saddens me deeply and somehow cheapens my childhood.

Siblings

My siblings gave me everything. Measles, hair-pullings, forced underwater submersions at the swimming baths, lessons in cheating, stealing, exacting revenge, the art of lying low when shit hits fans, petitioning for extra pocket money, how to reseal biscuit packets, how to blame the dog for everything, how to set sheds on fire, strangling as an effective non-elective method of aversion therapy for sweet thieves, the power of saying nothing, saying nothing while saying everything, bus pass forgery, pulling a sickie, nodding sagely at idiots, feigning death, hiding money, smuggling girl/boyfriends in and out, and how to look cute and get away with it.

How the old-school Black managerial class got things done

The old Black managerial class were finaglers, by necessity. They knew that coming forward with an idea to white colleagues and bosses was likely to get the idea knocked back. So, they boxed smart. Here's the footwork. You have an idea, you know it's a great idea, you know they won't think it's a great idea and you also know they will think it's a great idea if they think it's their idea. So, you set about getting them to think it's their idea. Two of you go into the meeting. You don't present the idea from the get-go. You present the foundation of the idea. Then, by a series of nudges, you prompt the white people at the meeting to do the thinking you have already done – you subtly build them a pyramid of thought and guide them up it, step by step, until they are almost at the apex, the only piece remaining – the pyramidion (the cap at the top of the pyramid) is the idea you had, way back, all along. And the white person who makes decisions at the meeting, guided by your discreet yet unerring nudges, climbs that golden pyramid you built for them and has that Eureka! moment, sees the cap, slaps the pyramidion onto the top of the pyramid and proclaims, 'Hey, guys, I've had an idea! Isn't this genius?' The Black manager listens avidly to their own idea being spoken back to them and duly proclaims the white person a genius for having thought of it. There is some downside to this. Now that it's the white person's idea, you'll be getting no recognition for it. But you chill. You are middle management. Who needs to claim credit for a new way of stacking warehouse boxes? Let the white folk puff themselves up and claim the credit. The art of management is the art of getting things done. In whose name didn't matter back then to old-school Black managers. Hats off to the old-school Black middle managers. They got things done.

Black North needs an army

The Black North needs an army. We need tanks, planes, rockets and gunships. We need to muster foot soldiers and march on London. We need to rout the Londoners –

including Black Londoners – and establish the Northern tongue as the new normal. We need to dethrone BBC English, dethrone Black = London, legitimize Black Northern accents, make them the new Normal, make received pronunciation the dialect and London Black speech the yokel tongue. We need to make London the province and Manchester the Black centre. A language is a dialect with an army, said Noam Chomsky. An accent is normal *sans* power. My extremely clever PhD researcher friend was at a seminar and answered a question. Nobody heard her because she comes from Blackley, Manchester and what they heard was how Blackley, Manchester sounds. They wrote her off as a bumpkin, a Black one at that. There followed some written tests – where of course her accent was not heard – it's the fun way they do some PhDs now – and she scored top. They were all puzzled when the results came out because they had confused sound with intellect. And their Dunning-Kruger selves over-estimated their smarts based on their own sounds and underestimated hers. They hadn't realised how power snuggles up so comfy and confident in their voices. The Black North needs an army. We need to speak this army into existence. March with all our vowels to London and take over.

Act Normal's two estranged cousins

Normal has two cousins, Mediocre and Average. Black people are not allowed to hang out with these cousins. We're only allowed to hang out with the good cousin, Excellent. This is stressful – given that most of us, present company included, are by definition normal, average, mediocre. Thank me later, it's true. Equality happens when we are given the right to be mediocre and it's no big deal, it's not a crisis, it's not failure. Meet Kwame. He's the mediocre transport manager, the average coder, the good-enough logistics guy, the adequate fridge deliverer. Meet Satwant. She runs a mediocre eyebrow-threading stall, Ugochi? She's an average dentist. Black Excellence is not normal. Black Excellence is the ineluctable effect of White Privilege. We demand the right to be mediocre.

The evolving language of bank robbers

'Don't try anything funny!' was a standard line in any number of 1970's TV bank robbery scenes churned out by scriptwriters not paid enough to craft anything poetic and stunning. I imagine the scriptwriters were told, 'Turn up, do your job, get paid. Don't get clever.' And, of the kids growing up, watching TV in that age, a percentage (bless their souls) went on to become bank robbers. And they took their cues from the TV robbers they'd watched and delivered the lines they thought bank robbers delivered in such situations: 'Don't try anything funny.' There were no linguistic issues. Everybody in the banking field understood the words and robberies got performed with excellent efficiency. Then along came film director, Quentin Tarantino and his Samuel Jackson robbers and their digressive, wavy, bank robber lines: 'The path of the righteous man is beset on all sides by the inequities of the selfish and the tyranny of evil men. Blessed is he who, in the name of charity and good will, shepherds the weak…' etc. And the kids of the 90s watched Tarantino and grew up and a percentage, bless them, duly started robbing banks using similar lines – flamboyance became the new normal. 'And yea I say to you, you verily shall be robbed, and woe is upon you if you do not fill this bag with paper gold…' It was OK. Everybody had seen

Tarantino, there were no linguistic issues. Except pity the 90's, left-behind kid, raised by kooky parents who kept old videos and had the old TV series constantly playing on screens. When that kid of the kooky parents goes off the rails and picks up a shotty, there is going to be linguistic dissonance, because he'll go into a bank and use one of the old TV lines: 'Don't try anything funny!' And the bank's Customer Facing Advisor is confused. This line was not featured on the Customer Facing Advisor training course. 'What you on about?' she'll reply. 'This is a bank, not a comedy club. The Frog and Bucket is three blocks down.' And the novice left-behind, child-of-kooky-parents bank robber is now equally confused, and responds, 'Oops, my bad. Hahahaha. See you later, mate.' Normal is a moving target.

Schrodinger's white people

Schrodinger's white people will speak fervently about equality while managing never to appoint a Black person to any position of seniority in their organisation.

Schrodinger's white people will play reggae music all day while lamenting the invasion of immigrants into England.

Schrodinger's white people will say this little brown baby is 'so cute, so cute' while identifying that same kid now grown as the perpetrator of a robbery without even opening their eyes to check.

Schrodinger's white people will be wheeled into hospital by a brown orderly across a floor being cleaned by a Black cleaner to be seen by a brown doctor, then have a plastercast set by a brown nurse and be given a prescription processed by a Black pharmacist only to say that immigration has ruined the country.

Schrodinger's white people will laud the initiative of Black people in setting up businesses, then call the police the moment a Black person pulls up in their Close in a white van, carrying tools which are mistaken for a shotty.

Schrodinger's white people will hold hands and belt out, 'I'd like to teach the world to sing in perfect harmony' right after a group of them finished shooting the Black members of that world in Sharpeville, South Africa (Schrodinger's white people: It's the real thing).

Schrodinger's white people will become professors theorising about the nature of racial injustice, while not having one Black or brown academic in their thinktank or department.

Schrodinger's white people will go to church and agree to love thy neighbour while never inviting that Black neighbour into their home.

Schrodinger's white people will agree that everybody is beautiful, while confessing they do not personally find the black body as beautiful as the white.

Schrodinger's white people will believe in the equal potential of all, then search hard to find the whitest school they can afford, to send their kids to.

Schrodinger's white people are your allies and not your allies.

The erotic thrill of trees

I had my first orgasm while climbing a tree. One summer, I climbed a tree in the woods by the River Mersey, which stretched halfway into the sky. It was in the middle of the woods and its foliage, after the first few metres, was so thick you couldn't see through to know where you were; you just had to keep climbing. I made it to the middle section. Here, the tree thinned out a little.

The heavy rubbing of the lower branches was replaced by the softer swish of younger limbs. The bark became softer under your hands and scraped less as you clamped on with your inner thighs. I could see for miles: the vast, heaving canopy of the woods; the river a piece of twisting tinsel; gnats pedalling bikes. I climbed on into the rising chorus of leaves, using my school-taught rope-climbing technique: body close to the trunk, thighs squeezing in for grip, hand over hand: stretch, pull, thrust.

The trunk had reached such thinness it was swaying now between my thighs, my body weight an unexpected disturbance for it. I knew this was the danger zone, peril adding to my excitement. I felt the tree, listening for any creak or the rush of a snap that meant a branch under my foot was overloaded or a branch held by a hand was about to give. The wind lowered. Me and the tree were in equilibrium. Another push from my feet, a further inch up, and then the sway began again. *Never look down.* I was in the sky. Hands firm. Chest and thighs clamped. We were one. This was divine. I braced to edge further up and, at my brace, this slow eruption in my groin. A dizzying euphoria come over me. It was disorientating and overwhelming. I clung on for life. Held my breath as the sensation ebbed away. It faded.

I regained consciousness. I slithered down, hands, feet in a jumble, confused, disorientated, in love with this tree, with trees. Later, I noticed wetness in my pants. Next day, I was with Ali, and he said he knew all forty-eight Facts of Life, and of course I wanted to know them all or at least one and begged him to share, but he said no, let's go conkering first. A bunch of us went into the River Mersey woods and threw sticks at the conker trees. It was strange, flinging sticks at trees, knowing next day I'd be wrapping my thighs around them.

Afro-pessimism 1: water skimmers

The swimming pool is Hockney blue. The sun shining down on it is Italian. Across the surface of the pool, a long-limbed water-boatman skates. I watch and think, this is how it is to be Black in Britain. The waters are warm, the pool inviting. The surface is buoyant. Go ahead, skate. But be aware that, at any moment, a drop of whiteness detergent may fall into those waters, and the surface lose its accommodating tension. Then you will plunge into those oh so seductive blue waters, and drown. And no matter how wide and deep the pool, the amount of detergent required to render those waters treacherous will always be proportionately tiny. The Italian sun blazes on. The boat-insect has started to struggle. I bend, dip a hand into the pool, scoop it up, and lob it into the grass. It shakes itself, heads straight back for the water.

In the running

I was always second or third at my favourite race – the fifteen hundred metres – until that sports day when Hilton decided to help me. The cleverest kid in the school – judged by test results – teaming up with the most Thug-like kid in the school – judged by expulsions from previous schools, suspensions, detentions, numbers of report cards etc. Hilton was a sprinter, and, from the last lap of the fifteen hundred metres, he ran alongside me, urging me, 'Keep going! You got it! You're winning! Keep on!' Finally, after all the years of being second or third, I crossed the line first. I won. For all of two minutes, I was the winner. Then I was disqualified for having received help. But really, I won. Because Hilton's act was the definition of friendship, and I never forgot. And all that came later, in no way eroded my sense of that bond.

Smiler

The white man does not smile. He has no need. People come to him and grin and genuflect and say please. 'Smiler' is a nickname often given to Black boys who grow up surrounded by white people. Those Black boys are smart and have figured out that the way to keep the peace with white people, who see their Black maleness as threatening, is to keep smiling. *I'm no threat, see, I'm smiling,* they're saying, *I'm keen to please.* Little white girls at school take home school reports which say, approvingly: 'Jemima is always keen to please, she smiles a lot in class and is a joy to teach.' Girls are taught by society to smile. Boys are not. Black boys teach themselves to stretch those face muscles upwards in the presence of white people. Power does not smile. White people didn't like Malcolm X because he didn't smile; they liked Muhammad Ali.

Me? I scowled my way through primary school. My school reports accordingly worried: 'Peter must learn to fit in better.' I scowled my way through secondary school. I was an irritant to teachers for this reason. We studied *Julius Caesar* at school. There was a line in it that I loved: 'Yon Cassius has a lean and hungry look... and he looks quite through the deeds of men.' I was Cassius. A walking X-Ray machine. But I was also a powerless Black boy. I conformed. I bit my lower lip and sucked my teeth and averted my gaze from stuff I didn't agree with. But I drew the line at smiling. Did it cost me? I was never a school prefect or the class representative for anything. I was not among the select who were called into the headteacher's office to have praise heaped on them on the eve of their exams. Yet, come the first set of exam results, I ended up with the best grades of my year. I threw off my scowl at 17. A new headteacher was appointed and in one of his first acts, he praised me to the heavens in front of the entire school for my exam grades and my attitude to learning. 'He demands the best and he expects the best,' the new headteacher lauded. Finally, I smiled.

In the second year of A Levels, I discovered a teacher was teaching the wrong syllabus. The Head of the relevant Department checked and said I was right, but to keep quiet because it was too late for the whole class to change course and that instead, me and my buddy in that class – a white boy called Harry – should quietly learn the correct syllabus in preparation for the exam. The two of us passed the exam having taught ourselves the correct stuff in a flurry of reading at Central Library, Manchester. Harry is now a professor of linguistics. Not bad for a poor boy from Moss Side. Harry was no good at smiling either. 'Why does everyone think I'm miserable, Pete?' he asked me one day. 'It's just how your face is,' I told him. Together, we ruined all the class photos.

Smelling the flowers

Mr Dahlia, the greengrocer didn't like us – all these Black kids taking over the avenue. *All these* was two families – us, the Nigerian-Danish kids, and the kids of the Ndlovu family, refugees from apartheid South Africa, their father having been a prominent member of the ANC and having had to flee. We played football in the avenue. On his return from work, Mr Dahlia would drive his greengrocer's van at us at breakneck speed, making us scatter. He'd get out of the van, laughing.

There was another Black family the next avenue along – the Taylors. The Taylor kids were older than us by about five years. To get along, they changed their first names from Kwako to Richard, and from Karaba to Tommy, though I refused to use their English names. Any ball landing in Mr Dahlia's garden was lost – 'confiscated'. Kids have a fine sense of natural justice. Our ball fell in the Dahlia's garden. We knocked on the Taylor's door and asked for Karaba because he was fearless. Karaba came out, ran into the Dahlia's garden and got our ball. As he ran, he began singing a ditty – a spin on a popular song. His version went: 'Tip-toe, through the dahlias!' We laughed our heads off. He grabbed the ball and threw it to us. The Dahlia's door swung open, and expletives showered out. We scattered with the ball, laughing our heads off, hailing Karaba.

Black optimism

It is a curse to be Black and an optimist. Because to acknowledge racism is to be forced to accept that we are dragging around a ball-and-chain. Critical race theory is a philosophy of pessimism. It argues that four hundred years of discrimination cannot be removed by the magic wand of a paper policy or two. And who would argue against that? Yet that sense of overhang, of shadow, is inimical to joy. How then can a Black optimist make their way in the world? There's no fun shouting, 'Woe is upon me, woe is upon us all!' There's no zing in declaring 'I'm going to live my life knowing I have one hand tied behind my back by racism, so help me, God!' There's no zest in being the grim Black person explaining stuff as best they can in the office team-building day's racism-awareness workshop. This is why the British Black ('We pulled ourselves up by our bootstraps') Conservatives appeal. This is why the successful Black person deletes the files that show they were helped along the way – deletes history, rejects Critical Race Theory – and proclaims, 'I did it by sheer force of my personality, by the sterling quality of my character, by dint of my exceptional intelligence and all-conquering talent.' It is real and normal – human – to walk this path. I sometimes invite the Talented Ones to a thought experiment. It goes like this. Imagine you were on a plantation in 1770. Where would your force of personality have got you then? Or try this one: imagine you were in apartheid South Africa in 1950. How far would the sterling quality of your character have carried you there? If you concede the point made, if you accept greater forces were at work then, it follows presumably, that it is your serious contention that those same forces have been completely extinguished now. Is that not counter-intuitive? You can invite them to the thought experiment. But the bootstrappers will rarely turn up. They have parties to go to. Signing up to be an aware person, conscious of the long-term effects of racism when you're successful is like having to leave the fun-fair to go sit by the sour bedside of your dying aunt.

Being somebody

I am a Nobody in the arts world (thank you, thank you, your polite refutations are appreciated but let the point stand, please, I beg). Being a Nobody is a useful position and it's from this vantage point that I have often encountered people who are Somebody – in green rooms, on staircases moving between TV studios, in media waiting rooms. There are Black Somebodies who don't recognise the Black Nobodies they used to hang out with because they are too busy trying to spot a Somebody bigger than themselves who can help them onto the next rung up. That's understandable. They probably have Impostor Syndrome and believe they will be thrown out of the Somebody Club imminently. There are others, though. Black Somebodies who still respect Nobodies. And they are gold. I met a famous Broadcaster-Somebody on a BBC staircase. I was stumbling around there because I'd dropped my lucky pen. She spent five minutes searching for it with me in the stairwell, then gave me her own and wished me luck. She didn't know me from Adam. I met a shy but Very Important Black Poet Somebody on a Central Library, Manchester staircase. He looked preoccupied and was being led by a librarian to stage lights but still he lifted his eyes and gave me a wry "wish me luck out there" smile. It amused me when I spotted a Very Famous Black stage-artist Somebody in the public bar of a theatre. He was travelling incognito: hood up, shades on, leaning on a wall looking round. Everybody was there to see him, but nobody had recognised him. Without blowing his cover, I sidled up and asked him why. He said he preferred anonymity, he was freer this way than when sycophancy surrounded him. This Somebody understood the benefits of being a Nobody. Of course, it's all sound and fury. The worms dine on the Somebodies and the Nobodies alike.

Getting your bearings

I asked where the swimming pool was in a town that I'd never visited. A long-chinned septuagenarian colonel gave me the following directions: Walk up this road until your reach the Black Boy pub, then turn right into Beads

Street. At the top of Beads Street, you will see a water tower, used to be attached to Arkwright's Cotton Mill. Make a sharp corkscrew turn there and you will be on Gold Coast underpass. That rises up to the Bonnie Prince Charlie Slept Here Inn which will be facing you. Walk along the bridge there, past Bonnie Prince Charlie Slept Here Too Tavern, then on to the Black Turk's Head bar, snake across the car park there, pass the Richard III grave memorial, and that's Plantation Road you'll be standing on. Keep going on that, past Sambo's Grave on your left. You come to a fork. Take the second passage, then the middle passage and then sharp left. The municipal swimming pool will be facing you. It's closed today.

The Black meerkat dilemma

Philosophy has many strange whorls and folds. There is one called the Meerkat Dilemma. It goes something like this (Don't @ me philosophers, imma give it my best shot here). The group as a whole needs to know when shit is going to happen. But the one who shouts, 'Shit is about to go down!' is the one said shit might target. Yet, if nobody shouts, 'Shit is about to go down!' the whole group ends up covered in shit. Somebody has to volunteer, for the sake of the group. But volunteering carries, potentially, a deep personal cost since the shit is more likely to hit you than anybody else. Bringing it out of theory and into the real world, the shit going down is usually something white people are *about* to do. The meerkats are the population of Black people who need to know this is about to happen. Would you be the sentry meerkat – the one to shout and therefore also the one most likely to catch the fire of the white folk if you shout out? It's a tough call. Black people take it in turns to be that sentry meerkat and speak up at meetings saying *Nope, this will turn out racist even if it is not the group's intention. Nope, this is just out-and-out racist. Nope, this is dumb on many racialised levels.* Speak up and you become the shunned one, the unpromoted one, the out-of-the-loop one, the one next in line for redundancy. Your call. You going to volunteer to be the sentry meerkat?

Why it is safer to be an amoeba than a stilt-walker

Lulu ran a fancy-dress shop called House of Lulu that supplied the extravagant outputs of her fevered imagination. She had an assistant Fina who was gorgeous. I was in unspoken thrall to Fina, and I visited the shop often. I let Lulu know how much I admired the kink and cut of her costumes, and we got talking and she hired me to be one of four amoebas coursing around Manchester city centre during a summer festival celebrating How Many Big Buildings Manchester Now Has. During costume-fitting, I fantasised about Fina and me as single-celled organisms making the leap to multi-celled reproduction and bringing on a revolution in natural science. In the real world, I walked around with three others that day in a person-sized amoeba costume feeling perfectly normal if somewhat hot. Amoebas bring out the best in people. I was offered water, bites to eat, and many asked to stroke my cell membranes – which I always permitted. Being an amoeba was so much easier than being a stilt walker. I learned stilt-walking as part of my Moko Jumbie Caribbean Carnival Band days. I made money on the side walking around locations on giant stilts handing out leaflets promoting events. I got a stilts booking in Bolton. My teenage son was with me on stilts (it was a family hustle), handing out leaflets from up high. A white man jumped out of a car and tried pushing me over. Another white man walking by joined him. They partially succeeded. I fell onto a post box. The first man ran back into his car, laughing, the second man disappeared. It was all over in five seconds. My son, who had been on the other side of the street during all this, clattered over on his stilts, shocked by the attack, and furious. *Why did amoebas generate affection, and stilts hostility?* I wondered. I started keeping notes.

Watermelon

I have great difficulty eating watermelon in front of white people. Throughout my childhood white people invested so much time and energy in their literature making us into these eye-rolling, big-grinning picaninny idiots who chomped on the big green and red fruits that I boycotted them for decades. Then I met someone from Iran, and they loved watermelon and didn't carry my cultural baggage. They were mad for it. Watermelon was in their fridge, on their kitchen counters, in their dreams and all over their late-night cravings. I was tempted. In my mind, I resisted. So much weight and volume, so little taste, those slithery pips that require spitting out making it an outdoor fruit rather than a dining room fruit, the crazy prices, the ecological damage of growing those things which drink litres and litres of water, the mess, the stickiness, the perfumy smell… My mind went on and on, but my stomach rumbled, and I gave in. Now I eat watermelon clandestinely. I only buy it from Black stores. I only eat it around Global Majority people. My daughters eat watermelon unproblematically. 'Deal with your issues, Dad,' they tell me. 'Deal with your issues.'

Sauna

"Black people tolerate heat better than white people" was one story that ran through my primary school summer playground. This was something I could get onboard with. I duly wore jumpers in the height of summer, feigned nonchalance when the sun blazed and stayed out under it while everyone else (read white kids) hung in the shade. *We Black people can handle heat far better than whites* was my message. Spin the clock forward a couple of decades and, with a pale friend, I step into a hotel sauna. It's just me and her. It's the first time I've been in a sauna – all my life I've avoided them. Within ten seconds, it's so hot that I can't seem to pull enough oxygen from the air. I'm surreptitiously gasping. A very white man joins us. He whacks the steam gauge up even higher. Steam pours out from all sides. The two of them are chatting and all smiles (as far as I can see through the haze of steam). Me? I feel myself crossing into passing-out territory. Blurting apologies, I stumble to the door, heave it open and fall out. The paler-skinned ones chuckle upon my exit. Outside that hot box, I feel an intense failure as a Black person. The two paler folks in there handled the heat better than me. Shame. My mind drips to that journey from Lagos to Ilorin on a minibus built for twelve and they'd forced sixteen of us in, and me in the back row wedged in a corner with a very large man who fell asleep on me and started licking my shoulder, and that was of no concern to me compared with the stifling heat of that mini-van and my desire to die, for God to simply come and remove me from this world because the heat was way too much, hell had to be cooler. I couldn't breathe, and then the slumbering man, bless him, farted, and the fart was highly noxious. The bus occupants were divided. Drive on! shouted

some. Stop! Open the doors! shouted others. And the
bus stops, the doors are flung open. I praised God. I'd
been saved from *cause-of-death: heat-exhaustion* by a large,
licking man's fart.

Guitar class with Kabir

There is probably a special region of hell where beginner
guitar classes happen. At sixteen, I went to Fielden Park
Adult Education Centre evening classes with my mate,
Kabir. The teacher was a bearded, bulky, white, folk
music lover in a flowery shirt. On borrowed acoustic
guitars, we strummed through learner classics. We were
teenagers with all the absorbent vulnerability that being
teenagers brings and in those moments, as me and Kabir
chugged along in 4/4 or 3/4 or some off-kilter variation
of these, we added our voices to the collective classroom
howl, and imagined our true love, her yellow hair
gleaming in the morning when we rise. I did wonder if
this morning girl had been bleaching her Afro because
when you bleach black hair and it goes wrong, it comes
out yellow. Mostly I imagined a wavy, flaxen-haired,
bare-footed white chick in a cream dress chewing her
cornflakes while looking at me with desire dripping from
every pore. Kabir at that time had grown a Dr Zhivago
moustache and was racing through white girls. Can you
smell my envy, even from this temporal distance? *Next
verse!* came the bearded shout. As we sang, part of me
was imagining Kabir serenading his latest in the *Yellow
Is the Colour* chords of D, G D, A, before switching up
quickly to the trickier minor chords of *Lay, Lady, Lay*
with its wet-dream closer of 'Let's go upstairs!' – or in
Kabir's case, since it was impossible to smuggle girls into
his bedroom because of his hyper-vigilant parents, or

44

'Let's go in that field near the underpass!' We were two average, out-of-tune Black kids in a class of average out-of-tune white kids learning guitar. Our guitar teacher cared, and I remember him with affection. Funny how an evening class guitar teacher you meet only ten times can stay with you a lifetime. Through most of my teens I yearned to deliver that line, 'Let's go upstairs' for real. There were plenty of girls I wanted to go upstairs with but we never quite managed the journey. I did not have Kabir's moustache.

Three humiliations

Today, I remembered three humiliations.

I arranged to meet a friend for a chat. We met at the Deansgate tram stop and wandered along the canal-side there looking for a coffee shop to sit and talk in. There were five new skyscrapers thrown up, inspiringly named Tower One, Tower Two... in Deansgate Square. We spotted a small coffee shop at the base of one of them. It looked fine to chat there – in the coffee shop, atrium side. We tried to go in through the Tower's revolving doors, but the doors would not operate for us. White people came and went – the doors worked fine for them, but never for us. After five or six attempts and watching everyone else get in and out successfully, a muscled security man appeared. He told us the revolving door was controlled by fobs and if you didn't have a fob on you the door stopped revolving for you. We beat a retreat from The Tower and looked for an outside bench. The grass patches in this Five Towers land were plastic and signs stated sternly if your dog defecates on the plastic grass, please clean it up. I realized this was another place ringed off by private developers for the people who had bought their luxury flats – meaning whites. We were dirt here, as in 'matter out of place', or 'a disruption of the existing order' as anthropologist, Mary Douglas put it. We were the shit the developers had put the signs up about. I thought of Milan and Paris, about how civic their urban spaces were, how porous and public, how nothing was controlled by fobs. Manchester's councillors were selling the soul of the city to the developers.

When I was starting out as a writer, I was friends with a novelist on a similar journey and during those early years we laughed together, stood on street corners people-watching together, shared dreams and jokes and had each other's backs. His career moved upwards fast. He won awards and became the talk of the town. Many years later, I went to a party in one of the Towers, and he was there. I waved to him; he walked past me, whispering 'Not now, Pete,' and began an earnest conversation with a TV producer. I was puzzled. Did he just air me? I moved my still-outstretched hand to my chin to save face. Someone sniggered at my scruffy shoes. I left the party and walked home.

Inside my council flat, I switched on my PC and tried a game of online chess. I was beaten in nine moves by someone going by the name of ISuckYourMothersDick.

Huggy Bear

You had to choose your stereotype. There were six on offer on 70's TV. Great athlete. Fool. Swivel-eyed Ogre. Happy Mamma. Tragic Mulatto. Fuck machine. I chose the fool. And of all the fools, I chose Huggy Bear out of *Starsky and Hutch*. Huggy was the Prince of Fools, the jive-talking, cop-informing, pimp-presenting uber-fool with

46

a face of rubber and a tongue as fast as Muhammad Ali's. And his clothes. They caught your breath and satisfied the maths of *style is greater than poverty*. Later, a friend was due a court appearance on heavy charges and asked me to come help him choose what to wear. He lived on a hard-times estate and ushered me up to his bedroom. Every outfit in his wardrobe was a million dollars. His case was hopeless and, as he tried suits on, I thought, at least you'll be going down in style. In *Murder Trials*, Cicero recommends that defendants dress in rags, the better to evoke the pity of the judge and jurors. Cicero assumed an even playing field, race-wise. If you're going to end up doing a ten-year stretch, which means your clothes, by the time you get out, are going to be out of fashion and moth-eaten, why not spend your last free day in something splendid? He had his day. He went to court in high sartorial flair, the coolest dude in court. He got eight years.

Make believe

We were not allowed television as kids, my father decided. It rots the brain. This was fine until high school. Then the cool kids with double knot ties talked loud in form class about the wow programmes they'd watched; your cool was measured by your take on these shows. I eavesdropped on the TV stories on the ovens side of the room (because our form class was a Home Economics room), then crossed to the sinks side and retold them – adding an embellishment here, subtracting a detail there, downplaying a highlight the first teller had ramped, inflating some other moment, thus ensuring nobody noticed my lift from the original teller. I found I could get away with my theft, no problem. This modus operandi bled into maths. Sometimes maths engaged me, sometimes it didn't – it depended on the amount of drama at home, whether I'd had breakfast, and who was sitting next to me in class. There was this one kid who did maths like it was tomato soup – just slurped it all up. We became desk buddies. Maths after that was easy – he did the equations, I fed him jokes and copied his answers, adding an error here or there to cover my tracks. We stayed friends. He ended up in jail having joined the family firm, importing heroin. I eventually did my own equations.

Instructions for teenage Black boys 2

Don't touch your pockets or have your hood up when the police drive past or are observing you.

Don't carry in your hands a vape pen, a calculator, a mobile phone or anything else that could approximate the silhouette of a gun at any given angle.

Don't walk too confidently.

Don't walk too anxiously.

Don't laugh too loud.

Try to add a white boy or two to your male friendship group if you don't already have one, especially if you are doing that 'boys hanging around on the street' thing.

Don't hang around with white girls.

Don't hang around on the street.

Don't slouch. Neither stand in a manner that might be perceived as aggressive.

Don't look proud.

Don't look furtive.

Try to look three years younger than you are so that the police can perceive you as the age that you actually are. You can do that by eating candyfloss or doing handstands against a wall or playing conkers.

Don't wear large or bulky coats.

Do not recite any rap lyrics especially not on social media, nor have any rap, grunge, garage, trap, mumble, gangsta, gangster, punk, crump or any other rap-related lyrics, songs, audio or videos on any of your apps or on any of your friends' social media.

Don't feature or appear in any of your friends' social media.

Don't carry a man-bag.

Assume every passing car is an unmarked police car and act accordingly.

Do not be boisterous and lively and rowdy and generally teenager-y in any public space except inside a football stadium at football matches.

Tidy your bedroom. That way, if you are arrested and the police go to search your room, they will know you are a respectable person.

Try not to bowl, or roll, or drag foot as you walk. Keep your back straight and your hips iced and have your legs move in a symmetrical fashion.

If you are hanging around outside with your male friends, and if it is at all an option, do invite a girl to hang out with you too.

Never get into a car driven by another Black teenager.

Never get into a car which is going to be driven down a country lane.

Don't drive a car.

If forced into an interaction with police, switch your phone to record as early as you can without attracting attention; turn on audio and preferably video, with real-time, passworded, remote cloud storage. If you speak, try to use an unostentatious received pronunciation – like the local newsreaders.

Do not use words or gestures which might be interpreted as facetious when interacting with police officers. Neither use speech or gestures with police officers which might be interpreted as sullen or combative or a piss-take.

Don't walk around with a book. Don't walk around with a gym bag. Don't walk around with a snooker queue bag, or a poster bag, or an artwork folder or a camera bag.

If you see a police gun pointed at you, drop slowly to your knees, hands high, then leverage your torso forwards and assume the snow-angel position, face down.

Have lidless eyes.

On eating birthday cake alone

One winter day, you will find yourself eating birthday cake alone in a bare flat while wearing broken shoes. A circuit breaker will trip, and you will sit in darkness, the only noise the rumbling of distant traffic as life passes you by. You will send messages, and nobody will answer them. The only messages you will receive will be demands for payment or else notices of the death of friends. Hunker down during this winter. Keep in mind, seasons always change. You will have summers.

Summers when friend after friend puts their arms around you, hugs you, bears you gifts and good wishes. And they will bring dancing shoes and drag you out, dancing, and you will leap and spin and feel joyous. This is how time seasons you. And the day your life ends, you will have a collection of shoes, including a pair of gleaming dancing shoes and only you will know the secret of who you danced with when wearing them. Those shoes will go to a charity shop upon your passing, to be bought by a young person who has just spent their birthday eating cake alone in broken shoes.

On eating bananas

I will not eat bananas in front of white people. This is because of deep childhood trauma. 'Haha monkey!' they used to shout at me in my infancy if I ate a banana. Depending on how I was feeling that day, I would laugh it off, fight it off, eat if off or ignore it. The monkey insult burned deep. It flared up big in my early teens with the release of the *Planet of the Apes* television series. Playgrounds exploded with epithets. It was the lowest hanging fruit for the school's little white racists.

I've noticed that baby boomer Black people try to get round the issue by holding the banana horizontally, rather than in the more natural, vertical way, then breaking off pieces and popping them in their mouths as if they were eating a segment of orange. For most of us, the taboo is too strong even for that. Intersectionality is relevant here. For Black women, the associations of eating a banana with fellatio make a dignified eating in public of this fruit doubly impossible. I asked friends, when was the last time you saw a Black person eat a banana in public? None could remember any occasion.

Instead, we eat bananas privately, at home. They are my favourite fruit. I buy them from a corner shop called Madina Superstore where they come in small bunches, unwrapped. I take them home and leave them in a wooden fruit bowl for at least three days, until the trauma of their journey floats off and they are fully ripe and firm yet soft. Then, let the light be low because the sublime semi-matt yellow of this fruit's skin is best appreciated in half-light when there are no reflections on its surface. And let that skin be mottled black because this blackness is a key indication of goodness. Now break one fruit off from the bunch gently. You will meet resistance when you attempt to peel it, but persevere. The rewards are heavenly.

Extra-curricular activities

There were various extra-curricular activities going on at and around my secondary school. One group of boys was rumoured to be wanking off men for money in public toilets. This led to an assembly during which the exasperated Deputy Head explained, holding back tears, why this was Wrong. The group I belonged to stole from shops. Not because we needed stuff. Rather, it was for the thrill. Which meant we often had stuff we didn't even understand how to use. We stole an opisometer from a maps shop. I know that word – opisometer – because our geography teacher, Mr Novac, taught it to us. He was impressed we had come to possess such an expert geographer's tool while being observant that we didn't know how to use it. Other teachers might have tried interrogation to find out how we came by it, which would have been a waste of time because we were experienced interrogatees and never cracked. Mr Novac was different. He spent half an hour showing us how to use our stolen geography goods (we had prismatic compasses as well). I owe my acute spatial awareness and advanced orienteering skills to our see-no-evil geography teacher, Mr Novac.

Hair wars: messy bun v messy Afro

White people got a style called Messy Bun. It is wild hair, just one notch up from complete bedhead. Messy Bun is spiky and swooped up and loosely pinned with pieces falling out here and there, and it's cool and legitimised by the designation, *Messy Bun*, because by giving it a name it's legitimised. Black folk are not allowed by white folk to have any messy style anything – there's no official Messy Afro style. Yet the neo-Afro youth often do that style. And they catch comments from white folk of 'That looks rough, can't you tidy it up, maybe you should even it out, make it all smooth and regular.' I ask on behalf of these youth, since when did white folk start deciding what cool Black people hair look like? Of course, some of the let's-not-make-trouble-here older Black folk often be siding with the Messy Afro critics, agreeing 'Yup, your hair is a mess, straighten that Afro up, un-clump it'. I would like to say to both the Black elders and the white headshakers, Messy Afro is a style, get over it. PS. I got no dog in this fight. I am bald.

Seducers: a brief, strange, obscure & probably misguided foray into biblical hermeneutics

(Bible hermeneutists please don't @ me, this is a thought experiment not a research project.)

Charlatans get a bad press in the Bible. There are eighty-seven references to them across the Old and New Testaments and all of them negative. Surely at least one example must be a mistranslation? The Bible only fell into English late in life. It began in Aramaic, Hebrew and Greek and found its way into the standard King James English version by way of a genius poet-translator called William Tyndale whose translation in c. 1520s was the basis for the KJV. If we accept cultural theorist Walter Benjamin's contention that exact translation is impossible, then each rendering into a different language places the text in a more and more tenuous relationship with the original. Maybe the text began with some Aramaic, Hebrew or Greek equivalent of prestidigitator – a word with positive connotations similar to magician, so holding an aura of positivity. The original translator, finding no direct equivalent, shaves off this aura by deciding upon trickster (even though trickster, to give it its due, does have positive connotations in some cultures e.g. some West African and Caribbean cultures) as the best translation. The next monk (were they not always monks and sages doing the translations?), transferring into their object language, picks up trickster and goes with schemer. The final translator, after uhmming and ahhing for a day, picks up schemer, and chooses charlatan. The die is cast. All the prestidigitators, both good and bad, are now tarred as charlatans. Do any passages of the current Bible work with a word more positive than charlatan for which there is at least some antecedent authority? Here's one possibility: The New English version of Timothy, Chapter Two, Verse 3:13. gives us: 'But evil people and charlatans will go from bad to worse, deceiving others and being deceived themselves.' But the earlier King James version has a different list: 'For evil men and seducers shall wax worse and worse...' Clearly, the 'seducer' of the King James version has become the 'charlatan' of the New English version. Moreover, the King James version places seducers outside the category of evil men: 'evil men *and* seducers' (my emphasis). The *and* allows the possibility that seducers are not always evil. Surely, therefore, it is not fair for all seducers to be tarred with the charlatan brush. Oh Happy Days when textual analysis washes the seducers' sins away. Seducers, thank me later.

Feeding the monkeys

The primary school photographer's call to me and my siblings sitting on the photographer's pose bench was *Smile, you monkeys!* I scowl-smiled, not knowing if he was cut from the same cloth as the white neighbour to our left who set his dog on us, or the white greengrocery store owner to the right who drove his van at us, or the white woman in a fur hat on the park bench who wrinkled her nose at us. He clicked his camera. Next year came round and I was older and when the photographer called his call, I refused. He muttered *niggers* as he waved us off having clicked us, and this clarified the point for me. That same day, after school, I strolled along the street to the zoo-man's house. The zoo-man's monkeys were out, and I let one of them sit on my shoulders and pick dead skin from my scalp.

The problem has always been white people

It is 1982. We are fresh out of school, and we beat ourselves up taking elocution lessons from our elders, improving our body language, calibrating our eye-contact time, getting succinct with our phrasing, dropping the erms and you-know-what-I-means in order to shine at the interview, get the job, win that promotion. Yet, however we developed our shit, somewhere in the back of our minds, we knew our fate would ultimately be determined by a table of white people who would say yes or no, depending on whether they ate cornflakes or eggs for breakfast.

Glass collecting

At the Job Centre, there was an advert for a glass collector at the Shoulder of Mutton pub. The boss at the pub said that was all I had to do – collect glasses. The role was available because the bar staff wouldn't collect them any more because it ruined their nails, and at the end of the night I was also to collect ashtrays. I wasn't going to be pulling pints or mixing cocktails or stocktaking or anything, I was to be a glass collector, and this was a job for someone who lacked ambition. The boss had flat eyes and shiny black trousers, and his bar staff were all pretty looking. I told him that was fine, I was the right guy, I lacked ambition. He hired me. It turned out to be my best job ever.

Cuttings room

I worked in an advertising agency for a summer. The work involved cutting out articles in local newspapers that had been planted there by advertising agencies. We cut them out to show their clients that the agency was getting results. Double-glazing. Golf courses. A pizza shop. It was boring as hell except for the local news items: The artiste, Foo Foo Lamar donated his Rolls Royce to a customer last night but is now sober and wants it back. Please dial this number if you were that customer. Another reported a local bridge which, if you walked across it, you got pregnant, and the proof was these three sisters. And there was the image of Jesus found in a loaf of bread. We were mostly university drop-outs around the cutting tables. There was a maths wonk who had auburn hair and a pixie tattoo and a skirt that rode up higher as the day wore on. Her name was Adele, and her job was to pass us the newspapers to cut up and check we'd cut out the right things. When she came round, she'd press her thighs into the tables we worked on. I'd get a hard-on and couldn't stand up till it faded. I worked a lot of overtime there.

Boxing ghosts

I'm a Saturday Dad and it's Saturday and I'm with lil dawta. We swerve the pond ducks and come across a man boxing in Alexandra Park. He's mid-twenties with a big beard, and, from his complexion, I guess Middle Eastern else Pakistani or Bangladeshi. He's shadow boxing very proficiently around a park fountain, one of the old Victorian style, three-tier fountains. He's definitely a pro or semi-pro. In his Adidas-striped tracksuit and white hand wraps, he looks ferocious, delivering sleek jabs and smart, lethal uppercuts. Lil dawta asks what he's doing. I grasp for an explanation that she can take in... He's, he's, he's fighting a ghost, I say. She's fascinated and stops to stare at him the way only a three-year-old can stare. He pauses his boxing to give her a little wave. Later, we're in the park rain shelter between two weather-beaten lions. The boxer starts walking up the herbaceous-bordered stone path that leads past us, having finished his training. I pick lil dawta up and point him out as he gets near to us. 'There's the boxing man,' I say, 'the one who was fighting a ghost.' The boxer hears me, grins broadly. He's alongside us now, pats lil dawta on her head, waves her a soppy goodbye. It's funny how the toughest guys are melted by lil dawta.

Fast forward fifteen years and lil dawta is in the boxing ring of life and on the ropes. The ghosts are coming at her determinedly, but she bobs, weaves, slips, flashes out jabs, uppercuts, holds those ghosts at bay. 'Go, Champ,' I shout to her, 'stick it to those ghosts!' The nature of the ghosts none of us yet understands. We all drag ghosts around with us through life. Some of us run out of jabs to hold them off.

Sorting depot

I picked up this job at a post office sorting depot in Leeds. It was full of National Front members. Working in a den of racists was fine with me. It wasn't much different from society at large. The bosses walked runways high above us, watching for thefts. The job was mind-numbing. You picked up letters and postcards, deciphered the postcodes then placed them into racks according to destination: East. Northeast. Kent. London. Scotland. And so on. Lower management figures stood behind you with stopwatches and fired you if you didn't sort fast enough. We sometimes picked up postcards that were sexy or amusing or wild and put them on the 'address unknown' rack for the next shift to take a look at.

Job centre filing clerk

I did an interview for a secretarial post. They asked how would you sort a filing cabinet? I said alphabetically. I got the job. My boss was the nicest. He was a wheelchair user, and he used to roll up with paperwork and ask me to file it. When I asked which word should I file it under, he'd say, well what do you think? Whatever I replied, he said yeh, I think that's right. It gave me great confidence in alphabetical filing. The job affected me. Two people fighting outside a nightclub, and I'd speculate one of them had their jacket filed erroneously by the hat-check boys and now the other is fighting to get their jacket back. I realised all my closest school friends became so because the school organised desks alphabetically by name – Richard Hao, Tariq Jahanbar, then me, Peter Kalu. People with last names beginning with A probably get hired by the lazy bosses who choose the first candidate on their list. They tested nuclear bombs at a site called Bikini Atoll. The first bomb they dropped there was called 'Able'. The second was called 'Baker'. My filing job ended when my boss scooted off with the Team Leader and Head Office archived the entire operation.

Stilts and philosophy

I landed a role with a promotions company. It was distributing double-glazing leaflets in Northern town streets and shopping centres. Sales engagement was boosted by the leafleteer wearing a bright silk costume while walking on two-feet-high stilts. Lunch was not included but transport was provided to and from locations, and the stilts were also provided. I needed the money. I lied on my cv about my stilt-walking ability. They drove me in a Ford Panda to Wigan. 'The windows of Wigan are 87% rotten,' Barry, the area sales manager said, while scoffing a vanilla slice, 'and we're going to make a killing here. You'll get cash in hand at the end of the day, and a five pounds bonus for every extra sliding door sale.'

I sat on a wall. They strapped the stilts on, shoved a couple hundred leaflets into my hands then drove off with the other sucker who was down for leafleting Bolton. I waved them off. I was confident. I had belonged to a circus once; it was a while ago, but I assumed stilt-walking was like riding a bike: once learnt, never forgotten. I got up off the wall. And wobbled like a new-born giraffe, knew *this might be a long day*.

If the window frames of Wigan were 87% rotten, the people of Wigan were untroubled by them. There were few takers for my leaflets. The stilts did attract the attention of Wigan's low life though. Two leapt out of a car and tried to push me over. I fell onto a red Royal Mail post box and clung to it. The duo found this hilarious, took photos, jumped back into their car and sped off. My leaflets were scattered and wet and useless now. I pulled myself upright off the box and tottered over to sit on the wall. I pondered my situation. I was dancing for coins. I could as well be beaten up and what did anyone care? We Black folk have always tapped spoons for a living. I knew a man in Manchester who played guitar for midnight clubbers. I could play harmonica, I could walk on stilts, it was the same difference. I was a song and dance man and as close to minstrelling as made no difference. Just another soft-shoe shuffler scraping a living in a street full of glass.

My mind turned to the existential. Jean-Paul Sartre says we emerge into this world from nothingness. The drama of life rolls over us. We experience struggle, joy, bills, break-ups, assaults. We go about our lives with as much dignity as we can muster, placing one foot in front of the other, riding out the humiliation, the jubilation and the angst. At the end, we die – roll back into nothingness. What do I gain, I thought, *pace* Sartre, by risking life and limb to proselytise the citizens of Bolton on the benefits of double-glazing? Was not the ground here too stony for the message? Was not the whole of life itself an invitation to walk on stilts, an invitation to precarity? I unstrapped the stilts.

I had no sooner unstrapped them than sales manager Barry pulled up in his Fiat Panda with a broad grin and a set of donuts. 'Well done, pal. Sales have been off-the-scale. Here's a donut. You'll be getting a ten-pound bonus for today. Same again tomorrow?' 'Sure,' I said.

On becoming ten

Our son was becoming ten, understand? He was growing up and he wanted his own party and not too much supervision this time; it's my party not yours. We organised a cake, drinks and sandwiches thing, bought invitation cards from Card Factory and sent them with him to school. We lived on an Oldham council estate and the kids at the school came from lots of different places but few from our estate – people tended to move out of the estate where we lived as soon as they could. Still, after a few phone calls answered, eight boys showed up, mostly driven to our house by their parents, and carrying the local cultural tradition of the small present for the birthday boy. Pass the parcel was played, cake eaten, fizzy drinks gulped. Then my son said they wanted to go play football in the local park and they were old enough to go on their own. Fine. They went. An hour later, they came bursting back through the door in a tumble of cuts and wild faces. I asked the obligatory *what happened*. Between gasps, my son told how the local boys had started a fight with them, claiming the football pitch was theirs, but it was OK because they gave as good as, and nobody needed the hospital or anything. This was accurate. They had scratches and bruises but nothing more cake couldn't cure. The parents of the eight duly picked them up. Next day, my son returned from school, and I asked, and he said word at school was that he'd delivered the best birthday party in the history of the universe; it was legend. None of the eight ever returned to our house.

It was my daughter's tenth birthday. She was growing up. She wanted her own party and something different because everything was so *boring*. Me and her mum had split by now, and I arranged a birthday party at a Manchester museum because it had interesting stuff in it, and my daughter liked the hands-on science puzzles and displays there – like you could push a huge rock with a finger or move an entire car with one hand. I gave my daughter the time and the museum address on invitation cards and sent her off to school. Come the day, eight classmates rocked up at the museum. They did the puzzles and stuff. Then, in the museum refectory, I ordered pizza for them all and – surprise – we sang Happy Birthday. A white security guard approached. This is not allowed. I asked what was not allowed. Holding a birthday party in the refectory, he replied. How does that work? I asked. What distinguishes a birthday party from eight friends visiting the museum? He was adamant it could not happen, and I had to break the party up, else he would. My white sister (yes, I have a white sister) was with me at the time. She took the security guard to one side and had a word. He walked back up to me five minutes later, saying, actually it was all fine, I could go ahead and continue the party. Eight ten-year-old faces relaxed and went back to their criminal laughter and singing and pizza.

Shadowlands

Late night, I get a text message from my 17-y.o. daughter. She's being held at this address by some guy she met at a bar, he won't let her out, can I come? It was a fifteen-minute drive away in the shadowlands of a small town. I pulled up at a terraced house fronted by wild privets, a short, broken concrete path, some steps. I take the steps to the white door, knock on the scratched gold letterbox. He opens. He's wearing a white vest, four-day-old stubble and a half-smoked spliff. He's about 75 lbs, medium height, right-handed.

'I've come to take my daughter from here.'

'She not leaving. She's with me.'

'That so?'

My daughter does not emerge as this dialogue takes place, so something is wrong because I know my daughter. I move closer to him. He squares up. He has a height advantage from the steps.

'OK. Come out here and we'll get to it,' I tell him.

He likes this idea and comes down the steps, hands high in a boxing stance, ready, and I say, 'Keep coming.'

He follows me down the path a little more. At which point, in a neat pivot, I duck past him. Now I'm standing on the steps and he's down there on the path with his spliff stuck to his lower lip which is now hanging because it has dawned on him that I've got the high ground, and that I'm now barring him from entering his own place. How did that happen?

'Just stay there,' I tell him.

I call out to my daughter again. This time, she emerges out of the yellow hall light, her face shiny wet. We walk past him. He shifts out of the way as we pass. Me and the daughter get in the car. I turn and look at her. 'This dating lark, eh?' Through the tears, she laughs.

Chicken run

Sociologist Pierre Bourdieu posits that the working classes, conscious of their destiny as meat in the grinder of capitalism, live more in the now than the middle classes and take more risks with their lives. Was that what was going on when we, as early teens, played chicken by seeing who dared dash across all six lanes of the dual carriageway? Or was it that school was so boring we couldn't take it without a shot of adrenaline, and we needed the buzz of feeling alive that came with dodging death? Speed forward twenty years, and, visiting a friend, I drove into a tired council estate. Two kids stepped into the road and stood there, daring me to keep going, to run them over. I braked, stopped and looked at them. Scrawny boys in fashion labels. They looked back at me, motionless. It was like I was looking at my younger self. I smiled, gestured I had all the time in the world. The road was pot-holed. The pointing of the houses needed redoing. Rubbish spilled out of black bags by open alleyway gates. One of the boys was wearing tiptop Nikes, the other a chunky silver necklace. L.S. Lowry would have painted them. One flicked an eyebrow up, signalling to me. I nodded. They parted. I drove on.

Tam and the imperious present

There is a grainy video on YouTube featuring Tam, the main dancer of a Northern male dance group. It's early Eighties and he's in a nightclub with his five dance group buddies. They start doing foot hops and spins. They are in floaty white shirts, and confident as they work through their routine. Now they do back hops, now slides, now front splits that segue into hip swings. They are impressive but not slick; they don't have the honed quality of Hollywood musical routines or contemporary big budget productions. The soundtrack is soul-swing, low-fi and mono. Their faces do not wax into smiles but instead crease with concentration. We see they are wearing matching two-tone shoes. The camera pans to the audience and people look through the camera like it's not there even though it would have been a bulky thing back then. Two young women – clearly friends – with geri curls and modest, tight dresses and matching earrings, wave self-consciously in a good-natured way like they know the camera holder. The lens swings back to Tam and his group of dancers. They spin out more footwork. Swing two decades and I'm in an arty room in a Big Glass Building at some city centre media bash. Tam is here with us, in the room. The spotlight shone so brightly on Tam all those years ago, and there is still the sheen of stardom about him, a glow of remembered crowds, cheering, tributes in all the locals and some of the nationals, adulation in the nightclubs, bodies pressing into him, wanting to touch the magic. Those good times all lodged in his body and the memories still play in his eyes, and he moves with only a light grasp of what colder eyes might see: the minor rip of his shirt at the back, the slight datedness of the jeans, the bartender waiving the excess amount he didn't have the funds in his account for. And this because his sweet de-linking from the imperious present, his minor delusion that those distant rays of fame still light him, is all our delusion, is all our heydays, and we, as much as him, want to keep it alive. He carries that torch for us all as we stack boxes and work tills and sweep litter.

The bins 1: survivor bias

We were scavengers. We went around bedsit land, rummaging in bins. We got to know house occupants by what they threw away. I found a functioning transistor radio in one bin. It was leather-bound and picked up Radio Moscow and the Shipping Forecast. It is the only radio I remember having in my childhood. I first tried out Ponds cold cream after I plucked a full, unused jar from a bin. That evening while applying it, I wondered about the lady's beauty regimen and why she had decided Ponds would not work for her. The bins also yielded jewellery, musical instruments, batteries, shoes, herb racks, holiday brochures, and porn mags. There was a glut of porn mags in bedsit land, so much so that a porn mag bin tour evolved. It usually threw up *Razzle*, a sex problems magazine called *Club International*, *Playboy* and *Penthouse*. One bin regularly supplied us with hairy armpits-and-pussies mags. We didn't know if this was because the purchaser loved hairy armpits and pussies or if, on the contrary, those were the only magazines they were throwing out and they were keeping the others (a phenomenon I later learned has its parallel in *survivor bias* theory). Sometimes we'd lurk around the front of the houses guessing who was hairy-pussy-and-armpits lover, who was big-tits admirer, who was belts-and-gags man, who was likes-it-up-the-ass man. To pass the time while loitering, we read each other articles from the *Club International* problem pages. We were the most sex-educated virgins of the area.

Paper rounds: ch ch ch ch changes

The clean white boys got all the paper rounds. We, meaning the Irish and the Black kids, pressed our noses up against the shop plate-glass as those white boys in there with David Bowie quiffs sniggered at us, picked up their newspaper piles from the altar of the newsagent's sorting bench, and slid them into their grey canvas paper-round bags. Paper rounds were lucrative. Early rising Black boys (this was only boys who did morning delivery rounds) had to make do with trying to assist the milkman, which, when you got lucky, and he let you ride his milk float, meant you got the bonus of drinking any milk on the doorsteps left from the day before and sometimes even a pint of the fresh stuff, and cream. The main newsagent was owned by Mr Collins. and he lived in a house on Moorcroft Road with sixteen upper-storey rooms. Today, the delivery business has more Black faces: Getir, JustEat, UberEats and Deliveroo could not function without their Black staff. I also notice small-time drug dealers are increasingly female.

Shiny pants and saki wine

My embrace of fashion came from my father. Not that he was a dapper man – he was an accountant, happy in a plain suit or dashiki. But he set up an import-export business (like 65.25% of Nigerians of that time) and once he'd got his business up and running, he began bringing home samples. He arrived one day with a pair of electric blue trousers in my size. Blue was the school uniform colour. I was twelve years old, and I slid them on. Next day, I strode along the school corridors in electric blue, telling anyone who asked that 'these are rare, export samples because my dad is a very big businessman who obtains such things, and you will not be able to find them in the shops.' I wore those trousers until I ran out of hem to let down. The next item he brought home was saki rice wine. It came in a display case with matching, lotus-flower decorated, ceremonial saki cups (as an adult, I've always enjoyed a drop of saki). Later, after my father's business crashed, bankrupting him and leaving our house at the mercy of foreclosing bankers, those saki cups still looked good in the sideboard.

Newspaper cuttings

My father's newspaper cuttings habit was just one sign of his creeping mental breakdown during the Biafra War of the 1960s. I'm guessing it made him feel useful – he was keeping a record of the injustices, and it was evidence being saved for a later United Nations war crimes tribunal. Or perhaps, in the early stages of the civil war, he was stocking the cuttings for the purpose of documenting the glorious path to victory of the unassailable Biafran army. As multiple members of his Igbere family died – in active combat as part of the Biafra army, and of starvation – and as this news trickled back to England, despair fed my dad's rages, and his clippings mania grew. We children were assigned related indexing and cataloguing duties. When the war ended, my father disappeared, leaving behind an attic cupboard full of scrapbooks. They went as yellow as his eyes, waiting for him to return.

Koi carp

I am in Umuahia, Nigeria and my father is explaining the excavation to the side of his compound's big house as the beginnings of a pond for koi carp which he intends to import and keep there. It's a ludicrous idea – koi carp basking in this patch of rusting zinc, trampled red soil, off from the parked-up battered tuk tuk, the abandoned Inspector Columbo car and the broken pump mechanism for the non-functioning on-site water bore-hole, just right of a straggly row of truculent English rose bushes – another of my father's *I Have Been To England* touches. Koi carp. The concrete bowl is full of rainwater and too murky to see your hand if you thrust it into the mud sludge, as years of leaf fall moulder with debris blown off the compound, all made pretty by a bloom of deep-green lichen. The excavation has steep sides. A rusted, reinforcing mesh scavenged from nearby abandoned roadworks forms a makeshift barrier to prevent kids, drunk adults and chickens falling in. I gently advise him. Koi carp are delicate, ornamental fish and they require clean, aerated water; they could not tolerate this. Besides, the starving local cats would have them. Even the birds would fancy their chances against such captives. He nods but disagrees.

After his death, I dream and, in this dream, the koi carp are there, and the water is clear as arctic melt. Elegant, flecked gold, fatted submarines cruise and flick. They are silver-moustachioed fish-royalty, gleaming as if enamelled, in a constantly cruising school. Dad is standing next to me watching this school. Now, he walks away, his gold and red dashiki shimmering in the sunlight, its threads flowing with life. The patio doors of the big house slide back. With a clunk of door lock he is gone, back to the other place. I look into the patio glass. Reflected koi carp glitter. I turn. There is only a mud pit.

Puccini, the complete bastard

What a complete bastard Puccini was for the local pub singers of Milan. They'd be, like, I mean, give us a break, Puccini. That leap from D to high B in 'Nessun Dorma', it's pretty much impossible. And there's no need for it either. It distorts the line. The line is in Italian, and, following Italian pronunciation, is meant to peak at the last syllable 'vin-ce-*ro*', not at the middle syllable 'vin *ce-eee* – ro.' So get to fuck with your 'vin *ce eee* ro' and write something sing-able, you arse.

Contrast Puccini with Andrew Lloyd Webber. Webber doesn't demand so much. Webber's song 'Argentina' is beautiful, perfect for pub singers, no strain. Webber is the patron saint of pub singers. He writes songs that the average pub singer can sing. And they do. How they do.

Bitter Ocean

Me and my 19 year-old daughter are mooching through inner city Manchester. Strands of International Mother Tongue Language Day musings are still hanging like glue flytraps in the empty corridors of my mind when we pass some graffiti, written in a Chinese language. 'This is unique,' I tell my daughter in Dad mode, 'because as far as I am aware it is the only graffiti in Manchester written in a Chinese language.' We are by some industrial units, off Ardwick, just around from where heroin users sit down on warehouse emergency exit steps to shoot up. 'What does it say?' she asks. 'That is the mystery,' I agree. Providence sends someone past us who looks Chinese. He's about 19, probably a student, dressed all in black, walking in a slow, no-bounce shuffle. He looks miserable. 'Should we ask him?' I say. My daughter screws her lips, dubious. I consider the context. A mid-afternoon, cold Sunday in February. On the edge of a bleak Manchester wasteland. Big balding, slightly dishevelled Black guy. Isolated footpath. Withdrawn young man giving no signal he has even recognised our existence, let alone seen us. 'Yes, let's ask him!' I say and bounce over to him, daughter trailing. 'Excuse me, can you read Chinese?' I ask. He stops, raises his eyes at us, sniffs, nods. He has a whisper of a moustache, and a touch of dry skin around his lips. He is neither enthused nor threatened. But through the bleariness, he has at least 10% of 'what is your hustle?' going on in his eyes. I explain. 'It is just that, we see this graffiti and we're curious, we don't know what it says; can you read it for us?' He glances in the direction I'm pointing. It's right in front of us, two-metres high, done in spray-paint calligraphy. He sniffs again, speaks. 'It says "Bitter Ocean",' he says. 'Uhuh. And what does that maybe mean?' 'It means the person

70

feels that the world is a harsh and depressing place which is vast and full of bitterness.' 'Excellent,' I say, thinking, there is a Chinese graffiti artist in Manchester who is also a top-notch poet. 'Thank you very much, you have solved the mystery,' my daughter says to him. He smiles, just a flicker, nods his head a millimetre at her, then trudges on.

Civics & Shakespeare

I am at the Manchester Poetry Library. Some minor poetry-related event has ended, and the refreshments are being released, including wine. Would I support a Black Shakespeare Trail in Manchester? I am asked. Filling my glass, I decline on the basis that the Shakesperean iambic pentameter is the voice of the white man, and it would be a deeply retrograde step to hold that up as the standard for Black people to aim for. I add that Black voices and Black poetics need to lean into jazz music and the musics of our African and Caribbean ancestry, not start imitating Shakespeare who is long buried and let him remain so. My interlocutor pushes back, insisting there is value in a Black Shakespeare Trail. A small crowd of Black, semi-sloshed poets has gathered around us, and I see they are not immediately repulsed by the idea of this Shakespeare Trail. I marshal my arguments, and the debate goes back and forth a little. Out of the corner of my eye, I see the white staff of the Poetry Library retreating, rather like the Homer Simpson meme where he slides backwards into the hedge. After more back and forth, a tribune of the crowd steps forward and proposes a resolution. She says, 'We accept there is value in the Black Shakespeare Trail, so let the sister do her Trail thing, Manchester is a big city, wide enough for that. And we also accept your Hotep vision of Black-centred aesthetics, and we acknowledge

71

your own disengagement from the Black Shakespeare Trail project, which should still go ahead.' There are nods all round and, in this way, the peace was brokered, the wine finished off and the crowd henced home from the Manchester Poetry Library. I was keen to get away as I had a vague, inchoate anxiety running through me. As I reached my bus stop, I identified the source of my anxiety: not two weeks ago, I had worn a Victorian bathing costume at a gathering in Blackpool to fete the new Roger Robinson / Johny Pitts book, *Home is not a Place*. If someone who had seen me in that bathing costume had also been present at the Poetry Library as I denounced Shakespeare, they might have come forward during the debate and derided the hypocrisy of 'this man who rejects Shakespeare yet only two weeks ago was seen walking along Blackpool Pier in a Victorian bathing costume.' These two facts, placed together and aired, would have fatally undermined my credibility. I waited nervously for my bus.

There is an apple in Iran

'Tell me about apples,' I said to her. She said, 'There is an apple in Iran, so sweet and creamy that you lose yourself when eating it. People travel from across the country to find these apples and nobody who tastes them is satisfied with any other apple after one bite of this…'

A visit to the opera / noises off

An Indian theatre company and an English chamber orchestra have teamed up to deliver the opera *Orpheus* as a hybrid thing. The music is beautiful. The lyrics are ancient. Captions on a screen fling up those lyrics.

The flung-up lyrics include 'fleeting pleasures' and 'nymphs'. I surreptitiously use my phone to search the meaning of 'nymphs' because I am unsure which way this opera is heading. The dictionary says, 'a large class of inferior female divinities.' Which has me thinking, was the original *Orpheus* poetry this bad? And in the next thought, does anybody here actually care? Attending opera is a performative thing. The formal attire, the regimented seating arrangements, the strict segregation of audience and performers, all mimic class and caste segregations. Hurrah for hybrid bourgeois art. To be here is enough: 'Last night, I went to the opera.' I can't wait to say this.

God has gifted us two bags of marijuana

A friend of mine was walking across a municipal park in Manchester when she spotted 'a small bag of weed'. She picked it up and carried it home and then to my place. After earnest dialogue around hygiene, ethics and risk, we smoked the contents. One month later, I was leaving my office in Manchester city centre when my eye strayed to the pavement edge and I saw a transparent square of zip-lock plastic no bigger than a thumbnail, with some green stuff in it. Another bag of weed. At her place this time, the same deliberations took place and shortly after, this bag's contents met the same fate. The two finds, coming so close one after the other, generated some questions: What percentage of cannabis carried in a public space is dropped? Is there a known ratio that could thereby allow a comparison between the amount of cannabis being carried in Manchester's public spaces compared with the amount being carried in other UK cities? Was Manchester merely average or was it an outlier in this field? I desired to test these speculations by sounding out a few acquaintances but could not see a way to broach the subject without appearing to be that social pariah, the drugs fiend. The question fluttered uselessly in my mind for a few weeks, before eventually being dismissed.

Church door

Mum hollered me, I hollered back, 'What?' She said, 'Come down!' 'What?' 'Did you paint your name on the church door?' 'What?' 'P.E.T.E.R.?' Recent sins came to my mind. I'd broken a row of knotty fencing pales at the posh girls school by the river, practising kung fu kicks. I lit the gas cannister in the shed in the field by the allotments. I threw stones at the neighbour's dog. I stole a bike's front-wheel. I told David his mum made shit bacon. But I didn't paint my name on the church door. I told her this. Not recently? Not ever. She gave me her unbelieving look. I said whoever did it was daft to paint their name – *their name* – and was I that daft? She reluctantly accepted my defence, which for once was true. An idea grew in me that there might be a doppelgänger out there doing shit and I was going to be blamed for a whole heap of stuff I hadn't done. On the plus side, this P.E.T.E.R. could be my perfect alibi from now. Motherfucker messed with my name and could now reap the consequences.

Paper job

Me and Hamilton got this nice paper job from a sweet-smelling old lady. She hoarded newspapers and they piled high in her first-floor flat. Our job was to stack them, arrange them in piles by width and date, and gather more of them for her from the outside world because she never left her flat. We went out and pulled them off doorsteps, out of bins, slipped them off shop counters. Back at the flat, we stacked and ordered the new ones into piles that matched the old piles. They bowed the planks of her floorboards and brushed aside her net curtains as they climbed up her windows, blocking out light. She never read them but said she needed the news to hand, just in case. She paid well, always in cash. Until one day she got out her cheque book and said we should go to the bank and withdraw money for her. In case. After that, Hamilton said it was *his* area (and with him living closer to her flat, this was true) and he was going to do her papers on his own from now. I was off the job, no hard feelings. We had a fight about this which he won. Fine. I picked myself up, dusted myself down. There were lots of sweet-smelling old ladies dotted around.

Blackface and cosmetic Blackness

I am six and hiding under the table because the *Black & White Minstrel Show* has come on the television and black-faced white men are golliwogging across the TV tube to a gaudy tune. I'm cuddling my little sister, and my fingers are spread across my face as I peep out. There is one real Black man among the blacked-up white people. I am sad for that Black man. We have all been that Black man.

White anxiety around racial boundaries – fences hastily erected and steadfastly defended – manifests itself in curious ways. Boarding a plane, white people have nanoseconds of regret when they notice it will be flown by a Black pilot. On demanding to see 'the manager', the appearance of somebody with melanin-rich skin, has them momentarily discombobulated. When the surgeon for the operation comes along and places their brown hand on the patient's white hand in reassurance, the white patient has a flash of misgiving where they wish that the person about to cut them open was white. All these are anxieties over race-mingling, concerns about the collapse of racial borders. The misgivers want to live in a world where race is demarcated clearly and in conformity with the stereotypes thrown up to police that border, where black denotes the bag-carrying, eye-popping, banjo-playing, watermelon-guzzling, dancing fool. And where white too keeps to its first class, front-of-plane stay-pressed lane. This is the ontology of blackface. This is the meaning of Laurence Olivier's 1960's eye-rolling, blacked-up Othello. This is the cultural work done by *The Black & White Minstrel Show*. Some white people are still doing blackface. They just aren't troubling the shoe polish manufacturers anymore.

Insulation piss

Knocking-on, we were asked by a lady with candy floss hair and a Volvo Estate to go up into her loft and lay down rolls of insulation. We shinned up the ladder and started the job. We'd hardly started when she removed the ladder. We asked why and she said they were an obstruction to her landing, and we had to lay out the entre loft with the insulation rolls and only when we'd done it all would she set the ladders again so we could get down and we'd be paid and given biscuits. She handed up a Tupperware bowl and said if we got caught short, we could pee in that. We laid the insulation all afternoon in the sweltering loft, and she passed up drinks. When we were done, we pissed all over the loft insulation then called down to her. She was crafty and wanted to come up and inspect first and where was the bowl? We handed the empty bowl down to her, explaining we hadn't needed it. She set the ladders again, candy-flossed up and looked around. Yes, she said, you've done a good job. It looks sweet and it smells sweet too. We nodded and we had our money and biscuits and were gone.

Raid on the synagogue (by way of St Augustine)

Mum was an atheist, but us going to church was a break for her, so every Sunday we were ordered to the Scottish Presbyterian up the road. In the youth hut, they had us singing and hunting prizes hidden in places linked to the Gospels, but the games were the main thing and often involved sitting on chairs and sitting on people who were sitting on chairs. We learned to recite Bible verses at the hut too. And sing church songs. Our Sunday School youth leader was Mr Benham. He was Scottish and didn't thrust a collection plate at you, unlike in the big church hall. One Sunday, by special arrangement, he brought in a Former American Gang Member Now Serving the Lord, who impressed us with his *dang* American accent, his tales of renounced evil deeds and his being Saved by Jesus, Amen. On the way back home, we spoke to each other in American and broke into the synagogue grounds, forced the door of the tuck shop and grabbed crisps, sweets and pop. The two Irish boys of our church gang led the synagogue heist. Was this a reaction to societal racism? Was this a religious war? The synagogue tuckshop sweets were sweet, is all.

Fresh prophets

Sometimes Black people ride a stereotype – work it in their favour. We've all done it. We shouldn't but we are human. Galt was a young gifted poet and guitarist. He swore allegiance to the Rastafarian faith, was a great cook and gave me excellent advice when I started out as a kitchen assistant ("Cut your finger early on in the evening so they don't keep you all night on chopping-onion duty"). He was both rootsy and modern, and in normal times, he spoke in a combination of Northern English, Jamaican patois and Rastafarian wordsmithery. But each year, at the time when the local university freshers' month came round, Galt saw an opportunity to get laid day and night, and he transformed himself into full Hotep. He began carrying a Rasta staff, wore a full-length, white, priest robe, bejewelled turban headgear, and a sun-gold Ankh necklace. Prophetic lines dripped off his tongue. Freshers were beguiled and enthralled. I caught him in full Hotep drip one afternoon, queuing in a chicken shop with his latest, fresher admirer. He winked and shoo-ed me away. He didn't want me throwing shade on his shine.

Old youth worker tribute

I was knocking around a northern mill town at a loose end between two engagements when I saw a poster saying 'An Evening of Songs'. I bought a ticket and took a seat in the crumbling, concrete-block Arts Centre. The poster proved misleading because it turned out to be not a provincial choir, but a youth club's talent night and the hall filled with rowdy youth. I don't remember any of the acts, but I remember at the end of it all, a grey-locksed youth worker got up and said he'd waited a lifetime to sing these soul songs in front of an audience, it was on his bucket list, and he couldn't duck it no more because he was retiring soon and might never have an audience again. He then warbled some old soul hits. He wasn't bad – in need of an autotune here and there, but aren't we all? What amazed me was that the kids didn't mock him. They cheered unironically as he sang the old soul songs, 'Emily' and 'So You Win Again' to a karaoke backing track. To see a jumble of kids – Black, white, brown, Goths, Geeks and Drill-Stars alike – cheering for this man as he gave it his all was a wonder. I knew then he'd been a great youth worker, by which I mean just an average bloke, who'd encouraged them and been there for them, and they were giving him all that love back. I went up to him afterwards and said, well done, Errol Brown would have been proud.

A dream of writers

I got on the train tagged Writers with a ticket for the station called Aspiring but got off two stops late at a platform called Published and I was surrounded by all these actual writers. I didn't know what to do, so I wandered around the platform trying to act normal. Someone hails me. I guess it's a ticket inspector and I'm going to be frogmarched onto a train back to Starting-Out. The arm-waver is a Big Influencer and says they want to interview me about 'how to write'. My suppressed answer is 'I haven't a clue' but I chat some nonsense to the camera: 'Writing. It's about how you select and place the words.' The interview ends and I slip away quick-quick because proper writers are everywhere and I'm sure to get busted. I nod mutely at Jackie Kay as she gets into a conversation with someone tall standing next to me. Kit de Waal is skinning up in a corner. Lemn Sissay is regaling a crowd of prize-winning poets with a joke involving a bar and a bear. I share a lift up to another platform with Irenosen Okojie and Leone Ross. I go back down in the same lift with Monica Ali, Courttia Newland, SuAndi and Helen Oyeyemi. Benjamin Zephaniah is not dead and is doing selfies with Monica Ali and Anjum Malik and I accidentally photobomb them. In the station waiting room, Bernardine Evaristo places a spoon in her cup of tea and stirs it and I use the same spoon afterwards and we swap a knowing glance. I share a taxi with Sharmilla Beezmohun and Linton Kwesi Johnson. Linton is after a promoter called Prince Marley – something about an unpaid invoice to raas. Ben Okri roars past us on his motorbike and waves at us, well, at Linton and Sharmilla actually. I go home and get into bed with Ignatius Sancho.

National Poetry Society Prize acceptance speech: Speeches I prepared just in case, No. 2

Thank you, thank you. Bit of repetition there, but for a legitimate purpose. Sit down Linton Kwesi Johnson, not you this year. Rest up Roger Robinson, Patience Agbabi, Mona Arshi, Jackie Kay. Next time, next time, next time. Wow. These lights are bright, aren't they? Words are all we have. It has ever been thusly. I'd like to thank the Atlantic dolphins whose communion with me was the inspiration for these award-winning poems. And the turquoise ocean in which they sported – a poet must be at one with nature, especially in these green times. And I also thank Homer whose long autobiographical poem *The Iliad* had such a profound effect on me. And the late Derek Walcott whose advice to me in an elevator

– "Fuck off" – was freighted with allusive meaning. I so understood the direction he was pointing out to me as a poet – to investigate the hinterlands. Thank you so much, Derek, thank you. Words are the clay from which life itself is moulded. We poets wet our hands and shape lives, shape futures, shape language. And now in my hand is the winner's cheque – symbolic of course as the money is actually transferred by BACS, I understand. It's sad there can be only one winner, and I know many of you here are disappointed. Sometimes life is a kiss, sometimes it's a bite. But let's all not fight, tonight. Yes, rhyme, but appropriate. Consider this speech a little love bite to you all. Thank you, no, please, too much applause. Thank you.

Happy End

I was cast as the Japanese character, Dr Nakamura in the school play, *Happy End* by Bertolt Brecht, with songs by Kurt Weill. Did I look sufficiently Japanese? My complexion was a Manchester late Autumn brown – and so passably Japanese because my skin had lightened in the absence of sunshine. My hair, though, was peak Jackson 5. The drama teacher (who was also the play director, props manager, set designer, stage manager, lighting director...) said if I straightened my hair, I might look the part more. Enter a girl, stage right, with hot comb.

Chandice's hot comb was a hefty chunk of sizzling metal that plugged into the mains. Me and Chandice had a thing going on. I wanted to bang her, but she said church first, church being the contraceptive deployed by believers the world over and highly effective. She leapt at the chance to straighten my hair though. This I was suspicious of – her enthusiasm – hot combs being lethal weapons as well as a key tool of the 80's Black boudoir. Nevertheless, the idea of the svelte, stacked Chandice buzzing around me with a lethal hot weapon was too great for the teenage thrill-seeker in me to resist, and we agreed to meet at her house on Albemarle Street, Moss Side. I knock. Her mother ushers me into the front room where Chandice awaits with her tool and grease. Her mother makes a short announcement that she is now popping out but only to the corner shop and will be back very soon, very soon. Chandice conks my hair all evening.

Not a single singing lesson was had by any of us for that school play. Yet we sang our hearts out. And after the first evening – when the lighting failed and a dog ran onto the set – the show was judged a success and we were school-famous which is the greatest fame of all, signing our names on T-shirts in lunch breaks, dismissing Year 7 fangirls and boys with the lofty waft of a hand. On the last night, in my last performance, as I began that tearful song, 'Don't be afraid (Fürchte dich nicht)' one last time, I considered my circumstances. Here I was, a Danish-Nigerian-British youth with Caribbean hot-comb-straightened, shoulder-length hair, playing a Japanese man singing a song translated from German to English, surrounded by an out-of-tune chorus of glottal stop Wythenshawe council-house kids. We brought the house down. No photographs remain of our performances of this play.

Dracula

Our maths teacher, Dracula, was over six feet tall and, we decided, hated Black boys. We named him Dracula because he had prominent incisor teeth and a saturnine face. He was on our case from day one and never let up.

We fought back in the clumsy way kids do. He singled me out for some reason. Every week, in Lesson 4, Monday, else Lesson 1, Thursday, he stood over me, shouting. In the end, I cracked – sobbed uncontrollably as he ranted about my proofs being inadequate. I was eleven years old. The Head of Maths appeared at the doorway and hauled me out, him too. I spent the rest of that term in the Head of Maths' class instead of Dracula's. I loved maths. But the possibility of being taught again by Dracula meant it was never an option when it came to choosing 'A' Levels. I got my revenge by keying his car. He accused me, but I pointed out to the Head of Maths that his proof was inadequate. She agreed.

Superheroes: Episode 1

Every Saturday I flew to one of the local cinemas. The Scala. The Trocadero (aka the Flea Pit). The Paramount. I sank into the fading majesty of those places – working class opera houses in miniature – with rococo frontages, ornate stucco interior ceilings, plush red carpeting, sprung red velvet seats and velvet-liveried ushers. Even the men who tried to grope you if you sat on the back row wore black ties and clean white shirts. It was in these grandiose, crumbling, faded Empire settings that I met my first celluloid superheroes. I was seven years old. I was no longer the shy boy with the scabby knees, holed shoes and tangled Afro. I was Superman! Spiderman! Batman!

The Pearl and Dean cinema advertising soundtrack – *Pah-pa Pah-pa Pah-pa Pah-Pah-Pah!* – accompanied by its spinning time-warp tunnel on the screen meant our superheroes were in the wings, warming up, the projectors were being loaded, the safety curtain was about to fly. Show time!

We were ready, sweating because it was mid-Summer, with radioactively glowing orange juice from the Kia-Ora drink, teeth-gluing popcorn, tiny tubs of ice-cream and as many bags of sweets as we'd managed to sneak in. The show started. We sank into the seats, eyes glued to the screen, ears drinking in the phrases dreamed up by the scriptwriters in place of swear words. *Holy Whiskers, Batman! Holy Long John Silver! Ker-Pow! Holy Understatement! Holy Ravioli!*

Enrapt. Agog. Enthralled. Breathless. We left the Scala groggy with Technicolor stimulation. One day, we tumbled outside only to see a boy chase into the road and get run over by a car. A man in the crowd burst forward and lifted the car up with his bare hands and the boy was dragged from under the wheels. The boy dusted himself down and hobbled off. The car-lifting man dusted himself down and disappeared. In that moment I knew superheroes lived not only on the Scala silver screen but among us.

Beautiful feet

I have beautiful feet, I have been told, repeatedly. I thank my mother and the Clarks shoe company for this. Recently, she said to me, when I die, with your inheritance money, buy yourself a fancy suit. I asked why. She said because you used to be so upset when I couldn't afford to buy you football boots. I have no memory of this, I tell her. I do, she replied, and I felt bad about it, so buy everything you ever wanted – everything I couldn't get you then, get yourself now. But you gave us everything, I think, but don't say, because you gave us love. Later, I imagine myself in pink and purple check corduroy trousers, gold velvet jacket and two-tone Dr Martens, styling it out like a Congolese dandy.

Mantlepiece pissing

I am told by one of my sisters how, aged three, I peed spectacularly while standing on the living room mantelpiece. Although I accept this as a considerable achievement, my mind turns to other acts of mine which might rank up there with my mantelpiece pissing:

I was doing 70mph in the outside lane of the Manchester M60 in my friend's People Carrier, having dropped him and his family off at the airport, when I hit the brake pedal and... nothing. No brakes. In that moment, I remembered a YouTube video about this situation. It told of how someone had used the handbrake instead and survived. Muttering encouragement to the piece of shit's hand brake, I pulled on it gently. It worked: I lost speed and didn't skid. I managed to get the piece of cheap shit into the inside lane, and from there onto a slip road. By now, it had decelerated to about 60mph. I dodged slip road traffic, sailed through the mercifully empty end-of-slip-road roundabout (God was smiling down on me) and swerved first left onto a town road. With a last burn of hand-brake lining, I pulled the piece of shit over. Thank you, YouTube.

As glass collector at the Shoulder of Mutton pub in Leeds, it was my duty to collect empty pint glasses, including those of the largest man in the pub, a Sikh with the heft of mountain-dwelling Punjabis. We glass collectors are paid to nip in and deftly grab empty vessels so that social embarrassment forces the now glass-less customer to buy another pint. Our skill set is very similar to that of pickpockets. The Sikh watched me approach from his corner banquette seat. He stiffened as my hand reached out. I gave him the Black nod quickly. Ritual forced him to nod back, and, in that beat, I had his empty glass.

I had some nice vibes going with Carrie, a Hong-Konger I'd met at a wild party in Kowloon when the end of the earth was being predicted by all, seeing as Japan's Fukushima nuclear power station had started melting down. We clubbed, got high, and I wrote her a poem. Then, after shaking off her bodyguard, we'd gone back to her apartment, a *pied-a-terre* in the middle of the maze of central Hong Kong buildings (her family home was in mainland China). She told me we could fuck, but I had to have a condom. No problem. Still high, in a feat my geography teacher Mr Novak would have applauded, I whizzed into the Hong Kong maze at silly a.m., navigated to an all-night pharmacy, bought condoms with a straight face and the correct currency, found my way back through the metropolitan maze to her apartment, remembered the flat number, hit her bell and got buzzed up. I was thinking that if Japan did blow up and take Hong Kong with it in a radiation storm, this was going to be as good a way to go as existed on this earth. At this point in the story, I draw the curtains.

Black fame, nervous conditions

Fame is precarious for Black people. White society only tolerates a Black person's rise upwards to acclaim; there are forceful terms and conditions. Black people who enter the rarefied air of fame understandably seek to stabilise their situation – to do what they can to ensure their giddy rise will not be followed by a vertiginous fall. One standard method is assimilation. This requires great effort on the famous Black person's part – in mimicry, and in acquiring powerful white friends who can vouch for their suitability as entrants into elite (read white) society. It may also require the acquisition of hallmarks of acceptability – a demonstration for white people by the famous Black person that they are willing to publicly commit to the project of whiteness, that they are white in all but skin. Such hallmarks may include taking up residence in a white area, sending their children to white (ideally Establishment) schools, vocally supporting an anti-immigrant party, accepting an Empire Medal (MBE, OBE, CBE, etc), and, most commonly, cultivating white cultural capital – a set of tastes in music and art as well as a set of postures, etiquette, mannerisms and professional affiliations – which authenticates their permit of entry into the circle of whiteness. Yet for all these efforts, the status of the famous Black person is still precarious. Challenges lurk around every racialised corner. One misstep holds the danger of descent, of a tumble back into Blackness. This is their 'nervous condition' – as traced by Sartre, Fanon and Dangarembga.

Porn delivery drivers

There is nothing more anxiety-inducing for a Black man than to watch white people porn – porn made by and for white people. The Black man features in this only as a stud with a huge dick who arrives to bang the white woman. The other category where Black men feature (and the results of this research were obtained by meticulous, cold-groin attention to detail while trawling through the UK's most popular brand of porn channel) is the delivery driver sub-genre. In this, the delivery driver turns up, knocks on the door with a pizza or parcel and gets dragged in to be fucked by (or to fuck) a towel-dropping white female who cannot pay for the goods by Apple Pay, Contactless, Cash, or any other standard way. This category of porn is almost certainly sponsored by delivery companies because never in delivery driver porn does the delivery driver sling your parcel in the hedge, or in the grey bin, or slide a 'you were out when we called' note through your door or drop off the goods at the wrong house. Moreover, all porn delivery drivers arrive on time and are able to dawdle for 5 minutes (or 30 minutes if you subscribe to Premium), and they even come repeatedly in the films. Delivery companies are clearly sponsoring delivery driver porn.

At Zippo's Circus: Miss Lala considers love and death

Love is a trapeze act – something best undertaken with loose limbs, dry hands and clear eyes. The upswing is great. The downswing is merely that necessary interval before the next upswing, the return clasp and the surge into the heavens. Sometimes you're so in the clouds with your flight into the canopy of love that you throw in a somersault, trusting your trapeze act partner to get the beats right, to know when to be in that exact sweet spot where they can reach out and clasp your wrists without any loss of momentum. Occasionally, the two of you get out of synch. Those powdered dry hands are not there to catch you. Do you fall? Does love suspend gravity? Is love particles or waves? Do we sink, or do we float in those moments?

Life is a trapeze act. We are all Miss La La (aka circus artiste, Anna Olga Albertina Brown), biting down on the suspended leather mouthpiece, hanging on in our tasselled, silk knickerbockers as the rope of life spins and hauls us up into the rarefied air of the Big Top ceiling. The rope loops us round and round and round... until the spinning stops. Then we cling to life by our clenched jaw and gaze down at the scenery. Or up to God. The trapeze rope becomes a hospital drip. Slowly the oxygen tank empties, the drip bag drains. The bleeps end. The jaw unclenches.

Dire Straits

Friends are those who still show up when you've got nothing and you're on your last legs. Bailiffs, speculating undertakers and gawpers will also show up in this situation and the difficulty is distinguishing which is which. When you knock on the door of some indigent friends, they don't answer straight away. They wait till you walk off because only then can they check you out – when your back's turned. They don't answer from the get-go because if you're the wrong knocker, say the bailiff or debt collectors, well, that's awkward. I'm used to knocking, then walking away. I turn as I reach the gate, and lo, the friend's upstairs window swings open and, 'Pete? I'll be right down!'

Quicksanding – a white, upper management technique

Quicksanding is a key section of the white, upper management rulebook. Promote the Black person when you've messed up bad and things are about to fuck up big style – get them in that quicksand fast. The Black person can take the rap for the fuckup when it duly happens, and whiteness can resume control afterwards, blaming the sacked Black person for what they – the white folk – fucked up. There'll be little resistance. Racialisation means everyone will be easy with upper management's 'the Black manager fucked up' explanation.

Clowns and the Theatre of Cruelty

The twenty-first century has seen a preference in Western politics for lauding opinion over fact, for throwing jacks over studying facts, for loving the walk and ignoring the destination. This is a stage set for demagogues. They appear first as sideshow clowns and they entertain bored and disgruntled citizens, throw bread which is eaten up to laughter and hallelujahs. Introduce spectacle. Revive the Human Zoo. It's a riot of a circus. Terrorising the weak is so much fun! Let's do this again. Quickly, these clowns become the main act, get to sit in the circus master's chair and crack the whip. Their reign transmogrifies from bread, circuses and zoos, into Theatres of Cruelty. Beware clowns. If we all end up behind barbed wire, we will have laughed ourselves there.

Guitar dreams 2: things that never happened

In Beginner Guitar Class, we strummed of love-sick white boys with white-boy problems, of empty big brass beds and green corn fields. The women in the songs were damsels and forlorn maidens. It was all very white. I kept strumming, but my mind wandered. It is still wandering. There was a Sikh guy running a guitar shop in Central Manchester at the time. I wonder about the Indian rhythms he might have brought to that teenage evening guitar classroom. And what if Tracy Chapman had ambled by, guitar on her back, and got us all 'Talking About a Revolution'. What if Bob Marley, having landed in Manchester for his Apollo gig, had taken the class and taught us 'Three Little Birds'? These things never happened: yellow was always the colour of my true love's hair.

First sex with another person

At sixteen, I got myself a foil-wrapped condom. It lived in the inside pocket of my glossy black, Grand Prix Racing coat. When I finally had a chance to use the thing, it was past its sell-by date. Sex proved trickier than expected. Like two spaceships docking in zero gravity. Finally, a seal was made. I looked up at her face, expecting to see the wide-eyed, thankful gaze that porn mag stars had. Instead, she was frowning slightly. *Is it in yet?* she asked. I nodded by way of an answer. Afterwards, we kissed, and I walked home, happy and sad. This feeling has hung around with me ever since about most things to do with sex.

I get more and more uncertain if this story about my first sex is true. When I tell the story to mates, sometimes she's smiling, sometimes she's puzzled, sometimes she's frowning, but whichever it is, afterwards, we always kiss. I guess it's the story of two virgins (or at least one), writhing in the dark.

Lean-them-up Jimmy

After we fled the police raid on the pub because we were under-age, we were at the bus stop when Jimmy began fingering his girl. I was embarrassed. It was the middle of the night and dark and all that, but nevertheless, what was I supposed to do? I watched, intrigued. They didn't seem to mind me watching. Jimmy told me later, you have to lean them up against a wall, to take the weight off their feet when you do it.

Anthony who saved us

We were unemployed and nobody loved us. We gathered in Anthony's above-the-shop flat and flopped onto his floor like wet dogs in from the rain. Soon, everything that could be smoked had been. Anthony reached behind the sofa and brought out his guitar. As he started tuning it, a sigh was heard from under a blanket. Anthony only ever sang bleak songs. Joan Armatrading. Tracy Chapman. Nina Simone. Yet his keening voice and the jangle of his strings eased something. Out there in the rain was Thatcher's world of finger-pointing, coal mine pickets and police. In Anthony's flat, as strings began jangling and his voice started on its beguiling drone, we sank into a revolutionary space – where we had dignity, where kindness reigned; our black and brown and white faces were oiled by Anthony's musical balm. If we got lucky, Anthony might even cook, because his skills were many-fold and he could conjure up a stew from old vegetables that was always flavoursome. Then we would eat while Anthony set the world to rights, quickly becoming England's next prime minister. Anthony was our hero and our saviour. And until his bitter fall-out with Lebanese Sidney over a garage-based painting-and-decorating service that proved unprofitable, his flat was our sanctuary.

Working for the man

To work for the man is to let a dog chew your bones and suck your marrow. Day by day, you feel the gnawing, sense the core of your life being sucked away. Yet, what to do – kick the dog? You need the money. You must decide on the size of the plate of misery you are suited to. Some dine big on the misery of work and spend the rest of their lives alternately eating and barfing it up. Their eyes become saucers of pain, and they sup their misery soup with a fork to make the experience more fully unpleasant. Some refuse to dine at all at misery's table. Instead, they waste away, partying on thin air until they crash. This group dies young with a beautiful corpse, a heroic biography and an empty work cv. Most of us are Goldilocks. We find the middle plate. We suck the work thing up for as long as we can. When we hit our limit, we retch, rebel, go rabid mad for a while before eventually coming back to heel, going back to working for the man.

Pounding yam

When we are coupling, a friend told me coyly over green tea, my partner likes to ride cowgirl style, that's what makes them come, whereas I only reach climax from doggy. And because we are basically inconsiderate lovers, once one of us reaches orgasm, the other can't be bothered switching round and being pounded till the other gets off. How do we fix this? My friend, I said, this is none of my business. I am going to pound yam. I spent the rest of the day pounding yam with my shoulder and arms, but with my mind I swivel my friend's and his partner's tangled body parts like a demonic Rubik's Cube. Why people come to me with these luxurious problems, I don't understand. They should be happy they are knacking at all.

Stokely Carmichael*

Stokely was our fifth black cat, and she was cool as hell – every morning she sauntered into the rose bushes of our racist neighbour's garden and took a shit there. In the late evening, she would sit on the fence and caterwaul at those honky people and their snow-white dog that they loved to set on us. The neighbours threw buckets of water at Stokely. Curses. Pelted her with stones. Stokely dodged everything and slinked off, as impervious and immortal as a pharaoh. When she was killed by a car on the main road, she was buried with full ceremonies in our front garden. One summer afternoon, the American Stokely had appeared on our snow-globe television. Both me and the cat Stokely sat and watched, rapt, as Carmichael took to the mic and threw off his jacket. He said, 'Black Power!' and 'We aint going nowhere!' to an audience of loving Black people who were all shiny-faced, chins high, lips firm, hair pricked, who were clapping him to the rafters. He wasn't done. He told on: 'Not one of those reporters here in this room is Black and they calling me the racist!' Stokely sticking it to the white man! We loved it. Telling it straight to that fine fine Black audience. 'The world belongs to you!' 'No more unpunished murders!' 'Be proud of your Black brothers and sisters rebelling!' Watching Stokely Carmichael, the white-shirted, shiny-faced truth-sayer, I felt pride growing in every cell of my being. 'Black Power!' I shouted, marching around the room, with Cat Stokely following. 'Black power!' 'We aint going nowhere!' Me and Stokely strutted the streets extra cool that week.

I came across Stokely Carmichael again in my twenties, as part of my All-African People's Revolutionary Party induction. I absorbed his name change to Kwame Ture. I was in awe of the constancy of his purpose. The unpunished murders continue.

⋆This item was sponsored by my cat, Missy, who considers dogs over-represented in Act Normal.

Ten Black nods

The tilt, with sustained upstroke. Have you noted this shit going down?

The tilt with sustained sideways downstroke. Yes, we have a situation. No, we don't move on it, not now, not yet.

The Black woman nod to Black man, responding to the Black man nod to Black woman. Yes, we both Black. No, you have no chance of dating me.

The waiting room nod. Yes, we are in a strange white environment but no, we are not going to have a meaningful conversation about this, let's just get our teeth fixed.

The party nod. I recognise your swagger and acknowledge its effectiveness in this situation and so will be deferring to you on what response we make should any white folk here pull racist moves.

The eye-blink nod. We going for a smooth and laid-back approach to this current difficulty. We don't going give them the energy of a reaction, we just keep rolling smooth, nuh?

The long nod. Get ready, this is going to kick off big, and I expect you to have my back.

The nod plus eyebrow raise. There are drunken liberal white people in the vicinity. Expect hugs, bad dance moves and expressions of love for Black music.

The nod followed by single, slow shake. This is a hairy situation, with aggravated, addled white folk, unless you have a stab vest, back away now. I'll take the heat.

The nod plus bland smile. I am unsure if you are Black-identifying, but if you are, hello sister/brother/they/other.

Carol singing and the expulsion of Michael

Miming was OK in, say, a six or even a five, but when you were a three, mime can't work and your voice breaking is just one of those things; you got to move on, we told Michael, but Michael resisted. I mean, Michael was a good mimer, and his face was still choir-boy cute and white as bakery dough, no pimples whatsoever, but he'd got tall, which made them look at him more and notice the no-sound thing. The no-sound thing wasn't good for business and the breaking voice thing was even worse because they laughed, and they didn't give us money when they laughed, they just closed the door, laughing, so Michael was out, nothing personal, just business. He wanted half the night's takings to see him through until he found something else. We said we'd give him a third like usual, which was generous because he'd been gold-fishing all evening. Then the fight, but we had the better of him and he sulked off, his jumper bloodied, his face smeared, and empty-handed. The rest of the night it was just the two of us knocking the doors, and we even did some harmonies. We did OK.

Tilt

I showed my new friend the magnet and pin method of robbing the Prestatyn boardwalk cascade machines. The arcade had anti-tilt alarms though, and patrols, and the cashier was the owner's daughter, so she didn't just do her job and change money, she had eyes, and you had to watch for her in her wonky plastic sentry box enclosure. Occasionally, she'd walkie-talkie the patrol about us, though on the days when her boyfriend dropped by, you could rob the machines blind and did she care? She only had eyes for him.

Pushing cars

During long hot summers, we sat on street corners and waited for cars to break down. The crestfallen driver would slide out of their car and look around, seeking help. No adults had time for that. The breakdown service, these ends, was us kids. Once they paid over to us some decent money, we'd give them a bottle of water for their radiator. If that didn't work, we'd plant hands on the boot of the car, bend knees and start heaving. 'Push! Push!!' the owner would urge from the driver's door where he was pushing and steering at the same time. When the car reached some critical speed, the driver jumped in and whacked a pedal down. The car would then either buck and splutter before roaring to life and shooting off, else buck then *phut* and stutter to a halt again. Sometimes, we'd be two hundred yards down the road before the engine fired to life. Other times, we'd just give up. 'Nah, it's dead, you need a new battery,' we'd say, then run off, keeping the money.

Blue lips

He used to watch me as I weeded the pink rose beds of the rich man's Edwardian garden for pocket money. Sometimes, I imagined the boy was smirking, though I had no clue why, maybe my clothes. He was the son of the people living in the mansion next door, I guessed. His teeth were in braces, and he did circuits of his garden on his Chopper bike. He looked lonely. Eventually, I went to the fence, just talking to him and, after I'd finished pushing in bamboo sticks for the runner beans to climb, I jumped over and we played together on his bike, eventually rolling around on his striped back lawn where I got him in a neck hold good and strangled him till his face started to go purple, his lips filling with a remarkable fountain-pen blue. I felt the same thrill I got from climbing trees. When he stopped gasping, I got off him and let him up, and we spun around on his bike some more. Next Saturday, he was watching me again.

Car crash

He'd taken the corner way too early, aiming for the private flats road and hit a boundary wall instead. We heard the bang and went there. It was a Triumph TR6, in beautiful chrome and racing red. The Triumph's front-end was crumpled like tissue paper. His mouth was open, and his blood filled it and spilled out, dripping from the driver's side doorsill onto the pavement. He didn't look alive. We ran for the thin vicar – the C. of E. one who lived in the avenue after ours not the Evangelical one who never answered his door anyway, because the thin vicar had a phone to call an ambulance. The thin vicar's door swung back, and he was unhurried and said be not afraid, death awaits us all. He went along his red Axminster hallway strip of carpet to the black metal-and-glass stand that held his black phone and kept an eye on us as he turned its face to dial. We left him dialling and dashed back. The driver's mouth was still open. Someone had had his jacket, and his shirt was all red and the blood was now pooled under the whole of the car and more. So much blood from one body. He'd run up the red carpet to his Lord who was waiting. I stared death in the mouth.

Superheroes: episode 2

One weekend, Marvel Comics burst onto the news racks. The Incredible Hulk! Fantastic Four! Spider Man! The X Men! I couldn't afford them new, so I got them second-hand. School-friends pitied me as the sad boy who was reading last week's comic and so didn't yet know if The Hulk crashed through that burning building and pulled out the Naïve Scientist who'd made a World Saving Discovery or not. I was late: in the way that light from the distant parts of our Milky Way can take thousands of years to reach us on earth, so the comic I was reading was ancient stuff to them, and they were dead to its thrills.

I didn't mind. Comics took me away from family dramas: my sister failing to return at night after a shift as a Bunny Girl at the Playboy Club; my Import-Export mad dad fretting over what to do with four thousand pairs of European-sized ladies underwear that had proved useless to prospective buyers in Nigeria owing to 'the generosity of Nigerian women's bottoms compared with those of the English' (his words); my brother's years' long auditioning for a part in some Juvenile Delinquent B movie involving off-road motorbikes that was private-screening in his head. I cast aside all this 3D melodrama for a 2D comic Spiderman flinging himself across Gotham's skyscrapers in pursuit of the villainous, pasty-faced jewel thief. Or the telepathic mutant X Men and their battle with the evil Magento. Or Superman battling villains who had taken over a spaghetti factory and were plotting to drown New York City (and therefore the Entire Civilized World) in spaghetti so they could rob New York's Central Bank of all its gold. Oh, Superman!

Heavenly choir

I was staying over at Malcolm's for a weekend. We were bored. We sat with the stonemason who was chiselling dead people's names into Italian marble and smoked a cigarette with him. Later, we shared a bath and next morning we decided to gob on the adults' heads from the choir balcony. They all wore hats at Catholic Church so it would merely be target practice and the rest of the balcony choir wouldn't snitch, Malcolm said. The organ began, and we opened our throats. I mostly gold-fished except the chorus parts because I didn't know the songs. The thurifer smoke only reached us by the end of the service which was a disappointment, and we were out fast because Malcolm warned me if his mum caught us before we got past those big church doors, we'd be doing a thousand hellos and God bless yous before we were allowed to leave.

Imaginary grandparents 2

No matter how much you walk towards a horizon, it always recedes. My grandpa was in typical reflective mood as he tied my shoelaces before school one Manchester morning. I understood the words *horizon* and *recedes* because I was about twelve at the time. Grandpa had begun tying my shoelaces when I started kindergarten and insisted all the way until I left for college. He hummed as he tied them, occasionally dropping in these sayings. Over the years, I watched his hands become more fumbly and skeletal, but he never failed to tie a good knot. And he always hummed. When he was dying, he made himself useful again. He got the nurse to bring forms to donate his body to science, signed them, then died that same evening. I've killed a few people since and watched others die and I never saw anyone die as neatly as grandpa did. Whenever I hear humming, I think of him.

Two barrels

Racism has many guns. Some are single-barrelled, some double. At high school, the darker-skinned pupils got the double barrels. In response, some Black kids became expert at mimicry – dancing white, lauding famous white cricketers and actors, sighing white sighs. This worked. The mimics were often adopted by teachers as class representative, holders of doors for guests, those Teacher's Pet kind of things. They scored better in tests and their parents' evenings did not end in tears. I was tempted to join them but lacked the stamina to mimic for more than a day or two and then it was back to detention and sit-where-I-can-see-you. It's been the same in adult life. There are situations where I know a cute reference to some aspect of white culture would put the white people at ease and I ought to make that reference, but I've lacked the energy to be cute. It has been easier for me, though, as I am, by shade, light brown-skinned in all seasons except summer. I've never faced two barrels.

Myself in a baronial 19C incarnation

I enter Marmaduke's room, smiling. He looks up, irritated: 'Why are you smiling – what do you want, you bastard?' I understand from this greeting that Marmaduke has recovered from his recent illness and is returned to his usual rude self. At this thought, my smile broadens. This makes Marmaduke even more wary. 'If you want paying back, you'll have to wait. I continue to be rather financially inconvenienced.'

'Your debt is waived,' I say. 'Worry no more about it.'

Finally, he joins me in smiling.

Whitesplaining the N. word.

'That must have been tough, right, like, when he used the N. word on you?'

'…Yeh, well…'

'But you know what? The way you should have answered is…'

And off they go. I half-listen to their whitesplaining.

Love, the cruellest idea

Love is the cruellest idea God ever came up with. Above flood, famine, disease and mortgages, love is God's *pièce de résistance* in the misery stakes. Walk a quarter kilometre in any direction, you will meet someone whose life has been wrecked by falling in love. Nobody understands misery better than the person in love.

Sakina & one hundred kisses

I'd gone to *mwah* you, but you'd turned your head slightly, so my lips planted on your cheek instead of in the air around your cheek, and we'd laughed and held the hug a second longer than convention. We talked and swapped numbers and in the Thai restaurant next evening, you said to me, 'You have hungry lips.' After the kiss at the restaurant door, you dabbed stray lip gloss from my lower lip, its dark berry colour making a flower shape on the tissue. 'Next time, a hundred kisses,' you said. You confirmed your name was Sakina to the taxi driver, and you were gone. We didn't meet for a few weeks.

We went ten pin bowling and ended up in your apartment. You had high ceilings, marble floors and Italian sculptures. I never knew clothing buyers made so much money! This time, for the first time, we kissed slowly and without clothes. Your shoulders alone I must have kissed thirty times. You were busy then, at a series of trade conventions. I landed a job at the local museum and wore my lanyard with pride. I took to eating lunch next to a Bengal tiger.

Glasgow was our first trip together. You sang endlessly in the passenger seat as we sailed up the M74. On a whim, we kept going – past Glasgow, up to Stirling Castle – and wandered among medieval tapestries and baronial fireplaces. You put a fist in your mouth to stop a scream when you saw the restored, panelled ceiling of the Great Hall, how beautiful it was. I tugged you behind a purple velvet curtain, where we kissed like knights, leaning against a stained-glass window. I imagined Sirs wishing each other good tidings before battle.

It became harder to meet you. This was the way of relationships, I consoled myself, they have to come down from the heavens, bills have to be paid. Finally, you're free and you'll meet me at the airport. We kiss briefly in the departures lounge, and I didn't know it at the time, but this would be our last kiss. You tell me Belgium is more than work, and you met someone and you're going to live with him in Belgium. 'But where are your bags?' I ask irrelevantly, my throat catching. You press my hands once more, then you need to go through Security.

I walk away, wondering. Many times, I've thought about you, Sakina. I had a hundred more kisses ready for you.

Acoustic Blackness

The Windrush generation's talking-to-official-white-people phone voice was a phenomenal mimicry of white BBC Pathé newsreader speech, mixed with poshboy GP bedside manner, and the occasional leakage of Patwah and Gospel. While being abundantly clear to the interlocutor that this was a Black voice, the sheer chutzpah of its performance usually got results. All hail the Windrush generation's phone voice proNunciAtions.

While we are here, Amen too to the minimum-wage, Black female backing singers wrapping warmth round the cold-white-male voice of the pop stars.

And let us hear it for Black men who keep their pitch up – holding off the bass in their voice in white workplaces in order to suggest amiability and non-threat and so counteract the stereotype of the dangerous Black male.

Now let us testify also for the Black women who go the other way and lower their pitch in white workplaces, speaking in. a. way. that. suggests. calm. and. ease… to diffuse the stereotype of the aggressive Black female.

And let us spare a thought for those of Black complexion who are not Londoners and who open their mouths to vocalise only to hear, 'You don't sound Black' and face that fork in the road of either explaining or getting on with what they were trying to say.

And lastly, may God bless fulsomely the code-switching throat gymnastics of those with intersectional identities who can translanguage at the drop of a hat and don't ever lose not one part of their flow, while doing so. God bless you all. Can I get an Amen?

Lucy, with a gun and diamonds

Lucy was crying in the passenger seat of my car about her boyfriend who had a gun in his bedside cabinet – which would be fine and maybe normal in America, but this was a regional city of England. We were not alone in the car, I indicated. Lucy gave lil dawta in the back seat a diamond smile and clapped when lil dawta responded by plucking a tune for her on her ukelele. The tune finished. For a second there was ⋆ silence ⋆. Then a sob as Lucy went back to crying and explaining the chaos of her life.

Dating when you have a small daughter

1

We're talking on Zoom, and lil dawta wanders into view. 'Who's that?' Tanja exclaims. 'My daughter.' 'What's her name? Put her on, put her on!' I do. Lil dawta gets chatting to Tanja. Half an hour later, they're still talking. I hint to dawta that she can chip now, return to playing hopscotch or whatever, but lil dawta's having too much fun; she and Tanja are laughing away. I leave them to it. Next day, when Tanja comes online, she straightaway asks, 'Put your daughter on, is she awake?!' I start thinking, Umm, maybe lil dawta needs to go back to her mum soon.

2

It's a Saturday afternoon in Manchester and I'm strolling in Platt Fields Park with Karine and lil dawta. Me and Karine have been getting close. She has roots in Haiti and I'm daydreaming we just need a couple more in-depth conversations about the revolutionary Haitian fighter, Toussaint L'Ouverture, then maybe we could go jogging in the evening and get all sweaty, and after that we'd hit the shower together and it might happen. Karine, however, is getting on like a house on fire with lil dawta. Lil dawta is saying, 'Let's go to the fair and get popcorn and candy floss!' 'Great idea!' replies Karine. She turns to me. 'Can we do that? I want to spend more time with your daughter, she's so much fun.' 'Sure,' I say, 'let's do that.'

3

I'm with Naz in a cafe. She says she's never ridden a bike. 'You mean, like, you've never learned?' 'Nope.' 'I'll teach you.' 'Yes, we'll teach you!' chimes lil dawta, demolishing her soft-boiled egg with a soldier. We arrive at Heaton Park, full of gentle grass slopes. Lil dawta joins in with the instructions and the pushing. Naz does well. After the lesson is over, she says, 'She's so good your daughter, she's thoughtful, a good teacher…' 'Yes,' I say, 'she gets it off me.' Naz smiles.

HMP Manchester

Prisons are crammed with storytellers. It is the hardest proving ground for anyone calling themselves a professional storyteller. All prisoners do is tell stories all day. I'm in the Strangeways chapel building – where the HMP Manchester riot started. Lifers are on chairs around me, muscled, attentive. The prison guard has exited and locked the door. 'So, you're a storyteller. Go on then, tell us a story,' they say. I understand them. I've hired bricklayers who can't lay a brick. 'Go on then, lay a brick then,' I've said. They are expecting something operatic, a black Brian Blessed. 'I'm not going to do the voices and that,' I tell them, to kill that expectation fast. 'You won't notice I'm telling you a story.' 'What do you mean?' 'I mean that stuff happens to me, like on Oldham Street three weeks ago and I'll tell you about it in this voice, my normal voice, like I'm talking to you now.' 'What are you on about? Just tell the story.' 'I am.' 'You're telling the story?' 'Yes, I was on Oldham Street a couple of weeks ago.' 'And?' And so the story starts. I carry on with no change of tenor, no flamboyance of voice, no change of body language. They sink into it and listen, rapt. At the end, when the twist happens, they burst out laughing: 'Na, na, not having that! Do another one!'

Smartarse

We did so much stuff about triangles in Mr Sporrock's class during the last year of primary school, we could have given the Ancient Egyptians a run for their money. Enough was enough. After three weeks of measuring Isosceles, Equilaterals and Scalenes, I refused to go outside to measure the sides of an equilateral with a tape measure and chalk and stuff. The formula was good, so there was no need, I argued. The teacher said OK, you stay here and keep measuring using only the formula. And I did. I sat alone in the classroom. With an occasional gaze out of the window at my classmates in the playground with tape measures. They were running around doing everything except measuring triangles. One looked up and gave me the middle finger: Who's the smartarse now?

Infatuation: a love story in five episodes

I meet Jada at a poetry evening. She says she's vegetarian. Somehow, I've already guessed because she looks so healthy – the brightness of her eyes, the way her skin glows. I swerve the chicken tikka option at *My Lahore* and buy us spinach fatayer. Later, in the park, she shows me her judo routines. This segues into a playfight, and soon we're wrestling. She's a good wrestler. Her body smell enthrals me. It's not flowery, more like a spice. I've never known a woman with this smell before. At my flat, as I'm sorting cutlery, Jada asks me, what am I thinking? Umm. What I'm thinking is, God must have understood all the heartache of my last break-up, and thought, here you go, kid, you was a bit hard done by there (God's a Mancunian), here's how I'm making up for it. I tell her, 'Nothing much.'

Jada sleeps overnight in my flat, but not in my bed up on the mezzanine level. Instead, she takes the sofa. And she has banned goodnight kisses, saying we can't rush things. Everything must be correct timing, like in judo. Next morning, she leaves early for her train.

Jada calls. She's back in town – a business meeting in the city centre, let's meet up after. We walk along the high street, hand in hand, and stop in a mini park to bask in the early sun. She rests her head on my shoulder and my left arm wraps around her. I breathe in the cinnamon-y scent of her scalp. Maybe we will have children together. She hops on a bus for her meeting.

Jada's meeting is over. I should meet her outside Selfridges, help her carry some of her shopping – she lives in the countryside, and must shop big when she comes to the city. She skips towards me, a hug. She's soaring with optimism about her job, her career, her finances, her approaching judo grading. She gifts me a silver bracelet. Just something she liked and thought it would suit me. I thank her and she blushes, looks away. We shop. She's running late for her train and we scramble for platform fourteen. On the platform, as the train pulls in, she allows a lip kiss. She surprises me with the kiss – delivers a tiny bit of tongue too.

The carriage doors clatter shut, a whistle blows and the train slides away. She looks directly at me through the train glass and smiles. She texts five minutes later. 'The hurried departure was romantic; to kiss then felt right.'

Another text. I won't see her for two months; there is a job offer involved. I think, is this God's cruel joke? At night, I'm restless with scrambled thoughts: lovers sigh because they are never satisfied, they want more; not seeing each other is painful, yet seeing each other is also painful, because the pleasure is intense, and you know it will be over too quickly and then you will inevitably part and be thrust back into an agonising life as separate bodies. Still sleepless, I try to conjure up some sense by playing my inner juke box of philosophical and theological wisdom:

Buddha: attachment is suffering: I'm crazy about her, that's why I'm suffering. I must detach if I want to end my suffering.

Bishop Berkeley: Nothing exists but what our consciousness creates. So, Jada is my own creation; why have I created someone who punishes me like this? Am I punishing myself – do I deliberately create the tantalisingly unavailable because it suits me to have an unavailable girlfriend?

Karma theory: Joy and pain are related and in universal equilibrium; someone somewhere in the world is deeply happy, seeing as she has made me utterly miserable.

The utilitarians: the greatest happiness for the greatest

number is the goal; in which case, if Jada's happiness outweighs my misery, is there not a moral imperative for us to carry on?

The Existentialists: In the face of the absurdity of life and the certainty of defeat, death, and God's complete and utter silence, we should continue nevertheless to keep on, even against all the evidence, or at least to act with nobility in the face of the desolate facts. In short, I should carry on loving Jada even though without any hope.

The Old Testament: You are here to suffer, you insignificant vessel of sin, stop whingeing!

New Testament: You heard the guy in the Old Testament, didn't you? Enough already! Try nails through your palms, that's proper suffering, unlike wanting another kiss with tongues. Stop flouncing around like some lovesick lesser god.

The Koran: Allah is The Merciful, but only to the true believers; non-believers can go rot.

The Nigerian Charismatics: Give us your money, then take out a loan and give us that loan money too, then we will sort your love problem out.

I fall asleep, grinding my teeth as various monks, angels, sadhus and relationship therapists chant over my tortured body.

Nine ways Black people cross public space

Tippety-toe. Lips sucked back. I know I am an anomaly and please pardon my transgression in passing through your beautiful white space. I am minimising my footprints to reduce as much as possible the dirt trail I leave behind me as I move. See? That wasn't too hard, was it? I'm through now and gone.

Invisibility cloak. If I think like a white person, act like

110

a white person and stay in character throughout, I can traverse this space as a completely plausible, actual white person, so help me God.

Victorian Promenading. Some streets (such as Liverpool's Bold Street) are Black information superhighways which paradoxically can only be walked at a snail's pace because, as you walk, you bump into other Black people you have not seen for ages and start talking and one thing leads to another. It is similar to the Victorian promenade tradition where young unmarried women would walk in coastal towns in all their finery and see what notes were slipped into their clothes by would-be suitors – except that the Black promenaders who are into this pickup aspect of the stroll, swap Snapchat, Instagram or other @'s and arrange their hookups that way.

Behold My Greatness. There comes a time in every poor person's life when they are done with being poor and wish to live it up. They push their day-to-day threads aside and pluck from their wardrobe multi-coloured cloaks and other splendid pieces and swan down the street in them, drawing envy, astonishment and admiration from all and sundry. This is also seen in uptown Milan where ancient white ladies stagger along the sidewalk in their best Magli and Prada, their clothes mumbling, *I still got it*. And they do. All hail the African flaneurs and the ancient ladies of Milan.

Full tourist mode. Yes, I am of the brown presentation, but I am acceptable in this space because I am a mere tourist and I have no intention of setting down roots, fucking your sons or daughters or opening a corner shop. This big sombrero that I am wearing, although culturally maladroit, is my way of coding all this for you so you can get my message at a glance. Please offer me directions to places I already know how to find and fleece me with trinkets.

Hand in hand. We are two lovers. Love is God's pass that allows Access All Areas. We are two entwined flowers, beautifying your streets. See how we gaze lovingly into each other's eyes? We are not here to steal goods from your window displays. We are not here to rob your town's vulnerable people. We are not here to sell you religion or cavity wall insulation. We are in love. As Shakespeare perhaps said, let the path of love be unimpeded.

Carrying a baby. It is sociological fact that a Black person carrying a baby is three times less likely to be seen as 'out of place' as a Black person of similar profile not carrying a baby. Seats may be given up, space made on pavements for easier passing, and smiles exchanged far more frequently for the Black baby carrier.★ It was not unknown in the past for Black people to lend babies to one another when a particularly difficult journey across a town or city is anticipated. This rule holds true so long as that baby is the same dark colour as its bearer. If the baby is white-looking, expect aggressive interrogation, queries as to whether you are a registered nanny and the appearance of police cars.

Faking a video selfie. Please be aware I am no ordinary Black person to be sneered at and followed by your local constabulary. I am an Influencer – fuck around and you may end up on my TikTok channel, so smile you beautiful motherfuckers, and treat me nice.

Walking alongside a well-dressed, senior white man. The senior white man is used to getting his way. He has experienced no different. Everything about him – the clothes he wears, how he holds his body, how he walks, how he smiles, how he offers his hand, how he speaks, the words he speaks, his gestures, his pauses, how he glances at his watch – all these actions sing privilege and hypnotise those around him to do as he asks without challenge. To walk alongside a senior white man is to slipstream this privilege, and find doors opening for you, chairs sliding out for you, the best views in restaurants, your word suddenly as good as your bond and the sun shining from your arse. This ninth method is the safest way for Black people to traverse public space.

*only applies to carrying one baby. Two babies or more induces panic

Wishing for a bird to fly through my window

H. was humming round the branch office, finding reasons not to leave. Now, she strokes my forearm, leaving her hand there just that little bit longer than a casual friend would. How she makes me laugh. Her little shimmies. The droll sense of humour at the Kafka nightmare of the paperwork we do, and her little ways to enliven it.

We cook up good all day, then finally she tosses me the keys to lock the office door and says, 'Let's do it – in the back room, now.' 'But I don't have a condom!' I exclaim. For this reason and this reason only, it's ruled out and her jibe is hilarious ('Call yourself an administrator, you can't even administrate a fuck!').

Then, over at her place, three days later, just as we get naked, she asks, 'Where are we going?' The question is a new thing – before it was 'This is fun.' I try not to answer quickly. The moment passes and she's stroking me again. We do it doggy style on her sofa, squishing the lottery ticket we'd bought earlier.

After, I'm driving back to mine, and I think, 'What do we have in common?' I like that she accepts my laziness. I love her ability to find short cuts for everything. She's lazy like me, just smarter. She's funny. And she's damn sexy. That's it. Is that enough?

This month, the boss has given her a pay rise. There's only the two of us in the office again and she kisses me carefreely. I'm suspicious of our happiness, unsure how long it will last. Then, at my place this time, not hers, her question again. Thinking harder, I take her point. We don't go out – to clubs, bars, restaurants, films, parties, dances. Nothing. We just come together in the office and pass the time entertaining ourselves. We fuck, in the office and at her place or mine. That's it. I recognise I should give her up, release her to fly to someone more suitable. Even advise her to stick it out when she gets bored in the new relationship, or when things get difficult, as that is her main gripe about *long-haul relationships*, as she calls them. She prefers quick fucking.

She gets promoted and will start work at another office soon, in another district. Just one last kiss that segues into one last fuck. And what next for me? I fend off the sadness, wishing another bird might fly through my window.

Ten smiles remembered:

Easing on my late grandfather's shirt. We never met, but now we share this shirt. It smells good.

Power cut at Riley's 8 Ball Pool Hall, around midnight. The *what-the-fuck* scowls of those winning. The equal, *wasn't-me-mate* shrugs of those losing.

Baby, finally burped and asleep, at 2 a.m.. The resulting smile that creeps onto my face has elements of mania, delirium and powdered milk.

M60 night, driving into a Stockport sunset with lil dawta, now a teen, Jacob Banks singing his Apocalypse song, somehow the Four Horsemen galloping by our side.

The last Sputnik smoked before we hike. The tent has

blown away. We shrug, slip through the field's kissing gate, and hike on.

After the court hearing. Rain sloshes my windshield. I'm at a Morrisons petrol station, parked up near the car wash. Through mirror shades I take in the banded grey sky. My suit wants to sigh off, my tie already adrift. I spot a nursery rhymes cd in the glove box.

My mother is finally booked to leave hospital. She is sitting on the hospital bed, dressed and ready. They have removed her drips and catheter, packed her bags, and ticked all the boxes on her forms. The wheelchair is being propelled towards her by a porter. 'Am I really leaving?' she asks. 'Yes,' I reply, 'you're leaving.'

Payment 59 of 59. The machine blips up a green tick. Nobody breaks into a dance. Nobody holds my arm aloft in victory. But this does not matter.

'And the winner is…' Her name is called. Daughter leaps with delight.

You come through the door.

An Ignatius Sancho tribute

Ignatius Sancho's letters show that on November 1st, 1779, acting out of a suspicion that God favoured beautiful beings, he asked 'a pretty young woman' in the queue before him to choose his lottery tickets.

In 2023, unconvinced my ugly hide was going to be favoured by the Most High, I asked lil dawta to pick my lottery numbers for me.

On November 16th, 1779, contemplating his empty shop till, Ignatius Sancho wrote words to the effect he despaired of being broke-ass poor.

On this day in 2023, contemplating my humongous electricity bill, I despair of being broke-ass poor.

On 18th July 1772, Sancho fervently counselled a young Black rogue on the error of his ways; subsequent letters show this counselling was of no avail.

On 5th July 2022, I spent two further hours mentoring the wayward K. His post-2022 crime sheet shows my advice had little effect on the course of his delinquency.

Conclusion: I am Ignatius Sancho. I merely lack a corner shop and a quill pen.

* *Ignatius Sancho (1729-1780), patron saint of Black shopkeepers.*

Heartbroken

I am heartbroken again. No one is interested this time. The first time, people cooked for me, took me out to the cinema, donated tickets to the football. The second time, they listened, but they were checking their watches and small pieces of not-advice leaked out: Sometimes your heart is a Hammond organ, Pete, and you've just got to unplug it. Women leave; that's a reality. Now – this third time – they are bored: About my new novel, Pete, can you review it on Amazon, and not all long and flowery, like last time, just say 'It's a good book, buy it'; that's what shifts copies… Yes, yes, of course once you've got over this latest heartbreak. Shall we say in a week?

Hat issues

One of my kids plops one of my hats on their bonce and immediately a pang of disappointment lurches up in me because I see the hat suits them far more than me. This is a frequent occurrence and is true not only for baseball caps, the natural crown of youth. It is also fedoras, bowlers, beanies, top-hats, berets, tams, pork pies, turbans, flat caps, even balaclavas. Whichever hat I wear, if they place it on their head, it instantly looks better on them than me. Maybe my head is not shaped so well as theirs, I started to wonder; they all have their mothers' genes for head shape. Whatever. I switch my sartorial energy to socks. They never borrow my socks. My socks always look better on me than them.

Unremembered acts

I have a face I wear when I want to discourage conversation. I don it most days on my morning commute, when the carriage is full of the furrowed brows of the anti-social. I also have a smilier face that goes with me on summer days, when long-gone friends signal they are about to return, after small triumphs with my laundry, when the digits in my bank account dance briefly upwards, after stumbling out of a sauna. I disembarked from a train one summer evening and made my way to the bus stop. The station walkway was merry with graduation parties, young men in tuxes, young women in frocks, chasing around, laughing, not a care in the world. I smiled to myself at their frolics. One ran up by me, leapt onto my back. I carried her, piggy-back style, back to her friends. It was simply a moment. Yet here I am, twenty years later, remembering it.

Goldilocks: a dream

Into the woods, super-white Goldilocks goes. It's where those who have managed to escape slavery have pitched camp. She walks into a shack. She would have known it was a Black folks' house because of location and because on the table were bare rations – not beans, egg, pie, pancakes and the stuff of other folk tales, just bare porridge. She's brought sugar and she sprinkles it and starts eating the porridge, which the Black folk have laid out for their lunch after having had the same for breakfast – no fish pie, no stew pie, just porridge (I am hungry while having this dream). Goldilocks shakes her sugary locks and works through the three bowls like Princess Entitled. She doesn't go to the second bowl and mix some of that second-bowl cool porridge with the hotter, first-bowl porridge. Nope. She messes through all three bowls, even sees the third bowl is a child size bowl and still gobbles it up. She nyams all three. We are not safe from Goldilocks, even in the woods.

Getting lost: 1

Getting lost while driving in the forested Derbyshire countryside, in the pitch dark, in Biblical rain, in a fifteen-year-old Ford Focus with my fifteen-year-old in the passenger seat is up there at the top end of the list of fun things I've done recently. To screams and laughter, I took a second wrong turn to add to the first. The road tapered into a bramble-hemmed track, broad enough – just – for the car. There are no streetlights on the track, no spill of house lights, no moonlight, only my Ford Focus's weak fog lights picking stuff out myopically: mud, bushes, trees, other green stuff, either side of us. *Do we carry on?* I ask. *Yes! Yes!* shouts teen dawta. The engine sounds game. On we go. The front wheels churn and slide. Branches lash the windscreen. The suspension heaves as we bounce across potholes. It's a horror movie, but we're laughing. The driver in me knows that if this is a dead end, I'm going to have to reverse though this twisting forest track and the odds will be against me. But I'm infected with dawta's teen spirit and keep going, thinking, what's the worst can happen? This is the Peak District not the end of the world; the RAC can tow me. We wail a mix of delight and disappointment when the track widens, and a streetlight veers up, and we are back in civilisation.

Oklahoma

Aged eight, I took a tin kettle from the kitchen, filled it with paraffin (from who knows where), lit the paraffin, then dropped a potato into the teapot's belly. My question: would the potato cook, given that the paraffin is presumably hot when burning – yet wet? This memory is all my own, though I have told it a few times so it may have grown some barnacles and decorations in the retelling. My error with the experiment? In order to get the potato out after a decent time inside the burning paraffin, I decided to kick the kettle over. The resulting flying paraffin hit my nylon trousers which ignited, and the nylon burnt into my left leg. Unable to think up a story to explain events that would find me anything other than Guilty of Stupidity in my mother's eyes, I hid the burnt trousers, burnt leg and the kettle, then skulked for three days till my left calf was fully peeled of skin. My mother eventually discovered all this, the way mothers do. Cue crying, shouting, and the hospital. After the skin graft, I was laid up alone in the house on the settee, leg bandaged, with my mother having to continue at her job washing dishes in the hospital. It rankled with me that I still hadn't found out if the potato had cooked or not. But I enjoyed the time off school, pootling around in the house. I got to sit in the usually off-limits Front Room where Mum's treasured record player lived. She had only one record I can now recall, *Oklahoma, The Musical*, for which the correct setting was 33rpm unless you wanted the singers to sound like they were on laughing gas or something. I laid up with my bandaged leg and listened to this record till the needle broke. When, ten years later, I stepped off a Greyhound bus into the bus station of actual Oklahoma, USA, I was disappointed because nobody sang.

Running the river

This river is fast, and you are in it deep. The waters swirl viciously. How you got here, you hardly understand. What you know is the undertow is pulling you down, and that you have low buoyancy. If you go under, you're not likely to make it back up, you'll become river.

In the throes of panic, a note of calm comes through the air. It's a radio late-show host. He runs the late-night phone-in, and his voice has that mariner quality, sounds like he has lived on rivers all his life. Look up, he tells you. What do you see? Sky, right? Notice you have not yet drowned. Take one hand from clawing the water and feel your chest. A life jacket. It's got you. I got you. We got you. Yes, the river's fast. Yes, the river's strong. But there's a bend coming. Let a hand fall into the water to create drag and you can steer yourself onto the sandbank at the bend. Till then, accept the raging waters. Till then, embrace the river's power. Till then, love the limpid sky, the mad charge of waters that you're swept up in.

Here it is, the bend, let your hand drag. Now, see how you are piloting yourself? You're doing it. You did it. You're on the sandbank now. Feel the grit under your feet. Press down into it and push up. Haul yourself up.

Let the water stream off you. You are no longer river. It's OK. It's over.

His name is Mike Njābá. He has been on the air at least fifteen years. The same show. The same time slot. I know he appears on TV somewhere selling loans, but I never watch the channel his advert appears on. I want to believe in the integrity of his voice, that he mediates the world truthfully into my bedroom; I've listened myself to sleep with him all these years: The man who gambled away his house and relationship. The son who killed his own father. The woman who had sex with her boss and now feels trapped. The youth framed on theft charges not knowing where to turn. The old lady who has outlived all her friends and asks why she should go on. The girl whose mother has beaten her every day for years and whose father beats her mother. The young man suicidal over his sexuality. They all call, struggling in the river. Their succour is his voice. It is the sound of pain taken up in a chalice, transmuted there and handed back as gold. I listen until the lap of the waves lulls me, tugs me under.

Kinetic Blackness

The invisible ball and chain attached to the right ankle giving a slight drag to that side as the young urban Black man pivots from left leg to right.

The languid, shoulders-back saunter of Queen Nefertiti ReBorn, often accompanied by the clanking of Ankh crosses and other Egyptian jewelleries.

The thunder-foot Black mother about to drag their chile out of some other person's house where they been hiding.

The stiff upper body posture and cold arm reach that

says this is a sundown town, so let's stay safe and do the white handshake thing because they watching.

The I've just got back from Glastonbury and am now adept at doing white people dance moves, including those hand flutters and the fairy hip swing and I got applauses in that mud field in Glastonbury so imma continue doing it as long as that applause lasts.

The Black legal-aid lawyer's wrecking-ball stride that says no justice, no peace – these walls of injustice must fall and by the power of my words, they shall, and we shall tackle the invoicing matter afterwards.

The athlete's head up, hands light, ball-of-feet roll.

The Trinidadian urban businesswoman's float.

The shoulder roll as you come close that says, don't be offering me no white person's handshake when we connect, this is shoulder hug and Black hand clasp time.

The eyebrow raise by which the Hotep tells you he will be delivering an eight-moves full Black handshake, and he knows you only know the first three moves because your soul is not Black enough – you having been spending too many lunches sitting at the white-people table so prepare for your public shaming.

Woman in headphones

I was walking home from my office job. It was late afternoon, my head was numbed from the drudgery of paper-shuffling, and I was in a herd of similarly numbed people, including one next to me with her head in her phone, ears in headphones, moving like a somnambulist in a *Day of the Dead* movie. As we reached the traffic light junction, I saw the green man in the black disc light up to indicate we could walk. But I heard a rev, and out of the corner of my eye, saw a white blur of car. The young woman, in her phone, took a step into the road. Breaking civic protocol, I took her sleeve and held her back. She startled, froze. The car raced through, a centimetre from her knee. I let go. She looked up at me and smiled. It was only a moment, yet it was everything. I thought about the thousand acts of unremembered kindness – civic gestures that occur between strangers in cities across the world every day, and I walked on to my bus stop. My bus, the Number 53, was there, and people were boarding. I squeezed into a seat on the lower deck. When next I looked up, sitting directly opposite me was the young woman whose sleeve I had tugged. Again, our eyes met. Another brief smile. She was reading a book. *Madness and Civilization*, by Michel Foucault. It was the same book I had been reading earlier in the week. I became suspicious. *Was I in a dream?* I let it go. Sometimes God toys with us, lining these coincidences up. The young woman was engrossed in her book. Eddies of her earlier smile still played on her face. Sometimes the world is a beautiful place.

Black laughter

It happened suddenly at a breakout interval during a Diversity, Equality & Inclusion Seminar at a mainstream theatre, let us call it Strawberry. There were three random Black people amongst the sixty-something attendees at Strawberry; they had found one another and gathered together to swap notes. At some point, as the canapés were being distributed, all three burst out laughing. The white people turned to us with frowns. We knew what was expected. We put our masks back on, quietened down.

It happened slowly in the job interview waiting room

of a company with impeccable public policies but a dubious reputation for (not) hiring Black people. Today was their Inclusive Hiring Day. The Black woman came out of the interview room, did an ironic, blackface jazz hands at us two waiting there, and we two laughed, or – step by step – we smiled, tried to suppress the laughter, but couldn't.

It happened, nervously, with a friend in a corridor of the courthouse, after the case ended and before the verdict, as we recalled the police constable's fake evidence and how our lowly, legal-aid barrister had torn through it. It was down to the legal process now; we had to await the verdict.

It happened at the board meeting when both Black board members took the same position, which the four white Board members opposed, and, after a beat, one of the Black Board members said, 'Is there possibly a race factor here?'

Afro-pessimism and Black Lives Matter

I did the Black Lives Matter marches. I spat my phlegm into the mic like so many others, denouncing the injustices. I raised my clenched fist and declared *The Time is Now* and *This Must End*. I enjoyed marching. It helped that Black Lives Matter blew up in the middle of lockdown. That added a libertarian *frisson* to our protest: defiance of the lockdown rules which everyone was so fed up with, and a perfect excuse to wear face masks so hindering the police evidence-gathering crews busy filming us for their Leviathan surveillance databases.

The sun burst out during the last march, adding extra, golden-hour zest: we were being lit beautifully by God. Moreover, the occasion was one of the few truly autonomous, self-governing Black protests I'd been on. It was youth-led and Instagram-organised: the Socialist Worker Party apparatchiks (bless them, many are my friends) who usually take over Manchester Black political things with their ready-to-go placards and solid Marxist slogans were replaced by fresh-eyed youths from the local universities and streets who came with all their clothing labels, home-made, hand-written campaign signs, chants both funny and serious, and earnest, heartfelt speeches. This was the realest march in decades. Change was happening. Black Lives Matter was a rattling of the sabre of civil unrest (this explains some of the delight generally in marching, for who does not like to rattle a sabre from time to time?). The rattling says: We are tired of walking within the lines marked out for us which have led us only to injustice. And now we've broken out of those white-painted lines. And you can no longer predict the path we may take. Behold the might of angry Black citizens on the move, and you better listen to our concerns. This time, we have brought the fuel and shown it you, but next time we may bring the match too, and then there will be fire. Do you want that?

And yet, on the philosophical front, I felt unease. *Black Lives Matter* strong-arms Black pessimists into a difficult ontological position. Afro-pessimists (and on bad days I fall among them) adhere to three precepts. 1. Nothing Black people say or do will ever overthrow the preening narcissism of white supremacy which has a Vulcan Death Grip on Occidental minds. 2. The imagination of racists is limitless and no sooner than measures have been put in place to counteract any one racist phenomenon or expression, a hundred other racist narratives and phenomena are dreamed up and implemented to replace it. Racism is ingenious, hydra-headed and undefeatable in our lifetimes. 3. Even if racism is defeated, it will be a pyrrhic victory since behind such matters as the organisation of society lies the deeper, metaphysical terror of the Meaninglessness of Life Itself, a terror to which all human lives are subjected. This third precept places Afro -pessimists in line ontologically with Heidegger's 'terror of nothingness', with Wittgenstein's 'pointlessness of all metaphysical argument since everything is meaningless and does not matter'* and with Karl Marx's philosophy of suspicion i.e. the sense that some elite will inevitably corrupt any political movement and use it for their own ends. To add a metaphorical veneer to the metaphysics, Afro-pessimists subscribe to the view that the wind blows forever in our faces, that we are mere leaves being chased down an empty street in an empty town in a world that God has long ago vacated.

Yet the sun is out, and the youth are marching and in full song. And to be in lockstep with the shining voices of Black Lives Matter youth is to suppress our Afro-pessimist misgivings, and, perhaps, briefly, to become young once more. And on that day, for the duration of that golden hour, I was young.

Moral philosophers don't @ me, these are shorthand paraphrases, philosophers not being noted for their brevity.

Theseus and the ship of institutional racism

There is a thought experiment called 'The ship of Theseus', first recorded by the ancient Roman/Greek historian, Plutarch. In this, a ship went off to war and had bits blown off it and some of its crew killed. The ship returned to shore, was patched up with new wood, and the shortfall in crew made good. Off it went again.

More war, more holes blown in it, more dead sailors. Again, it's repaired with new wood, dead and missing crew replaced with the present and living. After several hundred years of this, no wood from the original shiny new ship exists, and, of course, none of the old crew. Is the ship still the same ship? This was the question that the thought experiment asked.

Racism shares characteristics with Theseus' ship. Racism sailed out originally as a justification for colonialism and transatlantic slavery. Banks, churches, private corporations such as the East India Company and the Royal Africa Company, and plenty of governmental institutions all got on board with the message in support of transatlantic slavers, and explained away – as a collateral effect – the profits that the slave trade generated. Race as a concept then got busy perpetuating itself. Slavery was abolished as an institution by Britain in the 19th century, but slavery's intellectual underpinning and justification – race, with its beguiling flip side, White Supremacy – was too seductive to whites and they refused to let it go. In 1937, Churchill justified the dispossession of Palestinian lands by referring to them as 'dogs'. Here's Churchill huffing into the race ship's sails: 'I do not admit that a wrong has been done to these people by the fact that a stronger race, a higher-grade race, a more worldly-wise race [has] come in and taken their place.' Swap out Churchill and swap in the English race rabble-rouser of the 1960s, Enoch Powell. Here's Powell letting rip with broadside guns in Birmingham about the dread prospect of having a Black neighbour who didn't boil potatoes (Powell, to give him his due, does a nice side in Roman history here): 'I am filled with foreboding; like the Roman, I seem to see the River Tiber foaming with much blood.' *Plus ça change.* After Powell retired with full racialist honours and sailed off to his whites-only Valhalla, along came the ornately carved, highly wooden figurehead of the National Front's John Tindall, riding high on repatriation waves, in a fleet that included a Home Office policy of inspecting Asian women's vaginas for virginity before allowing entry into this Green and Sceptred Isle. When woodworm riddled Tindall and he dropped off the ship's prow into his foaming ocean of ignorance, the plank of wood known as Nigel Farage nailed itself to the race ship, singing, *Send her victorious, happy and glorious*.

So much for the crew. Planks got shuffled too. The Aliens Act 1905 was replaced by the Commonwealth Immigration Acts of 1962 and 1968. Then came the National Immigration Act of 1971. After this, the Nationality Act 1981. Followed by the Hostile Environment Policy 2012: as fast as one plank of racism is removed, another plank takes its place. It both is and is not the same ship of institutional racism.

Mamihlapinatapai
(a look shared by two people who want to initiate something, but that neither will start)

Funny how things spin. To have known you intensely in those seven hours stolen from your schedule, your email correspondence, your family concerns. You came into Ngum's Berlin apartment and were mercurial – something about you that I couldn't place. You had the squint-eye of the lawyer, bristling with clauses, rigour, ice and electric. And yet. Something in the turn of your lips, in how you moved around our mutual friend's apartment, a pattern that told me you would sit with me,

128

perhaps, if the ley lines were right. You'd brought a book, so I deduced you had rested here before. I didn't stir, and eventually you paused, then eased onto the sofa beside me. We talked about Ngum's letter to her boyfriend that she had been trying to write for days. Ngum was concerned about the new draft: was it too short now, had the soul of it been removed, or maybe it was too hot, or too cold? Of course, all the while, this letter wrangling fuelled our flirting. Ngum laughed at our brazenness. 'Hey, you two are supposed to be helping me with my letter!' You squatted on the sofa with your back towards me. I placed a cushion between us, so you could comfortably lean on me as you read. My hand slipped round you a little and, as Ngum drifted round cooking, chatting, composing, we arrived at this simple harmony: you reading, me editing one of my stories, propping each other up on the sofa.

I wanted to hold you fully. I found excuses to visit you, concocted with Ngum's eager complicity. I needed to edit some more, needed more space, some such excuse. You said yes, I could come up. Your apartment, in the same block as Ngum's, was zen-like except for the papers that lay in piles here and there, as if you had four cases on the go. I asked to recline as I edited, and you showed me your couch at one end of a room that had at its other end the bed. You brought tea, we chatted a little about Berlin. My eyes were on the bed.

You had a filled hot-water bottle in your hands. It had no cover. I was concerned you would burn yourself if you slept with it against your skin. You held it to your stomach as you talked. Midnight turned and I asked if I could sleep in the bed. I knew you were going to be up late with your cases. If you didn't want that, I could sleep on the sofa. You shrugged and smiled. Later, you tossed your hot water bottle under the quilt, slid in, and made me shuffle over. Your hair, gripped back by day, was now loose and made a soft black flag behind your face. The bed base had a slant, and the laws of science had you roll into me. Our skin touched.

– You know I have three defences to prepare in the morning? you murmur.

– Only three?

You squint-eye me.

– You're a distraction, you're not even meant to be in this apartment.

I fished something out from beneath my pillow and stretched its elastic.

– What's this?

– It's too bright here. Maybe I'll not need to wear it with you, though. What's it called in English?

– A blindfold.

My other hand was stroking your kinked hair.

– Here, this is practical. Goodnight.

Your goodnight sounds final, but your thumb presses into my cheek as you say it.

In the darkness, you turned into me. I sought your mouth, kissed you, your lips met mine. I felt the glide of your stomach, slipped low. Your hand caught mine, barring the way further. You stroked my skin, gently, then wrapped a leg around mine. I let my arm fall across you, and you snuggled your head into my shoulder. We slumbered.

Sometimes in your sleep, you'd be smiling and then you'd squeeze me with your whole body so hard – arms, legs, a grip that faded slowly. And you muttered things in German, in a lawyer's tone. As I dozed, I lost track of time and space and wondered where I was, when I was, who I was, reminding myself, it's me and H., who I've just met, and I'm in Berlin, in early March, and somewhere below, in another apartment, is Ngum, writing her love letter to her boyfriend, sleeping.

In the morning, you pack your briefcase and deny you ever smile in your sleep.

Life: a risk assessment

I was presented with this thought experiment by a drunk friend. If you had a choice whether to emerge into being or not (which of course is impossible in this rationalist model, since to choose you first need sentience and non-being rules that out but nevertheless…), would you decide, yes, to life, or would you think, 'Nah, all that drama on the path of existence, all the clown shows and indignities, all the heartbreak and rip-offs – can't be bothered with all that. Let some other egg float (or sperm swim) towards that one?' I tucked my drunk friend into bed, but her question stayed with me all night. We come from nothing. And after the short hiatus of life, we return to nothing. Is there an enormity to this? Or is it banal? I drink another cup of cider, and by a wayward path arrive at the thought that, for those who cleave to the 'enormity' side of this analysis, nature has ways of making us stick around.

One: progeny. After a bit of how's-your-father, another being is pushed into the world for which we often feel some tenderness and responsibility. We realise this new being is, like us, doomed to face the absurdity called life. Yet, what if we've got it wrong? What if life does hold some meaning, and we are simply unaware of it? Adopting such spiritual humility, for the newborn child's sake, we will ourselves to believe in life's unfathomable purpose. Our children take their cues

131

from us, and lo, we all go on enjoying meaningless life as best we can.

Two: the ageing human brain. As we age, our brain loses its vigour, including its ability to see a thought all the way through to an absurd end; bad things of the past fade away like the fogged rearview mirror of an overcrowded sports tour bus. As for looking forwards, our shrinking brain's understanding of the existential terror of nothingness subsides. We literally lose our minds, but with it our worries. So, happy days. Let us drink to kids and old age.

White-out

There are days when I have white-outs – when the overbearing, privilege-shrouded, ghostly presence of white people overwhelms me, and I have to avoid them until my blood pressure adjusts. It happens rarely, maybe twice a year, but is a rage that has no place in polite society or publishing.

All my abusers

Running feral, we developed radar about adults. The sudden arrival of a Boys Brigade commander at a local church had all the polite boys following him, till they all ran away. The football coach who liked to have only blond boys stop off at his house after matches, and those boys suddenly lost all enthusiasm for the game. The man who fixed children's bikes, especially those of girls, and the girls went into his house laughing and left mute holding a white, unopened paper bag of lemon drops. I rode my luck. A grope of my buttock here, someone pissing in my mouth there, weird drives in cars when the driver massaged my thigh while singing along to the radio. By the time I'd begun to grow pubic hair, I'd learnt what common denominator meant, and worked out that the danger for me was white men. I became wary of them everywhere.

Bus stop

We wait for the last bus out of the city centre. An Asian man in chef whites shuffles stiffly, absorbing the slap of winter air, curdled eyes avoiding everybody. An aged office cleaner, headphones hard-clamped to his ears, nods to a steady bass-line of syncopated dub. Five young clubbers are in minimal threads; three of them are standing in the betting shop doorway in a swirl of joking, hugging and phone-screen sharing. The other two are sitting on the pavement: a brown-skinned girl slumped in the lap of a white boy who has draped his arms around her. That the togetherness of these two is no bother to anybody at the bus stop is the beauty of the scene.

Why you should always pay your hairdresser promptly.

The text message pings in at about 2am: *can i sleep at yr place, I just bn attacked by my hairdresser cos not paid for the weave she tried pull it off my head, outside petrol station princess road i called police no credit to phone you.* This is the Blackest text I've received all year. I drive over and pick Elise up. She still has her weave intact, and she's victorious. 'I told them I'd pay them next payday; there was no need for this.' She sleeps in my arms, her weave drifting into my face.

The hammer blow of God

My friend, Jack approaches me. He's moved back from the Lake District, he says. I ask why. He tells me his story. He was out running along one of the rivers, with his fluorescent vest on, and all the running clobber, and this man steps out, waving his arms, shouting at him. He pulls up. The man hits him. With a hammer. On the side of the head. He doesn't go down. The man looks at him like he can't be human not to have fallen. Jack himself is thinking the same thought – how come I'm still standing when I've just been hit with a hammer on the back of the head? There's blood gushing everywhere. He's stunned. And still standing. The man with the hammer runs off. Jack goes along the river, hauls himself up the bank and knocks at the door of an Indian restaurant – he doesn't burst in, he is too English, too polite. When someone answers, he asks them if they could call an ambulance, but no, he doesn't want to come inside, doesn't want to make a mess of the restaurant carpet, what with all the blood. It would probably be bad for trade. Next, he's lying in a hospital bed, thinking he is soon probably going to pass into a coma, so he had better write notes to his loved ones – the usual stuff: how much he loved them, who gets what, the passwords to his social media accounts, that kind of thing. He wakes and discovers he is still alive. He has four staple stitches punched into the back of his head. He gets discharged from Westmoreland General after two days, and he decides to move back to Manchester. He's had a lot of time to reflect, and he's decided the hammer blow was a message from God that Manchester was safer for him. Anyway, Pete, I've got to get to the shops before they close; it was nice meeting you. As he walks off, I'm thinking, since when did God go around delivering messages with a hammer? There again, plague, pestilence, locusts, blokes with hammers – it's much of a muchness.

A Sunday blessing

I'm walking from the pub on a Sunday afternoon, and a car stops, its passenger window rolls down and a woman calls out to me. 'Hiya mate, I love your jacket, where d'ya get it?' I'm wearing a Puffa with a wild graffiti design. 'TK Maxx,' I say, 'I wanted something bright and jagged, keep me warm through the winter.' 'Cheers. Love it,' my sudden admirer says. She rolls the window back up, and the car drives on. I walk on, smiling, thinking: None of my mates will ever have this conversation, they wouldn't dare wear a jacket like this.

Three times I died and came back to life

1. I suffer from hypnic jerks – jolts the body uses to remind you to breathe when you forget. I experience these jerks most frequently when I have had a very relaxed evening, such as after looking at a particularly spectacular sunset. One sunset I watched was infused with a godly Madonna-blue. That night, I dreamt that Madonna sky again, in 3D. It took my breath away so much, my body shut down. Only my legs' frantic jerking alerted my partner that I'd stopped breathing. She slapped me awake. Since then, I have avoided sunsets.

2. The French have a name for the experience of orgasm, "la petite mort" – the little death. Early on in my sex life, that was what I experienced – a series of momentary losses of consciousness that were nothing to write home about: small deaths. Then along came C. and she killed me, and I realised I'd never really been living till then.

3. As I was reading Audre Lorde's *Zami,* time stopped. I entered into a singularity with that book. When, finally, I turned the last page, I was back in life. But everything was different, I was living a completely new life after that book.

La Dolce Vita: a monologue in the Italian style.

Enter a mixed heritage (Black African-White European) man, 61, in an Italian suit, including white handkerchief tucked into jacket breast pocket. He walks slowly but confidently to front of stage. He addresses the audience directly:

I am a middle-class man who is temporarily financially embarrassed. By temporarily, I mean my circumstances conform to the truism that money is made and lost in three generations. My Danish forebears were impeccably middle class. Look at the family photographs and you will see. Candlelight dinners with a white clothed, long table, chandeliers above, the most elegant suits and evening dresses, cutlery arranged with attention to correct detail. I know I have inherited this; it's in my bones. I always feel at home at such settings. My mother left the bourgeoisie of Aalborg, Denmark, and came to England with a small child. This migration was many things: a flight, a dash to, a liberation, an adventure. But, with her Danish teaching qualifications unrecognised in England and so reduced to manual work, she experienced a tumble into poverty, a fall from middle-class grace. After various adventures, she met my Nigerian father. Nigerians do not do class distinctions (or at least did not back then in the late 1950s). You were either rich or poor. My father came from rich stock. His father was a revered man in Igbere, descendant of one of the twelve original founders of the village of Igbere, in Abia State, Nigeria. My grandfather was short of stature but a tower of a man – a writer of thoughtful letters, an astute and determined trader, a dapper dresser, and wealthy beyond measure. His son – my father – was born with a golden spoon in his mouth. He was sent to England to study Accountancy (or Medicine, depending on whom you ask), became a chartered accountant, then set up an Import-Export business. Unfortunately, he did not have my grandfather's business savvy. After losing his money to the banks of London, he fled to Nigeria (or to Ghana first, then Nigeria, depending on who you listen to), but not before having four children with my mother. So here I am. My attitudes and understanding of the world are middle-class; my current circumstances locate me as poor. My own children, for reasons I shall not venture into right now, look unlikely to restore the family to wealth. So, I must do it myself in the small time I have left, if the family line is once more to know and become accustomed to *la dolce vita*: the chandeliers, the twenty-four candle dinners, the cutlery, correctly arranged. I dress well, you must agree, even if my suit is frayed here and there. The classic yet frayed suit tells my story. A middle-class man, temporarily financially embarrassed.

A doctor in a blown-up landscape writes a death certificate

She sat down at my second invitation but was mute. I poured some of my water into a cup for her, encouraged her to drink and find her tongue. I knew there was a queue of people beyond the door. I could hear wailing, an argument, the sigh of the fan circling above us like a lame donkey. But all of that went quiet when she finally

137

spoke. If there is a sadder story in the world, I haven't heard it. At its end, she asked: Which of the two would you have saved, in my position? And if you had known the life that the one I saved went on to live, would you have saved even him? As a mother yourself, what would you have done? At this, she touched my tunic sleeve, her hand wet and trembling. I couldn't answer her question, but I wrote her the papers she needed because I required no further proof than the child's finger which she took from her purse and showed me.

Me in a 19C incarnation

Man enters my study as I am examining a pinned butterfly with a magnifying glass.

Man: I heard your daughter sighing in the other room.
Me: Yes, she's in love.
Man: Ah. To other matters then…

Chess game 3

We had downed a bottle of my wine each and had another bottle on the go, so we were now Grandmasters, and Ali was scratching his stubble, insulting my wallpaper and declaring the game over, next move. 'You've lost. Phone an ambulance.'

'Do your worst. I'll take my chances.'

He moved his Queen in front of my King. 'Checkmate!'

I took his Queen with my King. 'Yeah, phone an ambulance. But not for me.'

He groaned, swallowed off another glass of my

premium wine, then insisted on a third, final game. It was small hours a.m.

'Fine,' I said. 'Some people just like getting licked.'

That final final game was interminable. He kept moving pawns one space at a time, like they were a Space Invader army. Eventually, the pawns began chewing the edges of my position, and I had to hop my pieces backwards to save them. He insulted my wallpaper again.

'Hey, forget the wallpaper. Look at my parquet flooring, you peasant.'

The game was relentless and dull, but he won, his pawn army finally rolling over all my positions. Smirking, he staggered up, drank off the final drops of my wine, then clattered off into the dark outside, all cock-sure and smarmy because he'd won. I went upstairs and collapsed onto the bed. The bastard had not only won, but it was also a double victory for him – he'd drunk off all my wine stocks; there was not a single good bottle left in the house.

Some three hours later, I woke to a throbbing pain in my left leg. I checked in the dark. The leg had expanded to twice its usual size. I tried moving, thinking it was trapped circulation. But the leg didn't deflate. The reverse occurred. It was growing larger. Whatever this shit is, it's dangerous, I thought, trying to stir myself fully awake. We were mid Covid epidemic; people were dying waiting for ambulances. I dragged myself downstairs. I had an automatic car that required only one leg to drive. I drove to within a hundred yards of A&E. I wouldn't drive all the way up because for sure it would get towed by the parking company if I left it there.

I tried walking the rest of the way but couldn't make it. Too much pain. I dialled Ali on my mobile. The bastard was an insomniac, he'd answer. Sure enough, he picked up. 'I'm fucked,' I said. 'Leg's ballooned. I'm a hundred yards from A&E; get me in there.' He was on his way. A cop car went past. I tried waving it down. It sailed on. I called out to some hospital staff clocking off, but in their eyes, I was just another red-eyed drunk. I dragged myself into A&E. They put me through straight away. Moments later, Ali made it to Triage. They wouldn't let him through, because of Covid. The doctor examining my leg was reassuringly confident in his diagnosis. 'You have a large blood clot in your leg. We need to operate fast; we're locating a surgeon.' At 7 a.m., after two changes of shift and no surgeon having been located, a different doctor – a consultant – looked at the leg again. 'You're lucky. The danger period has passed. If you were going to die, you would have died by now. Take one of these pills a day for the next week.' I laughed and limped off. No way was I dying. No way was Ali regaling everyone at my funeral with how his Space Invader Army rolled over my position and how that was the last chess game we ever played. I needed revenge first. Then I could die.

Jumping off

We jumped off things all the time. Car roofs. Window ledges. Riverbanks. For thrills for sure, but also out of curiosity, the way a baby chews a chair leg because they want to know what it tastes like. This body of mine, we were asking, what can it do? What happens when gravity battles the rubber of my bones? At what point will my bones no longer bend, and instead break? In adult life, there are similar explorations, though they are not conducted in the same visceral way. At which point do we cross from caution to cowardice? At which point do we exit bravery and enter foolishness? The dilemmas of adulthood are so much more disembodied. Sometimes, I yearn for childhood simplicity, to jump off something and see if I break a leg.

Cosmetic Blackness 2: channelling Prince

I was at work stuffing envelopes. In my imagination I was wandering around 2BC Egypt. I encounter ordinary people, rough-faced from the blowing sand. They look like Prestonians, but with more melanin. The Egyptians left us the story (which paradoxically I accept) that they were the most beautiful people ever to walk this earth. The assertion is made by their painters who, one must assume, were faithfully recording the skills with cosmetics possessed by the servants of the elite. I wonder if, for special occasions – embalmments and the like – the elite would have called upon the services of professional make-up artists; after all, this was to be their face not for a day but for a couple of millennia (Egyptologists don't @ me, I was up late last night and I've not had breakfast). The idea of transforming *myself* with makeup – becoming a better version of the current me – regularly appeals: to perk up my drab face with dabs of foundation, rouge, blusher. All children play this game, but permission to continue the practice into adulthood is withheld for the male of the human species. Actors are the exception. For men of the theatre, wearing makeup is normal. I remember, in my acting days, how I spent hours in green rooms, having paint smeared over my neck and cheeks in soft sweeps by skilled hands. The gunk slips and slides across my chin, brow, forehead, lips, eyelids, grease paint slowly colonising my face. The make-up artist's work is done. I look up into the mirror. I'm rapt at the more defined, yet Sphinx-like, more mysterious, me.

Nettle-stung torso

A fight was arranged by the river, to take place after Youth Club ended. The two fighters made their way there, bare-chested and surrounded by their shoulder-massagers, storytellers, tacticians, lovers, seconds, cuts-boys, pickpockets and witnesses. I was in Vinny's corner. We got down to the riverbank's lower level and the light was good, if fading. They went at it with fists and grappling. Cedric got a hold of Vinny's waist and threw him into the riverside nettles. When Vinny came up from this, his upper body was blotched with nettle stings. Cedric threw Vinny three more times. Each time Vinny got up. Each time, the nettle sting blotches multiplied. Until he didn't get up. Cedric headed back to Merseybank, arms aloft, his storytellers racing ahead of him to tell the tale of his great victory. Yet there was something magnificent about Vinny's nettle-stung torso. We hauled him up and got him walking and plucked bramble thorns from his sides. Vinny walked into the dark, torso gleaming, lips bloodied, head high.

Cliffhanger

We ascended steadily and by the time we reached the high point, even sheep were scarce. Ahead of us was a ledge, then a sheer drop. In the way God orders things, the ledge provided a panorama of Bologna in all its medieval architectural glory. I begged H. not to go and sit there, yet, defiantly, they did. I walked away, not wanting to feed any energy into their reckless act. And as I walked away, I thought of H's suicide ideations, the traumatic, rollercoaster life they had lived up to this date. And how affection traps us, because to love someone is to be vulnerable forever to moments when they go to the ledge. Yet, I would rather love and be scared shitless when they do this than not love at all. I cursed H. and all their ledges and opened my paperback and used the open pages as a base to roll a spliff. A shadow. H. was before me once more. My heart flooded with joy. 'Come sit with me, you enigma,' I said. We sat and smoked, then lay back and snuggled under the Bologna sun.

Bartender story

'Did you know I was secretly married to Prince?' she said. I nodded, thinking, Prince must have some backstage group marriage sessions going on after his concerts because she's the third person to claim marriage to Prince this week. I poured her drink – same as I poured the other two – on the house, in celebration of her marriage to Mr Rogers Nelson.

Breaking in

People who got locked out would send word and we'd arrive, agree a price and one of us would climb up, screwdriver their bathroom or bedroom window, slide in, two-step down the staircase, unlock the door and accept payment. Some of us continued this house-breaking line well into adulthood, though without owners' consent. Now I'm a writer-thief. I break into other people's ideas, steal the best of them, climb back out of their books. I steal from all the greats. I've just robbed Jean Genet.

The freelance carol singers

Out freelance carol-singing in a posh area, we found our way into an apartment complex off of a private street. Its atrium walls were whiter than the snow outside, and it had soaring, Hollywood stone pillars, marble floor tiling, and a mirrored ceiling. It was full of echo. We knocked on the spotless apartment doors, ready to sing our celestial *Good King Wenceslas*. Nobody answered. We didn't rush to exit – it was cold out – instead we chased around. I banged my head on one of the stone pillars and saw stars. Actual stars. They were four-pointed, and they rotated round my head like in the Tom & Jerry cartoons. I watched them twinkle and twirl as the other three chased around. I followed the cartoons more closely after that, because now I knew real stuff went on in them.

The first time I pulled on a nylon jumper and static sparks flew, I was in and out of that jumper all evening till Mum thought I had fleas. Ever since, I've loved nylons, from tights to Farah slacks. My inner child has watched the relentless dull march of the natural clothing movement with dismay.

Finding poets in Chapeltown

I was new in Chapeltown, Leeds and was giving up hope of ever finding any poets to join me in a poetry circle (that was my thing back then). Then I happened on the Mandela Centre. Someone had pinned a poem up on one of the pillars inside called, *Thru Malcolmz Eyez*. The poem was by Martin Glynn. Whoever pinned it, saved my poetry soul because it told me there were kindred folk here in Chapeltown, I just had to find them.

Radishes

I was the best nine-year-old radish grower in the entire world. I grew hundreds of them on the patch of grass at the back. Bulging, fat radishes. I declared it my contribution to family meals. On the third day, my family started to wave my radishes away. My older brother warned me, 'Don't come near me with no more of those f---ing radishes, kid.' I slunk off, reflecting that sometimes people didn't appreciate a good thing. I ate the rest of the radishes myself, one by one over the course of the summer. Now, I have become a writer and I write stories. My family are the general reading public. They wave my stories away: 'Enough!' I absorb their indifference with a shrug. I will reread every word of this paragraph, one by one.

The end of history x 3

C.L.R. James ruined history for the Black historians who came after him. You read any modern historian (a nice phrase, nuh, let's say anyone after 1980?) and immediately you can't stop yourself comparing their prose with that of C.L.R. They never come out of it looking good. C.L.R. James made his points with such style. Historians must go into any area C.L.R. has already written about with a sense of doom – holding no hope of capturing C.L.R.'s audience, who have dined on finer things. So too it must have been with Plutarch in Roman times. 'Here comes that conceited, swaddled, pen-wielder, Plutarch. Bottle your inks, fellas, nobody's gonna read our stuff now Pluty's about to scrawl on the subject.' So too in ancient Egyptian times. 'Here comes Kut. Down chisels, lads, back to the hauling of rocks. Once Kut starts chiselling histories, nobody will want our clumsy channellings; we'll be back on the slave market in the blink of an eye. He's a right wank that Kut, why can't he take a day off?'

The headmaster's TV

I am eight and in the headmaster's office. He has a TV with a twin-prong aerial. A girl is slumped in a corner of this office, crying into her hands. I am two years older than her, and on a chair. The headmaster is brisk with me. I beat Arnold up in the playground. Why? Because he called Rodrigo a nigger. If he used that word with Rodrigo, what business was it of yours? I thought he was talking to me. This was a lie. I punched Arnold in solidarity with Rodrigo. But I knew the headmaster was not ready for this subtlety, so I didn't bother. I don't remember the punishment. Only being surprised that the headmaster had a TV in his office. And that the girl in the corner never stopped crying, not even to hear my story.

Praise song for the zombies

I've seen generation after generation of Black folks zombified by a system that dines out on their brains. In this now time, as the young Black youth do their marvellous things on social media, exhibiting all their rightful swag and panache, the Black olders look out at them through marbled eyes. The olders have seen too much. They were there at the dawn of time, when white time was the only time. Their Black lives tick-tocked to the chomp of white teeth, chewing through their dreams, their ambitions, their dignity. They watched

146

white mouths masticate their hopes and spit out the pips. White teeth, lips pulled back, laughed in their faces. They endured this and survived; but it hollowed them out, ate through their brains and emptied their souls. They sit now in vinyl chairs by care home windows, gazing out on the nothing their lives became.

F.

F. was in my year at secondary school. We shared some classes. There was something beautiful in the lightness of his walk, the flight of his smile, the flutter of his hands, and his brown eyes so smart and edged with fun. B. another boy in my year, who I met in the playgrounds and hung around with because we both liked the same football team and I liked the way his red hair shook when he ran, declared F. our number one enemy, called him Gay Boy and decided we should destroy him. We set about it. His face became grey as tracing paper whenever he saw us. We would grab him, press him to the wall and draw a dick on his forehead. Everyone would crowd round and laugh. F. took his torture without begging. He had an older friend at the school who protected him as best he could, which was hardly at all, because in school there are infinite ways of torturing a person. I was one of three assistant torturers, but I never forgot F.'s beauty: even when torturing him, he was beautiful, sometimes more so. Once, I watched F. strolling in the playground with Roger, saw those wonderful shapes he made with his hands as he spoke to Roger, heard the peal of his laughter. I realised, just from looking at him, I had an erection. I tried to approach him on my own but, whenever I neared, F. melted away. Finally, B. was expelled, and his torture gang dissolved. The entire school relaxed, especially F. We three redundant assistant torturers caught our breath. We were never punished. We could have carried on, but without B., we lost the zeal for it. A way of life ended. We found other ways to kill time. Then this one afternoon, our year was on a coach, returning from a city centre art exhibition, and I took the seat next to F. He smiled at me accidentally – before he saw it was me. When he turned and looked at me, his face went that tracing-paper grey and he slid his arm, which had been draped across two coach seats, back into his body. I asked what he'd thought of the exhibition. Something in my voice, some hesitation, the shadow of an apology maybe, softened his hostility. And, sitting together, slowly and hesitantly at first but with increasing candour, we talked about the comic art we'd seen – then talked more, talked and laughed and fell into each other laughing all the ride back to school. He said I should call round his place at the weekend, and gave me his house number, because I already knew the street. When I got home, I went to my bedroom and cried. F. is the hero of this story, and I am the utter shit.

F, if you ever read this, there is nothing I can do or say to apologize enough. There is no point me pointing the finger at B., saying he was your chief tormentor; it was never my idea, it was he who sucked me into this campaign of cruelty. I've spent a post-school lifetime contemplating how weak and foolish I was to go along with it. We were 13 years old and who knows anything at that age, though we made out we knew everything. I learned the meaning of cruel, torturing you, F., and I never unlearned it; that's been my punishment – I still get a thrill from cruel things. Sorry is a shit word, but it's all I've got. Sorry.

Day of a flaneur: racial profiling

I was walking in the early evening and the sun was low. A couple in their mid-twenties, arm in arm, were walking towards me and, because of the way the sun was backlighting them, I could not tell much about them. In the first nanosecond of this uncertainty, I was bored and decided that when they got closer, I would look at her face first and guess from that, something about her partner. I looked. The degree of carefreeness in her eyes, the openness of her face, the happiness and self-assurance suggested to me she was walking with a white guy. I looked at the second face in the next nanosecond. Sure enough, she had a white boyfriend. They strolled past. I speculated whether white women walking with Black boyfriends held more tension in their bodies in this district of Manchester, and a more guarded or interrogative look as you passed them. Of course, the sample size – one – made all this speculation.

Later, I was walking some other part of the city and, in the same backlit optical restriction, I saw a white man offer a thumb-high handshake, the handshake traditionally associated with African and Caribbean communities but now spreading into general use. There was something slightly embarrassed in the way he offered it, which told me it was a Black guy he was offering the handshake to. I looked across. It was an Asian man (of – my guess – Pakistani roots) who he was offering the Black handshake to. Still later, I began thinking, did my presence affect the experiment? Was I a participant as well as a mere observer? There was no way of knowing. I ate beans on toast that night and went to bed.

The blue lights of Tokyo, the streetlights of Igbere

Yellow light was king in the houses of my childhood. Bulbs shed 40-watt yellow in whichever room you entered. School had plastic-encased white fluorescents that blinked and buzzed and laughed equally at those who could do the algebra test and those who could not. When I asked my father how he studied while growing up in Nigeria, he puffed his chest and said they had had no electricity, so he read his textbooks under his Igbere village streetlights in the street directly outside. Many years later, I visited the exact location in Igbere. There were no streetlights on this road. And there never had been any right there, his sister told me, laughing at my father's tale. Visiting Hong Kong, I noticed blue light is preferred there for lighting rooms. My Hong Kong friends call it Tokyo Blue and say it promotes a good mood.

Indian waiter

The casting does not go well. The call was for Chinese Take Away Man. I try out but am instantly stopped. 'The script says, "Chinese take-away man runs on, waving cleaver." It does not say, "Man runs on waving cleaver who looks vaguely Chinese." Next.'

Upon the nature of time

My mother, for reasons lost in time, kept two clocks in her living room. One was an hour fast, the other twenty minutes slow. While there, you did mental arithmetic to arrive at true time (should you want it) depending on which wall you were facing. This two-clocks consciousness of my childhood became normal and I took it into the wider world. Now, as age slowly Gorgonzolas my frontal cortexes, now and then my childhood clock algorithms start up spontaneously, and I become confused. The train station LED screen blinks 'Train now due at 17:00.' Might that mean four o'clock or 5:20 p.m? My phone screen says 'Dentist 10 a.m.' Does that mean 10, 11, or 9:40? Please forgive me if I show up an hour late or twenty minutes early. The cause is my two-clocks childhood.

Jonah and the whale

Our Scottish Sunday School preacher worked himself into such a fever over God's Grace in the story of Jonah and the Whale that spittle flew off his mouth and his Brylcreemed hair flapped left and right, and his eyes rolled up, only the whites showing. Absorbing the story, I spat at God for imposing this ordeal on poor Jonah, and for working the preacher up into a spit-spraying frenzy about it. Jonahs still travel the world and still endure whale after whale. They go from shipping container to lorry chassis to the bowels of a barge to a crumbling room in a HMO. I spit at SERCO and the tin gods in Government for imposing this ordeal on the modern-day Jonahs. I spit on the politicians who vie to conjure up more whales. Tents! Cardboard boxes! Ships! Prisons in a far-away land! I am consoled only by the certainty these Whale Evangels will depart this life in the tightest of boxes and verily will be swallowed by the earth.

Superheroes: episode 3

I was growing up. I threw away my comics and became a shoot-'em-up film fan. I loved Clint Eastwood's short-tongued way with words. 'Do you feel lucky, punk?' said Dirty Harry. Death Wish's Charles Bronson had the coolest line. 'Do you believe in Jesus? You're gonna meet him.' These were my new superheroes. Until they weren't.

Courtesy People's Publishing House, Beijing, one day I read *The Communist Manifesto*. Suddenly, I was repulsed by Individualism and banished the Eastwoods and Bronsons and McQueens from my mind. I joined the All-African People's Revolutionary Party, and dived deep into books such as *Capitalism and Slavery*, *The Autobiography of Malcom X* and *How the West Underdeveloped Africa*. Emerging from these, I doubly rejected the West's superheroes. I now understood, thanks to Malcolm X, that the white man can never save the Black man because the white man is the cause of all the Black man's problems!

Lisa and belonging

Lisa lived in the same avenue as us and she watched us play from behind her green garden gate in black shiny shoes and one ribbed white sock up, the other down. Later, as a teen, she would give birth to a brown baby, but that story happens outside of this one. Now, she's six and she stands watching and she can't play Hide and Seek with us because she has been told not to because We Don't Belong and what's more she'll catch nits. One afternoon, she calls out, 'I know a hiding place that's better than under the mattress, in the fridge or even the old lady's bin or anywhere else in the world!' We don't believe her. And only to show that she's right – because boys are so stupid – Lisa joins in, just this one time. And we can't find her anywhere till she pops up. She's been hiding in the boot of the sad hippy's car. And she wins. That evening, she gets slapped about the head by her red-faced father for playing with the coloured children.

Later, Lisa starts big school. We bump into each other on Burton Road after home time. She accepts gum and we chew and walk and talk which becomes our ritual after school. When we hit the corner, Lisa wipes her lip gloss off with her sleeve and rolls down her skirt, and does a finger wave at me before turning into the avenue and striding home. Later still, she stops walking with me and even going to school. I ask Disco Tony, who knows things, and he says Lisa's learnt to dance and is at discos all over and she has the legs of a runner and a lover. I nod at Tony's news, though I'm unsure what Tony means about her legs.

Pickups

I was neither confident nor knowledgeable about sex. I read a Pick-Up Tips column in a magazine and dreamt of meeting someone carrying a big column of books who spilled them onto the parquet floor of the library, and I intervened to help her pile them back up into her arms and one thing led to another and we ended up in bed. This was the most common way a man could get laid, according to the magazine. In the spirit of this advice, I approached someone in the city centre of Manchester and told her I was struggling to decide which shirt to buy, could she help me? We ended up shopping together and within a couple of days we were knacking, so the magazine advice wasn't far off. But I still knew nothing. Six months later, when Susan began moaning as we were in missionary, I was genuinely puzzled as to what was going on and was she OK?

Driving while Black: a rhapsody for cars

We worship our cars. After the lockdowns of plantations, colonisation, pass laws, segregation laws, Hostile Environment laws, Anti-Migrant Riots, all insisting we must stay in our place, we love getting in the driving seat of our car and zooming off. Freedom is sweet. Car-ownership is our normal. Rich or poor, we celebrate our freedom with wheels. Beyoncé owns a Rolls Royce Silver Cloud II, a Cadillac Escalade and a Mercedes Limousine. Prince loved his Pretty Little Red Corvette. Frank Ocean loves cars. Pete Kalu loves cars.

With cars, we get to see outside of our allocated space. Even the dullest things can start to show streaks of pretty at the right speed. But white people don't like us in cars. They think we can't drive. It's an idea bubbling in the white subconscious, fed by movies full of white driving heroes: James Bond in *Goldfinger*. Steve McQueen in *Bullit*. Michael Caine in *The Italian Job*. Keanu Reeves and Susan Sarandon in *Speed*. Batman in *Batman*.

The dream future is when we can go on road trips like the white boy, Jack Kerouac in his book, *On the Road,* in which white boys have four-wheeled adventures and never get shot dead. Till then, we resign ourselves to either driving wrecks that fly under the police radars, else driving pretty cars and getting pulled over by the police and handed a Producer (Hort1), else getting tailed endlessly by the same police.

There is an exception. We are allowed, and appreciated,

to drive delivery vehicles. We are allowed and appreciated to deliver white people to their destination. Like Morgan Freeman in *Driving Miss Daisy*. Or almost every taxi driver in a UK city. Every Deliveroo driver. Every JustEats driver. Many of the food delivery drivers are too broke for a car and are on electric bikes with strapped-on booster batteries. They fly past you, doing thirty-plus, dreaming of owning a Cadillac. We love our cars.

A still life painting: Alfonso, dancing

I was astonished, aged twelve, to discover that my limbs did not automatically fling themselves into the shapes I wanted them to be, as in the TV dance shows. I spent every evening after this discovery in my youth club's darkened dance room getting foot-light – honing my spins, kicks, hip shifts and hand rolls. Eventually, my moves became good enough to be seen in daylight and I started dancing in the sixth form lounge after school, to the sounds of 'I don't wanna be a freak (but I can't help myself)' (Dynasty, 1979, since you ask). Soon, I was getting invitations by the seriously cool kids to discos across Manchester and travelled as far away as Wythenshawe Civic Centre to roll shoulders and launch splits and kickups with the best. But let's cut back to the 12-year-old baby giraffe me and those dark room dance days at the youth club.

I was an OK dancer but there was one kid who was the star of the dance floor. His name was Alfonso. He was 'from another planet' good. In teen-hood, there are moments of intense pleasure that you never experience again across the whole of the rest of your life. Seeing Alfonso dance for the first time was one of those moments. Even recalling it now, brings teenage tears to the brim of my lower eyelids. The youth club dance floor is crowded; we are all chatting and fooling, the girls doing box dances around their makeup bags, the boys cutting around them with leg flicks and some lean-down shoulder rolls to Elvis Costello as he continued wailing about 'Watching The Detectives'. Then Bob Marley's 'Rastaman Vibration' dropped. The dance floor was game. Moves were adjusted. You didn't see Alfonso at first. Gradually though, the crowds receded from around him, the way that always happens on dance floors when somebody brings true shine to the proceedings. Alfonso brought the light: head flailing, locks flying, limbs dashing the ground, he became the shaman who scooped up all our council estate sorrows, all our can't-do-right-for-doing-wrong school woes, all our why-are-we-exiles-in-our-own-land laments. Alfonso. His blaze of limbs called out that we can't live in this hunched-shouldered, foot-hesitant, negative way. He shot his chin high, kicked up his knees, raised his hands to Jah, and danced up a storm that had us gasping, then cheering, then joining in. Irie! Jump up! Positive Vibration! Alfonso, the brilliant centre of a teenage dancefloor cyclone, channelling the ancestors for us all, the shaman rolling back the oppressors, grabbing down the future we deserved, that belonged to us, that we owned on that day, in that blissed, blessed moment.

Flight time

In my 20s, I had dreams of flying. I'd wake up and I knew I had flown but also knew that friends would dismiss this experience as the contents of a dream, argue that my body had remained on earth, in my earthly bed, pressed into my earthly mattress, held down by this earthly gravity. And yet. In the moment of the dream, I am flying, and *ergo* I flew. Of course, reading this, astrologers, Freudian therapists and Tarot card readers will by now be speculating on my life goals, my sex life, my relationship issues, consulting their charts and leaping to explain. I will save you time. In your 20s, all things are possible. All 20-year-olds can fly. Time plucks our feathers one by one.

Vast skies

I was in rural France with sixteen other gap-year teenagers from across Europe repairing an old water mill. We dug a pit, placed boards over it and tried to shit fast before the mosquitoes turned our arses raw. For the other – alimentary – end, fresh local fruit and vegetables arrived by farmer's wagon, and a rota for cooking was organised. In the afternoon, a farmer came on foot down to the mill, with a mini flock of ten sheep around him and said, choose one and I will bring it back as meat. We were brutes and quickly chose the juiciest one. The local radio station played endless *chansons*. The sky was blue and vast. Being at a water mill, we were by a river and the girls would sunbathe in bikinis on the riverbanks. I didn't join them because there was no graceful way of sliding over in my swimming trunks with a boner. The sleeping quarters was the mill's upper floor, but it got stuffy there and one night me and Laurence decided to sleep in a field together instead. The rumour for the next few days was that me and Laurence were fucking. I didn't mind the rumour, I really liked him and if he'd shown me how, I probably would have fucked him. Later, we hitch-hiked across France together.

Misty laundry

I'm nine and Mum orders me to take the family washing to the launderette. It means tugging a fully loaded granny trolley all the way down Burton Road. This view of me makes me laugh, my youthful doppelgänger skinny as a pole, scrunched face hauling my weight in four siblings' dirty clothes as well as my own. It is, of course, no exact memory but rather a construction delivered by the excellent narrative-making powers of the brain – how could I have seen my own face? – yet the detail is vivid, captivating.

This same boy snucks in with Sellotape to stick on the coins that you fed into the washing machines. When the metal coin box's stubby pin jerks back to release the coins and enrich footballer George Best, who I imagined owned the launderette (launderettes being the investment vehicle *du jour* for footballers), instead of falling, the money just hangs there on the Sellotape and the boy pulls it out and will spend the laundry cash on Chewits instead.

Now I'm back in the room of today. In a different Manchester launderette. It's early evening, summer. I begin loading my clothes into a washer. A pair of brogues rocks up alongside me, cracks open a washing machine, plucks clothes out of a bin liner, stuffs them into the drum, loads powder, works the dials like a Bond-film safebreaker. *Click click click click click clack click.* The brogues turn and exit, leaving my clumsy efforts in their wake. I see the brogues' body silhouette later, outside, leaning on a car, smoking Russian cigarettes.

Inside, I sit and watch women smooth laundry – socks with small holes, joke underwear and holey T-shirts with indifferent eyes. Three are by the spin-wringer, chatting in Polish. A fourth looks around, blankly. My gaze lifts to the View-Master of the shop window. Outside, two mothers with toddlers have congregated by the window and are shaking their heads; cars flick by; a dog wanders back, then forth, then back. Inside, the spinning dryers become explosions of clouds, the blowing white sails of ships, the party you once went to all those years ago where everyone would spin-spin-spin because that was the dance style.

A crying woman runs in with a bridesmaid's dress. She stuffs it into a large front-loader, sprays soap suds from the box with her fluttering hand, drops coins into the money slot. The machine clicks to life. She whizzes out again. Everyone in the launderette looks up into the fluorescents and attempts to write her backstory.

Football: three picks

We were a rabble of twelve-year-olds, playing early morning football at school. There was no sentiment on our tarmac pitch: you got picked last if you were shit, no matter what, and the fat boy was always the goalkeeper. Some turned up to play but were left on the sidelines because they would simply get in the way of those who could play. The game would run from morning, through first break, across lunch and into Games if Games was on the timetable for the afternoon. We were ballers. Mad for football. Conversely, there were the Games dodgers. You never saw the dodgers volunteer to play football, or anything else, and they found numerous ways to go missing during Games – sick, dog died, lost kit, religious restrictions, weekend appendectomy.

Aged sixteen, late summer, the mood was mellow and mentally fatigued. We'd been sitting exams all day. We broke into a game of five-a-side in the lunchbreak before the last exam paper. We knew it was the last game of football we'd ever play together, and the game was full of tenderness: half-hearted attempts at scoring, soft tackles, collapsing into each other's arms, the eternal goalkeeper playing centre forward, swapping sides freely, pausing the game entirely to allow someone to show off their keepy-up skills. Even the Games dodgers joined in, and we clapped their efforts, and they laughed.

In Cavendish Road Park, years later, Gary was on leave from the army and wanted to play a game with his mates before going back on patrol in Northern Ireland. We played with him and he scored two though his side lost. Then we sat and listened as he told us how he'd been dodging bullets in Belfast.

Spanish primer

Enrique joined our primary school and could speak no English. I was partnered with him in class. I got hold of a pocket Collins Spanish-English dictionary. It had a bright yellow plastic cover. Me and Enrique would to-and-fro mainly in English, but I'd pick up a word from the dictionary every day and his face would light up when I said the word well enough that he recognised it, and his happiness would be mine. I'd walk him to his house like this, then head home, and spend the evening thumbing through the yellow cover learning new Spanish words to try with him. Spanish became my favourite language.

Windrush America

The ultimate destination for many Windrushers was not England but America. Cue an analogy. You are in

160

the Caribbean and own this beautiful gleaming pink limo. A charlatan comes over from England and steals it. Vexed, you go over to England looking for the thief and your car. Everybody denies all knowledge of this charlatan, pleading, *We don't talk about him here, leave the subject alone, the car is long gone; here, have this bicycle instead.* After pedalling around England but getting nowhere fast and nothing but punctures and no sightings at all, you decide to take off for America because you're done with this bike, and there are plenty of cars in America and America is just up from the road from the Caribbean, so Americans are closer cousins than these robbing *we-didn't-see-anything, we-don't-know-him, we-don't-know-anything-about-this* people here in England. You book your ticket and go.

Fancy shoes

In Wales, my kung fu instructor was troubled by some guy who seemed to be making moves on his London-based side-chick, Rafaela, and he rings me and asks me to check the guy out since I'm in London. So, I went over to this place he gives me the address for, in London. It's a squat. The guy – Otis – was living with five others, none of them Rafaela, and he welcomed me. We play frisbee on a patch of grass inside the estate, then take acid and set off to see *Alien 3*. We skip over the Tube turnstiles and pay into the cinema and wow, what a movie. Stumbling out, we float our way back to the squat via the Tube again and I'm drinking cider when Rafaela walks in. I'm disappointed. Not with her – who wanted to be a side chick? – but with life itself, its squalid situations. The tension climbs. Glances bounce off the walls, some of them with threats. Otis says I should leave. I nod. I get up. Walking through London streets at 3 a.m., I pick up a pair of shoes by the bins outside a grand house. They are my exact size, and fancy as hell.

The weirdest game of football I ever played

September in that year was full of bailiffs, break-ups, roof leaks and storm warnings. The one joy amid the drizzle of misery was announced by Rupert. He said, 'Boys, it's mushroom season, time to pick them, before anyone else gets there; they'll be all puffed up and ready now.'

Out we traipsed in an orderly file to the Daisy Park football pitches, specifically the sloping side that runs off into the old railway line. Leading us in an orange cagoule, was Rupert, devotee of the Divine Light Ministry and Initiate into the Mysteries of Forcing open the Coin Boxes of Electric Meters. Rupert was soft spoken and sly, the chief tenant of a ten-bedroomed Victorian squat and proud possessor of sixteen Eviction Notices. Next, in combat trousers, walked Gerald, the care-home kid turned candle-maker with excellent connections to small-time cannabis dealers across Manchester, a self-taught martial artist and formidable numchuk swirler. Then came Paul, formerly of genteel Knutsford, owner of an incomparable range of knitted scarves and unchallengeable, bong-sucking lung capacity; Paul was prone to playing Lou Reed's 'Walk on the Wild Side' on repeat. Following Paul was South African Jim who could munch his way through a filled fridge, even the fermented stuff at the back. Bringing up the rear, in a green, army long-sleeve, was the scribbler latterly known as me. Someone in this crocodile of mushroom pickers has the cool idea to bring a football and there are echoes as the ball bounces on the pavement all the way to the park.

We found the shroom crop on the slope as Rupert predicted, and gazed in awe at their little brown monk's cape heads and mud-stalk stems, swaying gently in the ballet of lithe, humming green leaves of municipal grass, their brown, munch-me chant rising up from the mud to the stars via our ears.

Collecting was an undisciplined activity and some consuming occurred. Nevertheless, a decent crop was gathered into a communal polythene bag. Gerald suggested we now played football, and this was agreed to be a good idea. A game of sorts commenced even as the mushroom effects kicked in. There were no sides to this game. Paul quit quite early on, choosing instead to deliver a long harangue on the evils of meat-eating to an audience of ants dragging a dead fly by the kick-off spot. Rupert thought it was unfair on hands that only feet could make contact with the ball. This was agreed and the rules accordingly adjusted. Gerald noted the absence of a goal or goals and therefore the impossibility of scoring. Jumpers and coats were shed and three goals were thereupon improvised. General ball-kicking and throwing, chasing and fouling and diving and scoring commenced until the Manchester light faded so low it became too dark for the game, if by now there was one since most of us were by now wandering across the grass unsure of time or place or purpose.

That evening, as Lou Reed walked the wild side again, Paul began writing his Last Will and Testament in a corner – certain meteors were about to strike; Gerald's nunchucks filled the air with their steady hum, and me and South African Jim watched the dots on the TV cathode ray tube blink on and off.

We all dispersed soon after. Paul became a painter and decorator, much admired in the trade; and died by suicide in the 00's. Gerald signed up to Babylon and became a respected BT telephone IT Specialist. Rupert disappeared. South African Jim started a T-shirt printing firm in Valencia. I became a driving instructor.

Redundant interpretation of the text: The point being made is, we are all going to die, so why not live, first? We lived back then. We were young and fervent and wild and stupid and embraced all of life and lived it to the full, exulting in our physical abilities, gambling on our resilience, and trusting the leaps of our impulses and imaginations. Later, the remorseless turn of the world would beat us into submission the way it beats everyone on this earth into submission, the way the earth reclaims us all no matter how much fire we breathe.

Circus highs

Ophelia's speciality was shimmying up silk to execute double star drops and corkscrew flops and she was the best acrobat by far. Arturo the clown declared one day that he was gay. He was annoyed when nobody batted an eyelid. Rodrigo was a communist juggler and fire-eater who campaigned to rename the Student Union Building after a leader of the African Revolution. Cam the contortionist only ever slept with unicyclists. I was never sufficiently proficient in unicycling. I was the only Black person in the circus. The base of a human pyramid requires a strong ass and thick thighs. I was the go-to for that. I wanted to learn *commedia dell'arte* clown moves but never did. Instead, I learned how to climb the silk ropes and ended up twisting across ceilings with Ophelia.

Guy Goma Day

There are many Peter Kalus out there, including academics who are all more qualified and talented than myself. An academic paper publishing site emails me every so often asking things like: "Peter Kalu, did you write "Comparison of the properties of Cu-NBA's/ Ti Composite Wires...". Did you write "The effect of fabrication mode on microstructure, texture and..."

My answer was always "No, I am the lowly poet, Peter Kalu." But the questions kept coming. I began to wonder what would happen if I answered 'yes.' One day the devil got me, and I clicked that green 'yes' button. Before I knew it, I had a business class airline ticket to an electrical engineering conference in Arizona, a one-week premium booking at a Hilton hotel, a hire car, and a gratuity of $1,000 dollars, payable upon my arrival at the Conference. I had to look up the word 'gratuity'.

I found two phrases got me out of most tight corners. "I think there is a lot of sense in what my colleague said", and "that's a smart question. What do you yourself think?" A pressing need to visit the toilet got me out of the rest.

P.S. Guy Goma, you are a hero. Your circumstances were vastly different from the above.

Burnt shoulder

Aged two, I burned my shoulder by tipping over a boiling stove kettle. I know this because (a) my mother told me this is what happened and (b) I have a skin graft on my left shoulder. I have no direct recall whatsoever of the event. This absence of memory is hardly surprising given long-term memory is not laid up by two-year-olds (and I wonder now what drugs my school librarian was on when he told our class he could remember being born).

Through primary school years, I didn't think about the scar much; perhaps I was a little self-conscious, but I was a shy child anyway. It was at high school that my discomfort welled up: I decided it was a disfigurement that I needed to hide. All boys of my year did gym class together in shorts, socks and plimsolls – no tops. I sat bare-chested among the horse boxes and climbing ropes with my shoulders hunched, arms wrapped across my raised knees, hiding the shoulder scar. One afternoon, as we were all sitting there in the hall, a visiting gym teacher walked past and kicked my back – either as a way of telling me to straighten it and sit normally like everyone else, or because he, like the species of P.E. teachers in general, was a sadist and couldn't resist doing shit like that – or both.

The nadir of my self-conscious despair came one summer when the winning school T-shirt design had no sleeves. The white T with escalloped shoulders was undergoing a revival at the time. All my schoolmates said the T-shirts looked cool and they were getting one for sure. Poverty saved me. Everyone knew that Pete didn't do school trips, that Pete was on free school dinners. So, Pete for sure wasn't about to wear any school kit that wasn't compulsory, and wouldn't be wearing the new T. Still, I loved that James Dean T-shirt look, and I cursed my disfigured shoulder throughout the summer.

Time schooled the boy. As teenage self-consciousness left me, I saw that people didn't recoil with horror upon sight of the scar; their reaction was more one of curiosity. It became an ice breaker in summer social scenes. Someone would ask, 'How did you get that scar?' and I'd tell my story, either the truth, else the truth embellished for dramatic effect.

Now I have nothing but admiration for the scar, and for the surgeon who performed the skin graft operation that created it. The graft has never let me down. It restricts the movement of my left shoulder slightly, but it has never bled or peeled, never been anything other than magnificently resilient. The surgeon is probably dead by now, but I continue to thank those skilled hands that stitched my skin.

Long-ass epilogue to Burnt Shoulder

There is a saying from a branch of therapy called somatics, that 'the body keeps the score'. To consider the somatics of the event, where did the pain go from my initial scalding? I have zero recall of any pain – it lives on only as speculation. I can of course try to imagine the pain. And neuroscientists suggest that if we imagine something happening in a certain way repeatedly enough, we can convince ourselves it happened that way. The amount of pain I suffered as a two-year-old would become the amount I believed I suffered. I choose to believe I suffered no pain. Does my body tell me anything different? Is the pain that repeatedly springs up at the back of my left shoulder related to that original scalding? I don't know. I let the thought go, kiss my two-year-old self better, imagine no pain.

This is how it ends

Telephone wires criss-cross a mellow sky. I sip dregs of black coffee and slide through our photos. The poses we adopt in the selfies are our usual: you surprised, sunny, your hand waving to me; I stare my adoration of you into the camera's lens.

Your lips were fish, darting through coral.

You learn things about people in a strange order. Your first language was Dari, then Arabic, English and French. The book you carried was James Joyce's *The Dubliners*, in Dari. The poet, Tahirih was a Persian suffragette, and is underrated in the West. All the Middle East's problems would be solved if Manchester United's Sir Alex Ferguson became Secretary General of the UN. You did not feel feminine without your heels on. Your laugh told me you could skate down a frozen street, climb trees, lead revolutions.

Early on, sometimes when you spoke and I didn't understand your English, I would follow the movement of your lips, listen to the tone of your voice, the bursts of joy, the criss-cross of sadness on your brow, the defiance fading low like the faulty pilot light of your HMO boiler.

You quote Tahirih: 'You can kill me as soon as you like, but you cannot stop the emancipation of women.'

The life of an exile is such that even a religious cult can be a useful distraction. One room, no money, prohibited from working, under obligation to report Monday mornings to the Capital Building and each attendance a possible detention. You attach to nothing in this limbo, become an involuntary Buddhist.

At the final hearing, you told them that as a journalist you knew too much. If you returned, they would stitch your lips, run a sack around you and you would meet the fate of unwanted cats. They queried your credibility, assessed the translation of what you stated and deemed it poetry. *There are few hard facts in your depositions, only interpretations; there is no significant new evidence; it is not unreasonable not to concord with your interpretation of the scant facts you provide*. They must love Nietzsche, you sighed and reeled off a quote ('All things are subject to interpretation and whichever interpretation prevails at a given time is a function of power and not truth'). *We won,* you said. *The judge agreed with us.*

You sang Dari in the glow of the orange night-light, then stood at the window, looking. It was a cool black night in Liverpool, and the stars were out.

There is no time, only the eternal moment.

Your red-heeled shoes chucked under my bike welcomed me home one day. You learned I had no washing machine and turned in my sleep.

The thrill of a constant presence was balanced by the ennui of living with someone else. I thought about you each morning while on the ferry to work.

You called them sleeping tablets. I searched them. An anti-depressant. No big surprise.

Laura came to me suddenly at Sefton Park Festival, kissed my cheek. You were at a stall nearby, and saw. She was a friend, I explained. I'd helped her through the loss of her father. Artists are often tactile.

I returned late one evening. You mentioned her by name. I laughed and said yes, I visited her. She was having problems with a lawn mower; I got it started and then she wanted to talk – about her new boyfriend, the holiday she was going to take with him, how she felt about her father's memorial – things like that.

You turned away, lips pursed, and did that head wobble which meant 'I will think about it.'

That night was a hot night. I woke once, saw the serenity of your lips, the charcoal smudge of your eyelashes. I thought *This is the space-time fold, this is the here-now of infinity.*

The first time you slept downstairs, I didn't think too

much of it. Next morning, you said I should drive you back to your place by Sefton Park, with all your luggage. What was wrong? I asked after the car was loaded. Tears behind your sunglasses, you said a woman simply knows, and you had decided, and there was no point in more talk.

For once I hated my sat nav's precision, wanted diversions, road works, but our journey crossing from Swanside to Liverpool Eight was unimpeded. I parked up to drop you off one street away, as requested. Silence spooled and we followed it unravelling until it dissolved into awkwardness. You got out. I sat in my car a moment.

This is how it ends.

Trainee hairdressers love my high-top Afro

It's late March, which makes it National Trainee Hairdresser Level II Exam season. I am Afro'd. Therefore, I am in demand. My place of work is an office on a high street of hairdressers. The trainees stand in their doorways, all smiles as I walk their corridor of love. They eye my prized asset. Achieving Level II requires that the trainees have cut at least one head of Afro hair. 'Sir, would you like a free haircut?' 'Hello. Excuse me. May I cut your hair?' 'Wow. I love your 'fro. Can I cut it?' They shoot their shot. I choose the one whose smile I like most. A senior hairdresser observes as she washes, dries, snips, all the while telling me how beautiful I am, how my hair is gold, how proud and honoured she is to be styling it. It is flattery – part of the hairdresser's art – and very effective. With a final flick of an Afro comb, she is done. I admire my reflection in the mirror, thank her and leave. All that flattery. I file into my office and begin my allotted drudgery. A smile plays on my face all day.

Snow fight

The snow finally fell, and we became kidults instead of the Blood-sucking Descendants of Immigrants, Draining the Taxpayer's Purse. A snowball fight was duly arranged. We assembled in the Robert Adam Crescent bowl, along one of the pathways. Half a metre of the cold white stuff coated everything – the grass expanses, the Eagle pub roof that squatted in the middle of the crescent, the upper branches of mauled saplings. It made everything glisten, everything muffled and everything new. It was on. We scattered. Boom! Jimmy splatted Henry on the conk. Boom! Harvey launched a fat one that exploded on the back of Orson's trench coat. Whish! Dawn's missile whacked Jimmy's shoulder. Boom! Boom! Harvey was the cluster target. He'd lost (his version) or sneaked off with the final lump of Afghan Black (our version) in Gerald's flat last night. The missiles switched to Alan, who'd failed to share the profit on his short-lived candle-making operation that everyone had worked on, and we all had the candle wax burns to prove it. Wang! Wang! Wang! Akeem got it from all sides. He'd bedded Shenagh, then bedded Courtney the next day. For those of us not getting laid at all, it was too much: why did God favour this short-arsed, handsome, lithe, smooth-talking, clean-pored, bisexual unemployed sous chef? I took hits for my own sins: I'd drunk my home-brew apple cider off all to myself when it ripened instead of sharing it. I'd slinked away when Alan's flat needed cleaning after the party. In half an hour the snow fight was over. We ended it drenched, cleansed and knitting our escape ladders once more.

Brown moon bisexuality

Once in a brown moon, I have felt attracted to the same sex. When I was twelve, I fell in love with R., a boy in my year. We stayed after school for the table tennis club and fooled around. We played endlessly, sometimes with ping-pong bats, often physically, trying out headlocks and other wrestling manoeuvres from the telly. I never wanted to have sex with him – my desire for sex was a switch that seemed to turn on some years later – but I loved his company, loved the smell of him, and I think I would have loved to kiss him. Six years later, I fell for L. the French guy in rural France. I have no idea why I fancied him, probably the shapes he made with his hands when talking, and how we had such an easy companionship. We slept in a field together and scandalised the *Jeunnesse et Reconstruction* international student community – we were meant to sleep communally i.e. all sixteen of us under the leaking roof of the old water mill that we were renovating.

Half a decade later, I felt myself falling for Y., a Mexican Art curator – his velvet voice made me dreamy. But I am a lazy bisexual. I have never felt gay desire strongly enough to be bothered exploring it, or to pony up for the damnation and disapproval that goes with it in many circles. So, when the survey form inevitably lands after an arts event and asks me to choose a sexuality, I tick heterosexual. It's a simplification, but I also know that the survey form pushers do not want nuance. They want me to tick a box and not get cute with it. If only the forms had a seven-point scale instead of yes/no.

Head boy, duly noted

I was never considered the right type for head boy. I consistently kept bad company. My friends were usually in the sinbins that the school maintained to keep the 'unteachable' out of ordinary classrooms. I hung out with the school's petty thieves, latecomers, bullies and bullshitters, and, by association, I was a petty thief, latecomer, bully and bullshitter myself. I sat at the back of the room in most classes, appearing only to listen intermittently to what teachers had to say. *Effort B, Attainment A* was the usual mark of my annual report cards. Like my delinquent friends, I was often in line for punishment at home time. Our favourite punishment was the strap because it didn't take long. You stretched out your arms, placed one hand on top of the other, both palms facing upwards, and the teacher whacked your upper palm with a leather strap, between one and five times, depending on the sin, and how good or bad the teacher's day had been. It took thirty seconds each (we were punished in groups of a minimum two, a mean of four, and on a busy Friday afternoon, six), unless the teacher fell to lecturing us prior to wielding the weapon, in which case it could take as much as thirty minutes in aggregate, during which time resentment built among us as we had football to play, other shit to do. Some teachers used a cane across our backsides instead of the strap to the hands. This was considered by us an equally excellent – because equally quick – punishment. The two worst punishments were Detention and the Report Card. Detention involved remaining behind in some classroom in silence after school for an hour – a colossal waste of time. The Report Card involved a series of teachers writing snide remarks relating to your intra-class behaviour, class by class.

The head boy was always the pupil with the highest grades in Year 10. When the pupil with the highest grades became me, the school swerved the convention, and appointed someone else. I shrugged. My form teacher explained that, owing to the company I kept, there was a fear I would be *ostracised* if I were made head boy. I nodded, mildly amused by the teacher's smart use of the word *ostracised,* knowing it was the kind of word I would be distracted by and would feel compelled to look up to check its etymology.

The head boy shenanigans followed a pattern. Our school, like most, specialised in fake democracy. There was a position known as class representative. In theory, each class chose their class representative at the start of the school year on a show of hands. In practice, each year, we followed the form teacher's recommendations, did the North Korean politburo-style unanimous show of hands for that recommended person, and the teacher's appointee became our class representative. At the beginning of the last compulsory year of schooling, I'd had enough. I stood on a chair. 'We've had four years of fake democracy. This year, let's choose our own rep!' There was a clamour of agreement in the class. Shock on the form teacher's face. We looked around. And chose William. William was the kid who was most uninterested in formal education, and so most undeserving of any honour according to the school's system of honours. Yet William was also the kindest person in the class. He had never been awarded anything in all his years at school, not even so much as a Certificate in Tidying Up. Yet William passed one of democracy's key tests: general likeableness. It had to be William. William was up for it. To gales of laughter, we nominated him. On a show of hands, we unanimously elected him. William stood up to make (no doubt it was going to be shit) a speech. 'Sit down, William, sit down!' the teacher yelled over the cheering. She cancelled the election and, to jeers of 'Fix! Fix! Fix!' appointed last year's stooge instead.

When that year's mock exam results came in, the results showed I had achieved the best grades of my year in a slew of subjects. The teachers scratched their heads. There was no evidence I'd stolen any of the test papers. I could not have copied Waris in mathematics since Waris had been ill that day. My deviant classmate, Cathy could not have written my English essays for me – we'd been at opposite ends of the classroom. I was stopped in a corridor by one of the school's senior leadership team shortly after the results. He said it was customary for him to congratulate the highest achieving pupil in the mock exams of my year, and my attainment had been duly noted. I nodded, mildly amused by his use of the word, attainment. He swept away. I considered changing my name to Duly Noted.

Sweaty gyms

Posh gyms have extractor fans, air purifiers and professional cleaning staff. Working-class gyms stink. The more close to the financial edge these working-class gyms are, the funkier the smell. A friend asked me to pick him up from a boxing gym. It was old-school and had been open for over eighty years. I smelt the ghosts of Gene Tunney, Jack Johnson and Rocky Marciano wandering around, looking for bodies to inhabit. The uninitiated might reel upon entering such premises: boxers working up a sweat – skipping, sparring, punching bags, throwing medicine balls. The sweat drips to the floor, and rises as steam into the rafters, penetrates the plasterboard, the paint and brickwork, the canvas, the floor. It's stamped and pounded into the canvas year after year; and as the components of sweat decay and recombine, they create the Frankenstein of sweat that is the signature note of the working-class gym. I'm at home in that funk. It proclaims, *Here are ordinary human beings exerting themselves and stinking up the place while doing so. There is nothing that needs hiding or masking here, just honest sweat.*

Black pessimism: misery walks

Well-meaning historians are making every place in England miserable for Black people. Wherever you go, they are erecting plaques to Black misery. The beautiful waters of these historical docks? Slave ships pushed off from here. This wonderfully constructed red brick mill? Slave-picked cotton was woven there. Your splendid country home, with its unique, ribbed columns, pink, Italian marble floors, and soaring, vaulted ceilings? Funded by slave money. The glorious Norfolk countryside, its rich pastures and teeming wetlands? Enclosed by rich men who fleeced India and with the profits grabbed common land from the local peasants.

You get the drift. Misery everywhere. What is a Black person to do when we are separated by such a thin (though green and pleasant) skein from a congealed vat of historical misery? It reminds me of the urban myth that in any city you are never more than six feet from a rat. The solution is the same as for the rats. Ignore them. Turn a blind eye to a place's history. Adopt a blithe spirit. Black joy requires wilful ignorance.

The case against Pete Kalu III: sitting in his underwear

'And so he was sitting there, in his cum-soaked underwear, looking to roll a cigarette, and I placed my head in my hands and cried. I didn't need to get pregnant again. I'd told him that, yet he'd used no contraception. When he gets horny, all that goes out the window, and I accept it, I go along with it, but it's not right. My uterus needs rest, the doctors warned, and, with the fibroids, sexual intercourse is difficult. But he's only ever after his own pleasure. I've left him half a dozen times, told him he must move out, but somehow, he charms his way back in – I take pity on him, I let him back, and it starts over again. He's no good for me, all my friends tell me that, and I know it, I deserve better – someone who cares more and can express their feelings other than physically. And do practical things, like lay a new floor, cook. All he does is sit at a keyboard. 'I'm a writer,' he says. And if he's not typing, he stares at the ceiling. 'Reflecting, which is part of my writing process.' Yadayada. And he leaves me to clean up and all that, while he 'writes'. Have you ever read anything he's written? It doesn't even make sense, none of it. Who's going to publish that? I want a normal life. I want to come home from my job which is serving good food to hard-working people, ruining my hair in smoke and hot oil for them, and when I come home, I want that he's done something, like, in the real world. Instead, he's still sitting there, in his underwear. I ask and he says, 'I've retyped a paragraph.' That's all. It's not on. We are so over.'

The tobacconist is ready to see you

Imagine bedsit land. Four knocks rapped out according to a code gains you access to a bedsit littered with semicomatose bodies, paraphernalia overflowing with ash that you have to step over to find the customer armchair, nudge a random hand from the armrest, then listen to the ramblings of the freelance tobacconist as he vents his conspiracy theories, rants about a lost girlfriend, hatred of a famous musician (often the drummer of a rock band) before taking your currency, unrolling it, possibly holding each note to the light, pocketing it, then giving you some foil wrap of your tobacco which you know is short and may well be cut with other substances. Your inner monkey is nevertheless happy because you have sinned: evaded the authorities, broken some law, and will now inhale and draw your own pharmacological conclusions as to the composition and purity of this illicitly obtained material like the connoisseur you have become. The resulting intoxication is so much more pleasurable than receiving the same lab-grown drugs over the counter of a brightly lit pharmacy where the university-trained chemist can guarantee the purity and will quietly assess how far gone you are. The pear-stealing St Augustine of Hippo understood: 'Those pears truly were pleasant to the sight; but it was not for them that my miserable soul lusted, for I had abundance of better, but those I plucked simply that I might steal. For, having plucked them, I threw them away, my sole gratification in them being my own sin, which I was pleased to enjoy.'

Dad: skipping the ropes (warning: this is a long and morbid section. You may choose to skip it)

In death, my father looked healthy. From within the open coffin, he was smiling, eyes closed; his expression was serene, if slightly puzzled. He seemed smaller than I'd ever seen him. As I took in this shrunken, puzzled

178

shell of a man, I let out a sob. For his good times that came whizzing at me. For the boy who could sing his head off – he had the voice of an angel. For the student who could switch from medicine to accountancy and still succeed. For the man who could dance like there was no tomorrow. This man. With his affable kindness. His tendency to trust absolute strangers when doing business deals. For the Biafra activist who led marches of thousands of people through the streets of Manchester in protest. Who collapsed into rage as so many of his brothers died, as so many of their children starved, as so many of the surviving mothers and wives grew more and more distraught. I wept for the plight of this man – the first-born son of his father's first wife – who was meant to save them when the war happened. Who couldn't save them. Who lost everything – fortune, family and mind. Whose sense of agency was gone forever by the end of the war, broken on its wheel. Despised by family in England for his rages, for not showing affection either to his wife or his children, a man seen in England as having too much strut and too little heart, too unaware and unavailable. Shunned for long periods in Nigeria for having overstayed in England, having reneged on the childhood betrothal promise and left a young woman there to grow old, waiting; and for not having saved anybody. A man who could do no right. The ice man.
He skipped the ropes of Western culture and Igbo codes: barbed ropes that bled him with every skip.

The dutiful schoolboy who excelled yet lived in the shadow of his legendary father.

The rebellious teenager who ran off to a woman from another state and was rumoured to have had a child with her.

The proud, excited Dad, cooking egusi stew while

waiting impatiently for his fourth child to be born.

The headstrong fool who abandoned his car in the middle of Burton Road, Manchester rather than give way to the other driver who was *clearly in the wrong.*

The apostle of peace who never hit us, his kids (a low bar, but worth recalling), who said again and again after we fought the fights that siblings fight, 'Before you raise your hand, count to ten!' Advice that was impressive, though disregarded in spirit by him when he slapped the television off permanently one morning with his bare hands because it was on too loud for his liking, *for goodness sake,* he was trying to sleep upstairs.

Who had us cower from his exasperated disapproval if we did not learn instantly something he tried to teach us, usually mathematics.

Who left behind three wives, each angry with him in a different way.

I slowed my pulse and pulled my thoughts back to the good times. Walking up Burton Road with him, hand in hand, both of us smiling. Little six-year-old me, proud when he showed up in Manchester, and full of a six-year-old's boasts: 'I have a dad who does huge business deals, and makes loads of money, and see, he has a car, and he makes lots of money every week, way more than your dad.' Happy days when he stood in the avenue watching us play, his skin shining and his smile beaming.

The only Black man with a car in Manchester for miles and miles.

The Black man who had the temerity to buy a house in Manchester's richest (and so whitest) area, Didsbury. And who took the white neighbours' shock at, then disdain of him – and of us, his family – as a badge of honour.

Spin time's wheel and I meet him again in Umuahia,

Nigeria, thirty years after he left England permanently. In Umuahia, he was very much alive, and seemed the same man of my childhood, had the same puzzled smile and courteous manner, the same vigour and humour. He was more at ease in Nigeria than I ever remembered him in England. 'Stay for six months,' he suggested to me, then. 'Live here with me, I will build you a house here, right here.' Here being Umuahia, or more exactly, following his extended finger, a large hole in his compound, big enough for a small swimming pool, or a modest extension. The gesture was heartfelt. He had a straggle of English roses growing up the side of his large house, and an unplumbed English bath in one of the house's upper rooms. He was known locally now as the English man, his friend Richard, who lived in one of the outer buildings of the compound, told me later; he liked Marmite and English tea.

The good times. He was allocated so few. He had been one of the privileged people of Igbere, the first-born son of a chief. And he had departed this earth leaving only a mess. Yet, amongst all the debris, somewhere in there, between the planks of teak that comprised his coffin, and on the lips of some, was a good man.

The king arrived with a large entourage. He moved through the small crowd in the compound, his progress setting off a ripple of nods and bows and deferential smiles. He arrived at the coffin. I swallowed bile, wiped away my tears, offered a hand, then promptly withdrew it when my cousin nudged me to indicate this was not the correct protocol on how to greet a king. I bowed slightly instead, said how privileged we were to have him grace us with his presence. He answered in Igbo, then English, offering his condolences. His eyes spoke kindness from within the stiff collar of status. Having intoned some words at the coffin, and looked up to the sky, he spoke to everyone gathered at the compound in a soft, meditative voice, to regular murmurs of approval. The cadences of his speech were calming, the compound almost quiet. He finished to more murmurs, some soft exclamations. Then he and his entourage moved away, through the compound throng again, into the sanctuary of their 4x4s, and drove off.

That night, I turned in my bed. My father specialised in disappointment. With the remorseless attachment to misery that grief insists upon, I went through his dud cheques, his promises not kept. If I passed my exams, he was going to gift me a fountain pen like the one he gifted my elder sister when she had passed hers. The bounce? By the time I'd passed my exams, he had abandoned the family home. I never spoke to anyone about my disappointment over that absent pen. I bought myself fountain pens to compensate, still buy them. My mother gave me one of her few mementoes of him – a clay inkwell, glazed in mottled blue pigment. It sits on a shelf in my house. Again, my mother, bless her, doing her best to compensate for my father's deficits, and somehow intuitively finding something I would relate to. More bounced cheques. He promised I could join his Import-Export business after I finished school. He had fled England well before my last school year, his business having collapsed into bankruptcy. I imagined that my disappointments about him had settled like a sediment, or dust, somewhere in the territory of my heart, lost and been buried there, stirred into memory only by the great winds that came about upon momentous occasions like death. How was I to forgive him these and all other disappointments, and yet retain respect for the man? All winds abate, eventually, do they not? I fell into a turbulent sleep.

You can never have too many daughters

She is flamboyantly dressed and serene; her serenity is infectious. We glide through the Manchester rain to Ramen, a new restaurant in a London Street basement. Someone in monochrome clothing sitting at a table nearby asks if it's her birthday. A little micro-aggression, but effective. My daughter's glow recedes; I suggest we skip out, don't even order. We land at Archies, the American Diner. Archies' wall-to-ceiling shocking-pink is ostentation and glamour – she does not need to play small here for the monochrome tribe. Nobody does. A wonderful afternoon unfurls. First topic of discussion: men. I advise her do not seek depth, for we have no depth (as I advise, I can see all my ex's nodding in agreement). Next, housing. We agree on the infamy of landlords and the outrage of letting agents' charges. We move on to what is the right time to have a baby, if ever; how to build a career and get more pay; the difference between Nashville and Texas chicken wings; the sociology of design and its intersect with race and who will win the football league this year (she indulges me by listening to my predictions). By the time we step out, it has stopped raining. Sunrays dose us with Vitamin D. Daughters do that for you. They bring the sun. A man can never have too many daughters.

Heat

Me and Sonia spent six weeks working on an American summer camp together. With us both being English, we had a rapport, meaning ironic smiles, but nothing physical. One of our Dutch friends working the camp managed to charm a California stockbroker they met at

Lake Tahoe into allowing them to drive her pink Cadillac all the way from Milwaukee to San Francisco because the stockbroker preferred to fly back. Five of us took the ride – two English and three Dutch – one Dutch girl, two Dutch boys. Both Dutch boys fancied the girl and the Dutch girl fancied both boys and the three of them were sharing a tent to save on hotel money – and me and Sonia shared the other tent. We Brits smirked our way across America, unable not to listen to the various gasps and squelches from the Dutch tent, envious, but somehow never getting there ourselves – we'd fallen into a friendship-zone thing. After a week in the San Francisco house, with its palm trees and huge fridges, the three Dutch left and the big bed they'd been sleeping in beckoned. We played it casual. Sonia said we deserved some comfort after so much time on the smaller beds, and wouldn't be better if we wore no clothes in this bed because San Francisco was so hot, no?

A green hymn for the Black exhausted

Give me a Hallelujah. We are all exhausted. The harried Black woman trying to twist through the snide comments of her work colleagues and hold onto her job. Hallelujah. The plumber riding out comments as he fixes a tap for the housing association tenant who resents an immigrant *in her home of all places*. Hallelujah. The Black teens on the social media hamster wheel of reinventing themselves daily to stay one revolution ahead of the stereotypes that are chasing them. Hallelujah. The refugee delivery drivers delivering more, faster, at all hours, in all weathers, to all customers, politely, for a pittance, and the same tomorrow, and never enough to remit home. Hallelujah. Everywhere, we are holding it down, holding on, finding ways to be keeping on, hanging on. Hallelujah. And the request comes, *Can this be done in a green way please?*

How do we find the capacity – the strength, the elasticity, the stamina – to carry the green load as well as the others? Are we the donkeys of the world, to be stacked with all the world's burdens, burdens we did not create? In global terms, melanin-high people are the main sufferers of the environmental consequences that sludge-capitalism has dredged up. And while the world's natural resources are not infinite, neither are the psychic resources of the melanin-high community.

And yet. If we don't want to find ourselves dancing in the ashes at the end of the world, we too must address the climate emergency. Hallelujah. Our genealogy traces us out to every port of the world, so we can relay to the metropolis the green message as received from every brown village, every Black town, every melanined city. Hallelujah. *Think global, act local* is the mantra. Act where we can, when we can. The Black office worker can encourage less use of the photocopier. Can he? Yes. Hear me, can he? Yes. The brown plumber can fit water-saving floats into cisterns. Can he? Yes. The Black teens can hold green consciousness-raising events in schools and colleges. Can they? Yes. The delivery drivers can innovate ways of drawing more miles per watt from the batteries of their electric bikes. Can they? Yes. We can all drive less and walk more. Can we? Yes. In the past, collectively, we have stood up proudly for justice. Now, the Black communities living in the cartographical West, must stand up for climate justice. Yes. We must join hands to ensure ecological damage is reduced worldwide. Yes. And we must be vigilant that the eco-damage in the West is not simply contained and shipped across to our cousins elsewhere in the world. Yes. Let's act today to build a Black and beautiful, *and green* tomorrow. Yes. Amen. Give me a Hallelujah. Hallelujuah.

Generational trauma

My mother told me that she grew up in a household where she wasn't invited to learn to cook, and at school they laughed at her and said, 'No, you can't chop an onion like that, and now we'll fail our school inspection due to your useless chopping.' The criticism lived in her for a long time because she is telling me this story now, at age ninety-three, in her living room and her eyes are misting up. 'Don't upset yourself, Mum,' I say. She sighs, then tells of how her aunt said she was a very good carrot selector, praised her for her ability to find the best carrots from the garden for cooking. I feel my mother's continuing upset, despite her invoking the carrot story in an attempt to soften the onion story of humiliation. And I marvel at her mental gymnastics in swinging from the pain of her exclusion from the kitchen to her brilliance at carrot digging. We've switched roles and suddenly I'm her parent and I'm angry at the people looking after this motherless little girl, my mother, allowing the little child to suffer such treatment. Had they known how long it would stay with her, they would not have been so carelessly cruel. It had effects. When she had children – us – everything she fed us was from a tin or what could be put together simply – spaghetti and ketchup, minced meat, bread and cheese.

When I went to school, I experienced school meals. I was amazed at the heavenly crunch of the pastry on school cheese pie and the mouth fireworks of rhubarb and custard. At the divine slime of treacle pudding.

I begged second helpings every day I could. Now, in advanced adulthood, somehow, I have yet to learn to cook anything spectacular. I wonder if I've been holding out all these years in subconscious solidarity with my mother, assuming her mantle of indifference to matters culinary. I console myself that while I don't cook, I am a great appreciator of my friends' cooking: I have mountains of empty food containers in my kitchen cupboard.

Ignatius Sancho on books and dancing girls

Reading *Sancho's Letters*, I came across this line in praise of literature: 'The beloved book – the sweet pleasures of imagination poetically worked up in delightful enthusiasm – richer than all your fruits – your spices – your dancing girls –...' I thought, I get it, Ignatius, books are great, but steady on there, hold up, hold up. I'm as ardent a fan of books as anyone, but books have their limits and will likely not measure up to *all* of this earth's delights. Let us try an experiment. We place dancing girls to the left. We place the complete works of Shakespeare to the right. Now, on the count of three, which way will the general population jump? Which way, dear reader – dear reader – are you still with me?

A sentimental paragraph on childhood

Happiness in childhood is unalloyed. To marvel at the whirl of your fists in a fight, to notice for the first time the sharp *crunch* sound of knuckles on fleshy chin – whether you own the knuckles or you own the chin – is to learn something wondrous and new about yourself, the human body, and the world.

Cosmetic Blackness 3

On a visit to Hong Kong, that most vertical of cities, I was struck by the profusion of billboards wrapped around the commercial district's ankles. They displayed white-skinned, pointy-nosed Westerners selling handbags, shoes, clothing, perfumes, makeup and watches. The gweilos of Britain had ceded the landmass of Hong Kong, but white giants still leapt across Central, from billboard to billboard, signalling whiteness's enduring supremacy.

When photographer Mary Ellen Mark took a series of documentary photographs of sex workers in the Falkland Rd area of Bombay (now Mumbai), India in 1978, her subjects complained that she was photographing too many of them with dark skin: light skin to them was more beautiful. They liked to apply skin whitener make-up before work – or before Ellen Mark's photos. One sex worker, Champa, plied their trade dressed as an English lady, requiring the whitest of skin.

All three of the Black boys in my class said they could tell I had a white mother because my face was so ashy, *cho*, because I didn't put Vaseline on my face, and they'd had their faces Vaselined by their mums since they were tiny and they did it themselves now every morning, *cho*, and it was part of being Black which you clearly weren't, *cho*. Backed into this corner, I lied and protested my mum *was* Black, *cho*, and I bought a tub of Vaseline jelly so I could be like them – properly Black. I opened the tub. It smelled like car engines. I spread it on my face's *epidermis* (I paid attention in biology). Then made some shapes with it, finally rubbed it in. It felt good but it was too gloopy and smothered my pores and irritated my pimples. Worse, it went white in the freezing cold, and I became Mr Frost. I switched to a brand called Nivea for a while, but that was too flower-scented. Astra was white and watery, and it went transparent fast when you worked it into your skin. It would do. Astra meant star: a celestial body. My Astra sheen didn't match the glowier Vaseline sheen that the authentic, Black-mother-birthed boys achieved, but it did its job well enough for me to escape the ashy-skin jibes. The next Black kid I saw with ashy skin, I said, *cho*, for sure you got a white mother because your skin is so ashy, man.

My mother never wore make-up. For a long time, the women I dated were all makeup free. It took me years to accept and appreciate the beautician's craft, to see the skill that went into applying mascara, concealer, sculpting eyebrows, tracing perfect lipstick lines. In the Egyptian room of the Manchester Museum one day, it dawned on me that makeup was as old, at least, as the pyramids.

There is a photo of me somewhere in mid 2010s, in makeup, outside Three Minute Theatre, a Manchester club. I'm wearing a black velvet shirt I picked up in a Pakistani clothing shop in Longsight, Manchester. The shirt has thousands of tiny mirrors sewn into its fabric, giving me, in the photo, a princely, peacock aura. A friend (she's in the picture too, in similar makeup) had skilfully painted white circles on my face that resembled Australian indigenous people's art. Looking into that photo, I can see I feel ultra-relaxed in that moment, at ease, walking with ancestral spirits.

God, the Mother

Lil dawta had to go to church every Sunday when she stayed with me weekends (either for pious reasons else as a scheme to get her into a posh white church school, depending what milk you put on your cornflakes). I

189

followed instructions but the combination of cold, hard pews and Church of England vicar drone was too much, so when the Church of God, the Mother knocked on my door, I was ripe for signing up. The door-knocker's English name was Christine, and her friend was Mabel, and they were taking their mission to my area, and saving as many as they could. Christine was fit under her church weeds, and she piqued my interest. I managed to get a few words out of her that were off-script: she had been a University business student until she'd found God and dropped out to knock on doors for God, the Mother. My friend in Hong Kong, Z. was on my Zoom at the time. Z. heard her at the door and later yelled at me when I described her as Chinese. 'She's not Chinese, doofus, she's Korean!' Right.

Next Sunday, I took lil dawta along to the Church of God, the Mother. It was a warehouse in a rundown inner-city business park, and they'd laid the church wood flooring themselves, which was impressive. All the flotsam of Manchester was there – the unanchored, the unhinged, the hungry, the lonely and the curious, gathered up by the offer of free food, and you only have to listen to their Church of God, the Mother pitch as you ate. I passed recruitment levels one and two under Christine's tutelage that afternoon and was fast-tracked for baptism. I thought this would be by Christine and had visions of me and her in white robes and not much else, but the ducking team was three middle-aged Korean men in grey suits carrying a plastic jug of Blessed Water. So I was saved but not in the way I had wanted to be. Back in the main hall of the Church of God, the Mother, Christine showed me her phone and I proposed a pizza date with her, away from all this Church. She just had to give me her digits and we could text the where and when later. She nodded. Suddenly, Baptism men came between us. I never heard from Christine again. The Ways of the Lord are Mysterious. They are also sometimes cruel.

The gallery

You enter and you're stopped by a blue-shirted, lanyard-sporting security guard. He declares that you need to go to the basement and leave your laptop bag in a locker there. You and your friend are surprised; it's never happened to you before at a gallery. You shrug but conform. Once in the gallery, you wander round. An old white woman enters the space you are in. She carries a bag twice the size of your own. You shrug; she is old, you think – age confers some privileges. Five minutes later, two young white men enter, both with tote bags larger than your laptop bag. You look at the art. Matisse. Sherman. Picabia. Perry. It's all very white. And too large for either laptop or tote bag.

Tidiness

Tidiness is drilled into us from an early age. The best girls are tidy girls. Good boys make their beds. Correct handwriting is legible handwriting. My Danish mother taught me how to draw the letters of the alphabet before I began school, and I refused to relinquish her Danish loops when they were declared messy by a teacher. The ensuing battle presaged many others. My school reports noted Peter does not listen to instructions. Peter's desk is very untidy. Peter invariably fails to implement the method he has been taught. From querulous teenage years onwards, I have contended that just as black needs white, as day needs night, as silence needs noise to exist, so tidiness cannot exist without mess. Therefore, by maintaining my mess, I help the tidy people feel good about themselves. By providing mess, I validate the lives of the tidy. Thank me later.

Lil dawta and a picture of racial harmony

It's Saturday and I'm Saturday Dad again. I drive five-year-old lil dawta to the far side of Alexandra Park so we don't have to walk through the hooligan ducks who patrol the front – I haven't brought bread along for them and they get aggressive if you don't pay their bread tax. We shuffle through the rear iron gate and walk into the kids' play area. We've brought a plastic cricket set minus its plastic ball, a yellow softball standing in for the missing cricket ball, and coats, because it's October. There's a peep of sun. Lil dawta asks, Where are all the children? Its 9.30 a.m.. I tell her they're all sleepyheads. She laughs. She is happy to run around after the ball with her dad for a bit, but her head is bobbing every so often, looking for children to play with. Eventually a boy of about eight years old appears and saunters up to the apparatus section. He jumps on a spin pole. Lil dawta drops her ball game and sidles over to another spin pole. I watch as she soon gets playing with the boy. Two friends of the boy show up, aged about six and ten. Soon, they too are playing with lil dawta, taking great care to show her how to climb the climbing frame safely, and generally treating her like an adopted little sister. I sit on a bench, happy to half-snooze for a bit. The four of them end up playing cricket and football until, an hour later, the older boy's phone rings and the boys must go.

The older boy bends down to lil dawta and opens his arms wide. She gives him a hug, then the eight-year-old gets his hug, then his smaller friend. The three boys are white and lil dawta is brown. It's a picture of racial harmony that the borough council would die for. One day this will be normal, I think. Cue that Martin Luther King speech.

A blues: to be poor on a street corner with a baby in your arms

There were times when we were down, low down. Falling way down (now pick up the bass, hear the twelve-bar blues kicking in). Then we stood on a street corner in Chapeltown, Leeds, our baby in our arms, palms up. And people walked by with a judgemental sweep of their eyes at our wrinkled clothes, their lips curling. We were a disgrace, needed to fix up. Only the church people stopped, only the church people took pity. Mr T. and his colleague Neville took us to Ahmed, the greengrocers, bought us pumpkin and stayed with us to cook it into soup; and yes, they prayed over us but no, they never preached at us. God bless the Chapeltown church people. Now I'm driving my car and I pull up at traffic lights and there's a beggar with a paper cup in hand, working the junction. He is in rags, he has big, empty arms. He looks at me one second, then his eyes sweep past because my face has offered him no hope of money. I flip down the car vanity mirror and ask my reflection how did my face become stone like this, what journey did I make to become stone? I chastise myself that I should be more Chapeltown Church, less lip-curl. The lights change and I drive on, unhappy with my stone face.

Saturday dad: Lil dawta meets Batman

I pick up lil dawta and drive to Ashton Market, three miles away, for us to look around – there's usually plenty happening that a three-year-old can get into at Ashton's outdoor market, and I like the old school earthiness of the place. Today, there are two charity collectors on a pitch – thirty-something blokes, dressed as Batman and Robin. Batman is a big guy, tall, with a beer belly and red whiskers; Robin is less tall, less rotund. Their prop is a Reliant Robin car dressed up as a Batmobile; it's ludicrous and eye-catching. They're shaking big buckets, collecting coins. Lil dawta recognises Batman but has no idea who Robin is. She's a little scared at the sight of them, but also excited. As usual, she jumps into my arms, then urges me to go towards them. Batman is very friendly and has a good line of patter. He explains to me the charity cause and that they are travelling across the country in the Reliant Robin, raising money for cancer research. I drop him some coins. Batman smiles at lil dawta, shakes her hand and gives her a sticker. Robin is less extrovert, happy to wave at lil dawta half-heartedly, and has no stickers.

Maybe she picked up on Robin's awkwardness (who can blame him, ordinary bloke suddenly in green leggings playing Robin at a working-class market, while most blokes are in the pubs or at home preparing to watch the England v Israel football match?) because she decides she does not like him, though she really likes Batman. We leave the market. Later, she wants to find Batman again. I say, 'He has gone er, er, er... to the beach!' The beach is the most faraway place I can think of. She then wants to go to the beach. Back at my flat, she writes a letter 'to Batman but not to Robin' inviting him to visit her at her party 'but please don't bring Robin' (her letter consists of a series of very neat squiggles on lined, notebook paper). She falls asleep in the car on the journey back to her mum's.

Next Saturday, we go to Ashton market again. Batman is not there. I buy chips for us both from a market stall and we get mobbed by hungry starlings. Lil dawta loves the starlings, and the starlings chase the chips she throws for them. Later, she is in tears when, at my mum's, I try to draw Batman for her but fail miserably. We need to find Batman at the beach, she tells me, through the tears. As my mum steps in to heal lil dawta's pain by drawing a recognisable Batman, I quietly rue the day we set eyes on him.

Hallelujah tradespeople

Getting into the trades in northern England was close to impossible for the Windrush generation: roofing, bricklaying, tiling were all white, family businesses in the 1960s and 70s. In due course, white sons and daughters took over those businesses, and the trades remain predominantly white to this day. So, when Black people want a trades job doing – want a new floor laying, or walls plastering, or some roofing, or the like, done – they are often in the hands of the white tradespeople. And even though the average Black people's money is as reliable as the average white people's money, white people overall do not trust Black people. This is what racism does. So, we Black people have to pay above the odds for a job because that is how risk is managed and tradespeople understand this. Faced with this, some Black people get smart. The smartest get-smart I heard of was a Black couple joining a church because white tradespeople worshipped there. The couple joined and went through all the hallelujahing and embracing and

Praise the Lord-ing, and We are all Brothers and Sisters, let's hold hands-ing. And in the euphoric afterglow of that religious experience – often in front of the priest or pastor or deacon – they quickly closed a deal with the church-going electrician for him to rewire their small extension at a brotherly rate. For the believers, God finds a path where there was none, Hallelujah. God bless our brothers' and sisters' Holy Tradespeople smarts.

Where old cars go to die

My father's car sits in his Umuahia compound. It is a wide Buick, its once glossy black paint coated in Umuahia's red earth dust. *Your dad had dreams once*, this big, wide car proclaims. I imagine Dad passing it day after day in his final years, memories flickering to life in a wagon wheel illusion. *I'm young once more: preparing to see the Japanese Minister regarding the importation of Honda motorcycle engines into Nigeria; I straighten my tie before shaking hands with the undersecretary to the London Minister for Trade in the matter of Export Credit Guarantees. I'm…* The gleaming windscreen of the future was clear in his suit-and-tie days. Now, chickens cluck around the Buick's deflated tyres seeking grubs, and the compound's shack tenants brush past on their way to the incontinent compound standpipe.

The Ford Focus Sport is on Daisy's Longsight driveway, freshly waxed so it gleams in the sun. It's her son's, she explains. He dived from a boat off the Canary Islands, and they say the currents took him. But he was always a mischievous child, and he was wanted by the police. There is a beat as we both absorb this. She continues. She thinks he's decided to disappear for a while until the

196

police stop looking. The car's been here for a good two years now. She doesn't have to pay road tax when it's parked on the driveway. Every so often, she sees a police van waiting at the corner in case he nips back to visit her. She smiles and confides. He's way too smart for that.

They cubed it. I couldn't pay the compound charge and then, with the wife rushed to the hospital because her waters broke and she had to stay in because the baby had jaundice, I plain forgot and by the time I remembered, what could I do because they'd crushed it already? The baby though, I have a photo on my phone. Isn't she the spit, just the spit of me? Cost me my car, she did, but hey, that's life, isn't it and I never liked that car anyway. Look. Isn't she cute?

The big wheel

I pick up four-year-old lil dawta and we head off to the train station for a trip to Blackpool. 'We can find Batman there and invite him to my party,' she says. It's two weeks since we last saw him, yet she still remembers and still wants to see the Ashton Market charity fundraiser a.k.a. Batman again. The Blackpool train is a crawler. I've brought a bag with a change of clothes for her in case of weather changes or accidents, a ham sandwich, a colouring book and felt tips. The train is crowded with other families of all shapes and sizes who boarded at earlier stops so there are no seats for us. Maybe somebody will give up a seat, not for the guy but for his sweet four-year-old? Maybe. I walk with pleading eyes. No luck. This train is rammed, and everybody has sharp elbows. Mid-way through the train, I decide to head us back to the first carriage because at least there was some space there and everyone without a seat is moving forwards. We work our way against the flow and get back to the first carriage. There is some floor space by the carriage doors, blocked off by a couple and their tandem bike. Me and lil dawta wriggle through to it, sit there on the floor. She does felt-tip drawings happily through an hour of stop-starts all the way to Blackpool.

From the station to the beach is a ten-minute walk. There is a mini negotiation with lil dawta who wants me to carry her. She wins. I carry her on my shoulders into central Blackpool.

The North Pier is quiet. She spots a carousel horse ride and is fascinated. 'Let me on, let me on!' OK. Lil dawta chooses her ride and I take the horse alongside her. Hers is mechanically raised up and down by the carousel mechanism, while mine is fixed and I have to bounce up and down on as it goes round if I want it to budge. She loves the race which she wins at a gallop, though she would also have won at a canter seeing as both horses are bolted to the carousel floor. Haha. It's good fun.

The West pier is the one most people are strolling along. We join them. Lil dawta spots the shape of a Big Wheel from a distance and wants to go see it. No problem. We get to the Big Wheel. I look up at it. It must be a hundred metres high, minimum. It's a clanky, ancient thing with metal cages that are not completely enclosed, unlike the new 'glass pod' Ferris Wheels, such as London Eye. I look for the sign that says, 'No little children allowed'. There is none. I look at the queue. A father is in it, with a baby in his arms. Little children can ride!

Lil dawta really wants to go up in it. I can see how it will end if she does: she gets in, and it goes up high. She becomes petrified. I have to flap my arms and shout to get the wheel workers to get us off prematurely, as lil dawta screams with fear and is traumatised for life. Not to mention what her mum will make of it when it gets back to her. But what the hell. I pays up, and we gets in and the thing clanks upwards to the sky.

Revolution One. We are at our cage's peak distance from the ground. Lil dawta is loving it. 'I can see everything!' I am holding her in my lap.

Revolution Two. She wants to break free of me. 'I can do it myself!' She stretches her arms out and laces them round the cage's front metal bars. I calculate fast: she is thin enough for her body to slide through the bars. She's a fast kid and can have occasional tantrums. If she wriggled and then shot off from out of my arms, she would catapult through the bars and plunge to a certain death – either in the sea, else mangled in the wheel's structure, or in the stalls below. To avoid her doing any sudden moves and reduce the likelihood of these calculated outcomes, I comply with her frantic wishes and slowly release my hold of her waist. She's instantly right at the bars, her face pressed through. I'm terrified but trying to talk as if I'm totally chilled. 'Yes, it is a nice view. Yes, that is the sea, all around. And the people below are so small. Yes, it's lovely.' My stomach is in my heart. My heart is in my shoes. With every small turn, I look for how much closer we are to landfall.

Revolution Five. The wheel has stopped. With us at the wheel's apex – the highest point we could reach. Lil dawta is loving it, fearless as the cage sways in the wind. I am rapidly writing my will, wondering why we have stopped. Is the machinery bust? You hear of accidents. Could I climb down with lil dawta clinging to my back from this height? Would it be better to wait for the fire brigade, or would that commotion panic lil dawta, and maybe then she would slip through the bars and well, see earlier speculations. I decide God is cruel – to stop the wheel like this, with a hyperactive, fearless three-year-old, at its peak. Lil dawta meanwhile is in seventh heaven, looking all around, looking down through the bars, waving to the people in the cage across and slightly below us. I calculate that if she slid and I snatched at her to save her, I'd have to grab a leg because all her clothing is elasticated, and she'd plunge and – see earlier speculations. I sit on my hands. 'Yes. Hold onto the bars. Good girl.'

At last, we're moving again. Only straight away to jerk to another stop. Are clowns running this wheel? Is someone taking the pee? Lil dawta likes the swaying of the cage high up in the wind. The sun is beating down because the clouds have cleared. Isn't it nice, Daddy?

Another short lurch. I figure it out. People are being let off, cage by cage. We stutter lower, reach ground level and they crack open our cage. 'That was good, Daddy, let's do it again!' she cries. I'm less keen. 'Not right now, maybe next week. Let's go get ice cream instead.'

Lil dawta is all beans on the train journey home. We have almost an entire carriage to ourselves. I bought her a huge Spiderman colouring card from the train station shop, and we colour that in. 'We did not see Batman,' she reminds me. 'We will have to go again.' 'Yeah, right.'

Fire

Chris worked with my mother as a domestic ancillary, meaning washing dishes, at the local hospital. She had three shiny-faced children, and they lived nearby in a flat on Burton Road, just opposite the big church. Chris would flit in and out of our house, always with a big smile and sometimes a pat on my head and say how my hair looked good and like hers. Then, one day she came in, distraught, and bolted into the front room followed by Mum. The front room filled with wailing. We learned later she'd lost her children in a fire. All three of them. My mum was inconsolable for weeks. Chris moved away.

At the petrol station

It's late. Under the brim of the fierce, cold lights of a petrol station's forecourt, a group of Black teenagers are chilling. The usual fist knocks, shoulder surfing, laughter, breakout chats. I scan to see if one of them is my son, forgetting my son is now all grown up. Parking at pump 1, I give them a general nod and know my presence here will provide, at least momentarily, a modicum of protection. *From what?* Only white people ask me this question.

Saturday dad: the roller-rink.

It was the summer holidays and boredom had set in. We needed something new. Lil dawta was seven and wanted to skate. I saw skates advertised on Freecycle by a lady called Betty in a place called New Moston. We drove up. Betty was in her 70s and had gold earrings and a beautifully tended garden of African marigolds. She was enchanted by lil dawta in the car, who was munching on bacon ribs. She said she'd had so much joy with these skates in her youth and had kept them all these years but now the time had come to let them go, and she could think of nothing happier for her than to give them to the little girl. She pointed to said little girl who had bacon fat all over her face, which made me and Betty laugh. She called out, 'Send a photo of yourself on the skates!' to lil dawta. Back home, lil dawta had eaten off all the bacon ribs. She was looking at the skates and laughing. 'Dad', she said, 'these are ancient skates.' It was true. They had red leather flaps that laced up over the toes, and a heavy, steel undercarriage with a Frankenstein bolt through the middle. They'll do. I lashed them on lil dawta and she tried them out. She did OK: stepping more than rollering. 'Let's go to the park,' I said. In the park, she clung to me until I got tired and sat on a bench. Then she did the width of the path on her own. This expanded to short lengths, then all the way around the park. Haha. Look at me, Dad! Look at meeeee gooooo!

The local roller rink was ancient and legendary. Charlie Chaplin once skated there, a pinned-up newspaper article said. It was an oval-shaped, brick barn, with inside walls painted field green, and a corrugated, fluorescent-lit ceiling. They had buckets out to catch leaks and skaters had to swerve round them, which was part of the fun. It was run by a family of uncles, aunts, nephews and nieces. The skates room smelled like old boxing gyms and had shoes piled up everywhere. I rented a pair of kid-size 11's and tied them to lil dawta's feet.

'What about you, Dad?'

'Next time,' I said, my mind recalling my own childhood: me and skating never clicked.

On the rink, lil dawta said she was going to go round 'three times only.' Instead, as I cheered from the sidelines, she did a dozen circuits. She made a new friend, and the two of them went round, hand in hand. I finally pulled her off the rink at six p.m.. 'We can return tomorrow,' I said. 'Wow, it's weird standing still,' she said.

Next day, lil dawta told me she expected me to skate

this time. 'It's more fun if we both do it,' she insisted. 'OK. As long as you don't laugh.' She promised not to: 'I'll help you, Daddy,' she said. At the rink, we get our skates on. I flounder for a while before I start to get round with the help of the rink's sturdy sides, and with only a few stumbles. Lil dawta flies round, showing off, doing all shapes and stuff. Then she starts helping the learners – big or small – she's becoming one of the roller-rink family. Her friend of yesterday appears, and they spin round together. I think I'm improving. 'Film me, film me,' I tell lil dawta; 'my friends need to see my newly acquired skills!' She takes my phone, points it at me as I do a circuit. Then she shows me the footage. I'm wobbly as a three-legged chair and stiff as a rusted ladder. We laugh. 'But you're doing good, Dad,' she encourages, 'keep trying, you're doing really good.'

Lil dawta's friend, Elly lives locally and has a dad who is on nodding terms with me. Next day, he joins us on our walk to the rink. He talks more to me than he ever has before – about how he used to roller as a kid, and he thinks he still can. 'I'll give you some tips, if you need them,' I reassure him. Lil dawta snorts at this, and Elly giggles. We get inside the rink and the daughters are excited. Elly's dad straps on his skates and pushes off. He topples like a drunkard at first. Then suddenly he's making long swishes with his legs, counterbalancing with an outstretched arm, rolling along on one foot, turning effortlessly to skate backwards. He's Nijinsky! A smile lights his face. His daughter's mouth is agape. 'Dad!' she says in wonder.

I cling to the rink's wooden sides and look around. A sixty-year-old Nana is being propelled by a team of three grandchildren. She's panic-laughing, somewhere between petrified and exhilarated. Two teens glide past in

Goth T-shirts, holding hands bashfully. A small-legged, large-bellied Black man is skating in a line with his three brown daughters. Five youths are playing tag at twice the average rink circuit speed, sometimes whizzing round against the counterclockwise flow. In short, everybody is giving it a go. *You got this*, I tell myself. I push away from the protective sides and try a few glides. *I got this.*

That night, dozing, I remind myself to send a thankyou note to Betty who gave us those ancient skates. Sleep does not come fast, and I muse instead. The rink was a godsend. The magic was how it unfroze people from their weighted adult selves and let them experience the pleasure of vulnerability and falling and laughter and wobble and accomplishment all in one small oval under erratic fluorescents and in between rain buckets. It was a training ground in civility. People crashed into you, and you knew it wasn't deliberate; they apologised, they helped you up, you swapped smiles. The rink turned stuff inside out. Big bears of men became puppies. Quiet unassuming people became whirling tops. The family who ran the rink were all skilled skaters. Their four-year-old zoomed through the crowds like he was born on skates. His older brother tucked his arms behind his back, Charlie Chaplin style, as he glided across to help fallen people up. The rink has gone now – demolished. In its place is a glass-faced municipal multiplex, and the beautiful skating family has been replaced by council employees, the rink's donut of outside grass landscaped into a car park.

I see the ghost of Charlie Chaplin gliding across the rink, young Betty pirouetting on her red wheels too, tossing her auburn locks. Slowly the rink, and my memories of it fade to black and white.

Troubled kids

Zach, the most troubled kid in the school arrived at our class newly expelled from some never-to-be-mentioned other school. He was told to sit next to me and quickly became my new best friend. I wondered if the teachers had planned this. If they had, then, as a social experiment, it produced mixed results. We were two Black kids brimming with creativity and potential. He taught me shoplifting, the Cruyff turn, credit card fraud, kung fu leaps, shifting stolen tyres, and chirpsing girls. I taught him biology, pickpocketing, maths and, occasionally, geography. He wasn't often in school because he was most of the time suspended for one delinquent act or another. He was a brilliant footballer though, and for all the most important school football matches, he would be temporarily unsuspended – in order that the school could win the match – then resuspended. I would like to think there is a parallel in adult life. Maybe it's those fake pop groups where the singing is done by others in the studio, but they put the prettier faces out to lip-synch through the tours and do the media stuff. Maybe the leap should be bleaker – a generation of hollowed-out, zombified 70's Black kids, forced to navigate a demeaning education system. Occasionally, we would rebel, and Zach was the rebel leader. The teachers, after punishing us, would lecture, "The universe is kicking you in the teeth for a reason. Do better. Try to act normal, like all the other (read *white*) kids." Unlike me, Zach never learned to lip-synch. Take us out, Milli Vanilli.

Me, Jess and Marco smoking cigarettes behind the Old Vicarage

It was an early evening; the sky was red as ketchup and the river low enough you could see the shopping trolleys – it hadn't rained all summer. We'd played 8-ball pool and when the youth club closed, we wandered aimlessly. We came up off the riverbanks. Jess said her dad would be necking the whiskey now; he hid the bottle from her mum in a high-up box she couldn't reach. Marco's sister would be on the mic warbling that 'Silly Games' song, which was ear-splitting even when sung well. I said I'd have to dodge the neighbour's dog if it was running loose. Marco had two cigarettes left and suggested we hung out behind the Old Vicarage. He passed me a cig but not Jess; Jess had to smoke his, he said, laughing, and she had to lean in to get it which she did, using her tongue to take it off his pouted lips at the third attempt. After he lit it for her, she had a puff and coughed and that set him off giggling. You laugh like a fairground ride, she said to Marco, and it was true, so I laughed at what Jess had said. You laugh like a banjo, Marco said to me. True! True! You laugh like an accordion, I said to Jess. We all laughed again, and round it went, and each time more absurd, until we were sitting in an orchestra, laughing so much, and Jess ends in Marcos's arms and she's laughing into his chest, and he looks at me, like stares, and then for a moment Jess does, from inside Marco's arms, and then I said I had to get back. Marco said, Don't go, Pete, but I could see in his eyes he didn't mean it.

Decimal points

Vital fucking things. The difference between ten quid and a hundred quid. Between misery and joy. Vital things. So, what do they do? They make these vital fucking things the most hard-to-see sign in the entire signifying code. It's a dot. Your life is hinging on the position of a tiny dot.

'Here's your writer's advance, Pete – a cheque.' I'm seeing a one and four noughts. 10000. Where's the decimal point in that? Is there a decimal point in that? 'Happy?' my publisher asks. I poker-face the bastard. I'll do my actual face after I've identified the fucking decimal point.

If I was there when they were deciding this decimal point thing, I'd make the decimal point a boulder – as hi-vis as it gets. A well-placed decimal point can kill you. It's a bullet. Dush. Smack. *Cause of death: a decimal point.*

Knife throwers / work

I was in my office checking supplier invoices and daydreaming about throwing knives at my work colleagues, as all office workers do, when it struck me the world divides neatly into the knife throwers and the knife thrown-ats. The knife throwers bring razzmatazz, patter, and fill the tents with punters. That's a lot of work, a lot of work, they tell you. The knife thrown-ats merely have to stand there and do nothing much other than risk their lives as the pointed steel blades come whizzing at them. 'Isn't this dangerous?' 'That's the whole point, it's dangerous. Trust me, you just stand still, look pretty, and we'll fill our boots with gold,' the throwers say. Boxers are thrown-ats. Two lumps trying to rip each other's heads off. Their promoters are the knife throwers, always in the ring afterwards in their shiny suits, eating the mics, talking next steps, and wasn't that a spectacle, as the wreck of torn flesh and broken eye sockets glances up from where they lie prostrate on the canvas, having smelling salts waved in their face, else slumped on their stool, trying to feel their face.

It is written somewhere in the laws of circus that the thrown-at must be a girl in a spangled leotard and the thrower a white bloke with long black hair and a flamenco dancer's shirt. In folklore, the thrown-at becomes a child, hence William Tell and the kid with the apple on his head. 'Go ahead, Dad, I have faith in you, and wow, your Flamenco shirt looks so cool.' 'Thanks, kid.' Whoosh. The original knife-thrower was God (Old Testament version) starring the Stupendous Sensation, Abraham & His Son! 'OK, God, just so I got this right: I take my son up the mountain there, and slit his throat but everything works out OK?' 'Yup, that's it.' 'Thought so. OK, yeh I'm good. Let's get up there, kid.' It's always the dads, signing off on such deals. William Tell was pulling that shit with the apple while the kid's mum was visiting relatives or planting crops or something. You can't imagine the mountain kid's mum taking the deal. 'Nah, sorry, God, come up with something else. How about we don't eat cheese on Tuesdays for a test of faith. Deal?'

The Office Team's clock cuckoos lunchtime. I get up from my desk. The other staff side-eye me. I have done zero work. I give zero fucks.

The shack

It is shoe-horned into a corridor of a crumbling city building, an old skool Jamaica food shack. There's only one customer there when you arrive. Her order keeps changing but the cook is patient and, like him, you lean back and wait. A white man strides in with a phone to his ear, makes eye contact with the cook. The first customer finally pulls away and awaits her order. The white man steps to the counter and begins telling his list. The owner slows him, points to you as the queue. The white man smiles through this correction, steps back; it's cool. You order. A young Black man enters, heads straight to the counter and starts talking – in patois – about ital food, how the owner should serve it exclusively. It's part jest, part earnest and the owner is fine with it. You make your contribution to the conversation: what's cooked here tastes good, though ital is fine too. The young man nods, the owner smiles. The white man waves his phone – he has an urgent call – and exits the corridor.

Voyeur

Every day after school, walking Plato meant a lot of stop-and-starting, what with his territory to be marked, new scents sniffed and stuff. As Plato cocked his leg for the fourth time on Moorland Road, I looked up and there she was – showering behind a frosted glass window. The glass was scalloped so created optical effects, and as she moved, the hips bulged, the buttocks squished, the right breast shrank, an elbow expanded, and when she shook her hair, the whole pane kaleidoscoped. Next day, same time, same thing. A routine established itself. I never thought I'd see her with her clothes on. Then, one time, she was late. Me and Plato waited. A car pulled into the block of flat's car park. She smiled at me as she got out of the car and walked into the entrance of the block of flats. I felt embarrassed to watch her shower that day.

Afro-pessimism 3 – silent disco

Heaven knows what internal soundtrack some people are moving to, deciding that, although their skin is black as onyx, they are in fact white. Yet, to give them room, have we not all, at moments, drunk the Kool-Aid of racial delusion? The logic of their dance is elegant: the world is populated by white people and by Black people. White people are the good people. I am good. Therefore, I must be white. Running this in reverse holds up too. Black people have had a hard time. I've had a hard time. Therefore, I must be Black (analytic philosophers and syllogists don't @ me, I've not yet brushed my teeth). So, let's live and let live, leave people to spin their own vinyl, dance to their own beats, synth their own sounds, however weird the plug-ins they're using. Let's just enjoy the parade. There they go, we might think, the deluded ones, jogging along in their own silent disco. Let them dance. Let's all dance. Let's do the St. Vitus' dance, sashaying along the loopy runways of life, across the infested waters, crocs to the left of us, crocs to the right. Heaven help us all. Take us out, Stevie Wonder.

Delight and liberty – the simple creed of childhood

Guy could hawk his snot and gob it out with such force it flew ten metres. He danced like Alvin Ailey and there was always a girl on his arm. His family was from Grande

Terre and spoke French creole as well as English, and his eight brothers and three sisters made them a clan. Their skin was dark, but their mother was not a nurse, and their father did not work on the railways, which caused confusion for some in the neighbourhood. Once, while walking my dog, I came across Guy on a street corner, kicking some other lad methodically. The kicked lad was in a ball on the pavement, yelping. I asked Guy why and he gave me an explanation of which I have no memory; all the while that he calmly explained, Guy continued kicking the lad on the ground, never missing a rib (his football skills being legendary). Having heard the explanation, I agreed the kicking was deserved and walked on with my dog.

Afternoon tea at Alice in Wonderland

Soaked from incessant rain, I am five minutes late for a meeting with my dear friend at the Richmond Tea Rooms, an *Alice in Wonderland* styled cake cafe in the Gay Village. My friend waves to me; she has a table by a pillar already. Her sandy-coloured Marie Antoinette wig is slightly askew, showing a fringe of luxurious Afro hair. We hug, say hi, and I settle into my pillow-pimped, doily'd chair. Already I know she is back on heavy medication. The slowness of her responses. The smile that freezes across her face as if the next thought is snagged somewhere along the neural pathways. Yet it's there, she's there. It's simply a matter of waiting. And she's the same drop dead gorgeous and effervescent as when I was dating her and we enjoy chatting that old flame chat: skirting around are you seeing anyone else now, remembering good times and daft things we did together, what became of some mutual friends, family health, trips taken. We talked of nothing and everything. She is happy. The ice in her neural pathways maybe gives her lips a numbness, so cake sometimes stays unnoticed on her lips or falls unremarked onto her butterfly-motif red dress. And sometimes her laugh is loud and comes many seconds after the conversation's cue. The cake shop clientele were stealing glances, and now throw stares that harden. *The crazy Black woman with the sideways-on wig, aren't you embarrassed to be with her? What are you two Black people even doing here?* What lurches up in me surprises even me. *Go fuck yourselves* I stare them all down. Then settle into my frou-frou seat, laugh louder, deeper, spill cake, remark on the beauty of her blue nail polish, love her story of the photographer who tried to lure her to his 'studio' but couldn't answer her question on depth of field. When finally, we both leave – for the glamour of Primark where we will both choose warm socks for winter – the princess is on my arm. And it's me who feels sorry for those in the cafe who sniggered at her, at us, for we are royalty, and they are nothing.

Burning mattresses

I burned things as a kid. Boxes. Sheds. Crates. Cars. Everything looked better, burning. How wild is fire. How attractive. It was hard to burn mattresses – the wadding was so compact, but when I managed, I appreciated the rising stink of evaporating piss, the slow speed of the head and foot ends, contrasted with the faster ignition at the middle. The skeleton of twisted, shrunk, blackened mattress springs afterwards. A car burnt down began as a black skull. Then, if it stayed long enough, rust took over and browned it; the lushness of the early rust's freckled ginger brown emerged magically; that brown changed hue week after week darkening into crinkled, knee-cap brown until finally firedot lichen latched on. As an adult, I've seen other adults burn things. Relationships mainly. Spark them up, waft the smoke, watch the flames take hold. The glint in their eyes as the fire leaps, debris flitting upwards in the warmed air. How the flames shoot, how giddily they observe the hidden energy released. Then the cold after. The ashes. The purity of those ashes. Some people like to burn things.

My tribe, the stoics

There is plenty of choice out there because philosophy has many tribes. But of all of them – the hedonists, the somnambulists, the existentialists, the logical positivists, the continentals, the nihilists, the mystics, the militarists, the pessimists, the pragmatists, the phenomenologists, the negritudists, the optimists… – my tribe is the stoics. Life is to be endured. We are all stuck in an eight-roller car wash, getting flailed, pummelled, sprayed and mauled by events. Occasionally, we may glimpse a ray of sunshine, but we know the water jets will start up again. Relationships will rupture, bank accounts empty, our bodies fail us. But it will be OK; these things happen. We persist. The crying baby has to exhaust itself and falls asleep eventually. Our flight is delayed but in the scale of things it's not important. A glass of wine sweetens most regrets. The sun will rise – if a little dimmer and colder – tomorrow. All things eventually pass. We can only endure.

Sister's boyfriend

Down in our cellar, my sister's boyfriend boasted how with his bare hands he could chop through this cast iron stove pipe easy, and he only didn't do it out of respect for our mum, his hands being fully trained in karate. My head tilt at this nudged him further, and next he said he could swim right across the River Mersey any day of the week, any weather. I dropped my jaw and followed it with an eyebrow raise. Right, he said, to prove it, he would do it that afternoon, and he marched up the cellar steps and out of the house. I spent a few hours daydreaming about him drowning in the River Mersey. It was a great disappointment when he returned, saying he'd swum it and here are the wrinkles on my fingers to prove it, see? And I realised it was hard to drown a fantasist, and my sister would have to get rid of her boyfriend her own way.

Getting lost 2, Part A

Getting lost is an intrinsic part of becoming an adult. So much so that the British have something called the Duke of Edinburgh Award in which they take their older children into the countryside and abandon them without maps or phones, confident that, though lost, they will ultimately find their way home. The scheme is highly successful with no more than three children per thousand not finding their way back and only one or two permanently lost each year. Trust your instincts, the scheme advises, channel your inner homing pigeon.

So. You are lost. What to do? Advice has been available for millennia, boiled down in Psalm 137, as preached by Mr Bob Marley and his Wailers, who faithfully sang, 'How can we sing the Lord's Prayer (i.e. be happy) in a strange land (i.e. when lost)'. The advice from 137 is to find a river (Babylon in the advice, but any river will do), sit down on the banks there, and weep. There you go. Weep. Accept your situation – deal with your issues about being lost. And only then – once you have confronted your grief and processed it – will you find your song: find happiness in your new circumstances.

This essay will now take a wrong turn.

I was wind-surfing a lake in Milwaukee. The sun was blazing, the surfboard responsive, its sail full. I sped across the waters in a supreme demonstration to the drunk Americans on shore of my newfound surfing skills. Except I couldn't figure out how to sail *into* the wind as opposed to *away* from it. Soon my original launch point on the shore was a speck. The sun's rays beat down on me oppressively; my heart sank. My 20-year-old body lay down on the board and wept. I was lost at sea. Through my wailing, I heard a shout. I looked up. A grey-haired couple in a pedal boat approached. They spoke American but we were able to communicate. They towed me behind their pedal boat all the way back across the lake to my original starting point. There, my blessed friends suppressed their mirth at the ignominy of my arrival and clasped me to their chests, handed me beers to arrest my dehydration and we sang with joy, toasting the grey couple, who joined us in our celebratory drinks.

This essay is lost.

The maths exam had come at the end of a week of exams, and I was flummoxed. Every route I took failed to solve the problem. My mind became fevered. There had to be a key, some formula I had forgotten, or correspondence

I was missing. Maybe to turn the problem upside down would help. Or to look at it as if into a mirror. Yes, the mirror, where everything is still there, but flipped. This was the way through, and out, surely? I wrote my answer down, checked it as best I could. Then left my paper on the desk and walked out of the hallowed exam hall, silently praying to the exam gods.

I'm with E. in Manchester and we're lost. She laughs. 'I so love getting lost with you,' she says, 'it's divine.' We fall into a bar, then a cafe, and meet a group of Senegalese students heading to an international swimming gala; we learn from them the Dakar slang for 'have a great time', then, as the sun sets, we entertain the Italian cafe owner's claim that his is the only authentic Genoese cooking in the city.

Now I'm with D. in Leeds. He's thunder-faced as he realises that we have driven two miles into a dead end. He blames the information we received, the false position of the sun, the absence of distinctive landmarks, and, finally, he blames me, the incompetent driver. We retrace our steps in silence. He vows never to ride with me again.

This essay is spinning its wheels.

My brother is a racing pigeon with three compasses in his head, like those migrating birds have, each compass finely calibrated by his years as a lorry driver. I, on the other hand, am expert at getting lost.

Getting lost 2, Part B – lost continents

The West's plundered wealth rested on the concept of folk being lost. *Finders-keepers* was the principle on which all colonialism was built. To no avail did local

216

populations remonstrate, 'We're not lost, thank you, and have no need for you to find or discover us. We're fully self-discovered and have no further needs, though thanks for passing by!' Not that the Colonials had any three-compass brilliance at getting around. Columbus got lost – hence his designation of the Caribbean as the (West) Indies. Dr Livingstone was lost for so long they sent Dr Stanley to find him.

I experience a chain of memory associations. The tombstone in an overgrown Whitehaven cemetery that commemorates a boy 'lost overboard at the Bight of Benin.' J.M.S. Turner's oil painting of *The Zong*, the slave ship from which enslaved Africans were thrown overboard – 'lost' like so much lumber in the argument of the owners' (failed) insurance claim. The thought that, even now, unless careful, you can still be thrown overboard and drown in seas of whiteness.

The courtroom

I'm in a courtroom. I'm called to deliver the case for the defence. I clear my throat and begin. Your Honour, Anyaso Anyogo Kalu did get some things right. Exhibit A. He brought home one pair of sample trousers in my size. These nylon pants were shiny metallic blue. I wore them proudly to school, and to the eagerly awaited question from classmates, namely 'Where did you get them keks from?' I puffed out my chest and said, 'My dad does Import-Exports and these trousers are samples from Japan; you can't get them anywhere in England.' The school allowed them; they were the correct school uniform colour, blue, even if a shade brighter than strict regulation, and their shininess made them different though arguably not a breach of school uniform policy since that policy added no adjectival qualifiers to 'blue' and being silent on the matter of shininess. Looking back, I see now that the school was kind and showed leniency, sensing that this boy, at this time, needed to wear these trousers. Sometimes teachers are clairvoyants, gods. I strutted around school in my nylon, electric blue trousers and spoke my father's name with pride. Was it an irrational allegiance? What made me so loyal? All boys want to be able to boast of their fathers.

The judge clears his throat.

'OK, Exhibit A enters the record. One pair of nylon, metallic blue trousers. Do you have an Exhibit B?'

'No.'

'Your case rests on one pair of nylon, metallic blue trousers?'

'From Japan.'

'Your case rests on a pair of nylon, metallic blue trousers from Japan?'

'Yes, Your Honour.'

The judge kisses his teeth. 'Court is adjourned.'

Dads' race – ignominy

It was a family tradition that I would turn up to cheer on our child or children at their primary school sports day, and then I'd win the dads' race. I'd been supremely fit in my 20s, and, even if I'd put on a few pounds and swapped my weekly five-mile jog for arm calisthenics with a glass of red wine, I was still no slouch. I duly turned up at my eight-year-old son's sports day, cheered him on (did he win? I think he did, I don't recall – shame on me) then raced. And lost. I wasn't even second. The appalled look on my son's face when our eyes met after my failure to cross the finish line first has haunted me to this day. *The shame you've brought on me, Dad. Do you understand?* he seemed to be silently telling me. I understood. In the days before, he would have been boasting the way all kids do: 'My dad is going to burn up the grass all the way to the finish line, leaving your dads panting to stay in sight! My dad is fast as Olympic lightning!' What a fall from grace for both of us. The ignominy. I absorbed his disgust and embarrassment. Then I shrugged. Such is life. We have to learn to stomach these things. My son wasn't having it and turned away in disgust. I'd ruined his life. In the days after, our relationship changed. He began finding my shoes for me, he looked concerned if I suggested I was going to climb up a ladder or in any way exert myself. 'It's OK, Dad, I'll do that for you, you stay sitting down, you don't want to overdo anything.'

That Christmas, I visited my sister. After eating the turkey, roast potatoes and roasted parsnips, swerving the Brussels sprouts and sampling the Turkish red wine as a matter of politeness, me and the teen nephews went to their garage which housed their gym machine to burn off some of those calories. I was astonished to find that both the muscly nephew and the skinny one could bench press more than me. Being good kids, they were embarrassed for me, and called out to their younger brother. Surely, I could press more than little brother? I had a sudden pain in my left shoulder which meant that unfortunately I could not continue. We should resume it another time; tell your younger brother he need not come. Little brother turned up anyway. He bench-pressed way past my top weight. I shrugged. I have developed a range of shrugs. Old boxers understand all this. Ask them and they'll tell you, defeat is inevitable, we all get knocked down in the end. Nobody can out bench-press time.

Elation

In his book, *Piece of Light*, Charles Fernyhough suggests emotions can cue emotions. In the example given, depression as an adult can cue memories of being depressed as a child. I'm not keen on chasing thoughts around depression, so I flip the direction and decide that if Fernyhough is onto something, then this associative recall should work for the opposite mood – elation – too. I summon times when I have been elated. For a few minutes, it's a depressing exercise. Tumbleweed. Then a memory pops up. Watching my father cook one day. It's mid-summer and he is excited about the imminent birth of my sister, and I'm feeding off his excitement. Is the memory accurate? The age gap with my sister means I would have been two years old; memory does not lay things down long term at that age, Fernyhough reminds me. I decide the *dad cooking* memory is probably a confabulation – the brain creating a single narrative from different sources. About one element of the memory, I'm certain. I'm convinced I've seen my father happy cooking. I smell okra and sizzling palm oil, and I see a stove. But the when and why of this moment may have been assembled from other elements of my life. Perhaps my mother told me how excited I had been at the imminent birth of a sibling – finally, somebody I could boss about and pass the blame onto! I consider this, on reflection, unlikely. If it is true, as Fernyhough advances, that we remember the past through the lens of the present and so what we recall now is closely related to what we want now – perhaps I confabulated this scene because I want to have been excited about my sister-to-come, and I also want to remember my father as happy about that too.

A trichologist dreams of hair

'Keep your hair on!' is a phrase that has unfairly dropped out of use. The phrase is versatile, corresponds well with the causes of hair loss and pleases wigmakers (a much under-appreciated profession, big in the seventeenth-century and due a revival). Hair, except in the case of the lucky few, leaves us eventually, falling out along with our dreams. We shed the beautiful horizons our youthful ambitions painted for us as we slept. We cast off intimate relationships and with them, the futures we might have shared together. We lose even our children. They grow up and choose their own path in life, and all the ways we dreamt for them when we cradled them in our arms, fall away. It's a competition between head hair and dreams to see which fall out first.

On the absence of Black people kissing

I woke up this morning and realised I had not seen two Black people kiss all year. I don't mean teenagers because teenagers are always sucking each other's faces, and I don't mean at Gay Pride events because sucking face at such events is a necessary political act. And I don't mean footballers because the amount they earn for kicking a ball around, I'd be kissing everybody too. And I rule out carnival because carnival is a one-off special event where licentiousness is an established norm. And I don't mean at music events because music is a known hypnotic that induces kissing. With these five exceptions, I have not seen two Black people kissing all year.

Hallucinations (another morbid section, but shorter)

My father's last quarters. The double mattress on a low wooden platform. The bedding ancient and stinking of pus, shit, rot, flies. A small dresser by the bed with scattered pills, a Marmite jar, an asthma inhaler, herbal supplements. Spools of sprocketed accounting papers. Boxy, 70's era computer screens, with ancient dot matrix printers in a heaped pile by a rusted guillotine. Letter-headed paper for his accountancy practice in a pile. Beyond, on the periphery, in an empty, dust-filled next room, an unplumbed, cream-coloured, fibre-glass English bath, grimy, and held up by worm-riddled wood supports. I turn my gaze back to the bed quarters, look up and across. Wiring follows the door frame, then runs up into the ceiling. I go over to the bed, lift the pillow. Under there, more medicines in the form of blister packs, and a book: *Technological Advances in 19th Century England and Nigeria.*

It's then I notice the wardrobe. Something pulls me to it. I open the wardrobe door. The air in here is of the man alive, the scent of the father I remember. Musky, herbal, boiled okra and beef, cedar aftershave. That trip to Osaka he made, the businessman supreme, oiled skin, cool cologne, box-fresh shirt, carrying a hefty cheque book and a business plan including robust profit projections. This is him. The clothes maketh the man. Here in this wardrobe, my father is alive and in his prime.

He clambers out from the wardrobe in his red and gold dashiki, looking slick and fired up, and utters a greeting to me. Without waiting for my surprised reply, he goes to the bed, picks the book up, riffles the pages until he reaches page 184, and opens this page out wide for me, points. *Read this,* he says. I look. It's a blank page.

Lazy bathing

When I was a young father and the house was chaotic with small humans – dancing, crying, falling, fighting, shouting at the television cartoons – I would sly away, saying, 'I'm going to take a bath.' The bath those days was downstairs, through the kitchen. I'd lock the door, get in the hot water with a book of poems and stay there for an hour, sometimes two, despite protests. 'If you're that desperate, piss in a bucket, the English managed that way for hundreds of years!' I'd tell the small humans. If I was lucky, and my wife was in the mood, she'd slip me a plate of food. A hot bath, a book of poems and a plate of rice and peas. Sometimes, life can be good.

Heroic suffering

I suffered heroically in my childhood. I can't remember any specifics, only the sense of heroic suffering.

Billy the Kid, part 1

The Western film genre was America's last cultural stand as the heroic white man. In my childhood, I watched the 70's film, *Pat Garret and Billy the Kid*. It was without any Black hero, but I gulped it down. The mesmerising life of Billy the Kid – what's not to like? The hippy musician, Bob Dylan was in the film. He played a small acting role and gifted the film its defining track, 'Knock, knock, knocking on heaven's door'. I hear the song now, through the *wah wah* and *flutter* of experience as an obituary to the white Western version of history. The myth had to be buried, was how I interpret Dylan's lyrics, however long it takes. It's been five decades since

Dylan buried the Kid. Every so often they try digging the mouldering body back up.

Billy the Kid, part 2

I loved to ride out in the posse of big chinned, pale-skinned celluloid cowboys. James Coburn. Kris Kristofferson. Wayne Bridges. Paul Newman. Robert Redford. I shot all who came at us. *Kepow.* I drew every gun, bled every drop of blood. Leapt with them off cliffs to a heroic death. *High Noon? Bring it.* Back then, I didn't know that it was about rugged, heroic, *white* individuals and that I, as a Black kid, wasn't invited. Until one day in my sour teens, I noticed, and stopped loving Westerns. I spent a long time in the wilderness, wandering alone on my horse. It wasn't until another Bob – Marley – released 'I Shot the Sheriff' that I dug up my gun and rode back into town and started shooting again. Me and Bob, we shot the sheriffs.

Schrodinger's ring

That a ring existed and was our mother's and was lost by a sister who had been playing with it is accepted by all. We then enter the science of wet memory. The ring was lost either between floorboards in a rented room in Clyde Road in the early years when our parents were broke (i.e. not the later years when our parents were also broke), else dropped into the brickwork of the Clyde Road house's garden wall. The ring was either 21-carat gold, or a beautiful but – from a metallurgical point of view – valueless, metal hoop. Mum either bawled her heart out for three days non-stop upon discovering its loss, else did not notice for several weeks and when she finally did, shrugged and carried on. The story of the ring has been repeated sufficient times that the original recall of sisters and everyone else is now inextricably affected by subsequent attempts at retrieval and retelling. The ring, meanwhile, as metallurgical phenomenon, is somewhere and indifferent to all these attempts at recall; it exists, either smelted down and its atoms redistributed into other jewellery or the National Gold Reserves or else it's still in roughly its original form, and remaining in the cavity of that garden wall or under the Clyde Road house original floorboards or in neither of these two places. Yet its residence in memory has multiplied: from two sisters to all siblings, and now to you, the reader of this paragraph. In that sense, the ring is eternal. I have toyed with the idea of going to the Clyde Road garden wall – it still exists – and tearing it down to see if the ring is there. Yet, what would that achieve? The ring is now a story, and its discovery as an object has no bearing on this story, might even kill the story. The ring's indeterminacy is the story's lifeblood.

This Brussels sprout awaits me

I've tried to be the ideal Christmas guest, pulling crackers with my hosts, complimenting their furniture, their children and their choice of electronic devices and wallpaper. I've spent several minutes asking enthusiastic questions about the Victorian tiles used around their eco-complying wood stove. I ate the turkey breast slices even though they were medium rare and so skirting with gastric upheaval. Yet the Brussels sprouts was a fork too far. I couldn't swallow. I made some excuse and fled to my room. From an early age, I have not been able to stomach those pellets of green grossness. Ever since my punishment for opening my sister's presents was being forced to eat all six sprouts on my Christmas dinner plate, I have hated them. I will wait here until my hosts call me down, then feign some personal disaster – an aunt has died, or some such – to get me out of the house and the situation.

Short lament for the offspring of Windrush generation bus drivers

Irish men dug roads in my childhood, and they chatted to us while they stood in muddy holes, fixing pipes and cables. Now there are big utilities companies, and you see their descendants' names on the trucks – Gallagher, Murphy, Byrne, Joyce. The first-generation West Indian men were bus drivers and bus conductors, and they were great, chatting to us and throwing us off the bus when we tried dodging the fare. Yet their descendants don't now own any transport companies or have their family names on fleet liveries. This saddens me for some ill-defined reason. Amen.

Brothers we must cherish each other more (after Audre Lorde)

I am at the dojo. My Wing Chun (translation, 'Sticky Hands') instructor intones, 'When you place your hands against your opponent's in the start position, you can read from that physical contact everything that is happening at all points in your opponent's body, and you can sense by pressure variation, their intent – to attack to the left or right, to feint or manoeuvre.' Martial arts are a favoured male touch mode – giving tactility the cover of masculinity, holding simultaneously both affection and aggression. We love our sparring partners.

There are other channels of warmth where men feel free to touch. Barber shops are famous as locations of connection between men: handshakes, shoulder bumps, back slaps, are common among clientele at barbers, and, beyond the banter, sometimes in quieter conversation, dreams are affirmed, the aftermaths of relationship breakups assuaged, a soul is revived, a steadying hand supplied. The barber trims head hair, shaves chins, then holds up a mirror and wills the customer to see their best self in it. On Sunday League football pitches every week of the season, a goal is scored, and men slide through mud to embrace each other, and when a final is won, they hoist star players up onto their shoulders, sing arm in arm in the dressing room, while the losers rest their heads on each other's shoulders in consolation after a nightmare defeat. Yet these are tactile exceptions. British manhood generally eschews tactility.

It was never like this in our boyhoods. Piggybacking, two-on-a-bike, flinging each other up in the air at the local swimming pool. Else we'd just chill, lie across one another, chewing gum, sitting on a garden wall, watching the world go by. We held hands when enemies neared, rested arms on shoulders, legs on legs, slumped into each other easily.

We have lost touch with touch as men. We might clasp one another's shoulders before entering a bank to find out whether our loan application can be accepted, or squeeze an arm before entering the Visa Application Centre, or rock a shoulder before entering court to learn of our fate. But tactility is mostly gone. To touch skin with another man, outside of very special occasions, rarely happens. Brothers, we should cherish each other more.

Addressing the Igbere village elders, seeking my father's exculpation

'My apologies for my father's failure to ever reside overnight in Igbere in the many years since he returned to Nigeria from England. His reasons, if he had any clear reasons, he never shared with me. But what I do recall is his fondness for Igbere, his allegiance to this village and his unwavering sense of belonging here.' With this line, I had crossed over into fable or necessary fiction, for my father had never once mentioned Igbere to me in any more than a glancing way. I continued on the rhetorical path I'd started, garnishing the theme. 'There was never a week I saw him when he did not mention his love of his village, the beauty of life here, the wisdom and resourcefulness of its inhabitants...' I paused. The elders were attentive, respectful, and, most importantly, agreeing in their wisdom to participate in this fiction – we all knew that I was at least gilding the lily. These men were wise and educated, all of them at least bi-lingual. I broke out of my story to pick up three bottles of whiskey I'd brought along for them – the gifting of whiskey upon key occasions was an important tradition I'd been informed, and one I totally approved. 'Please,' I said, 'let me pour this for you before I talk more, because the more you drink, the better I will sound!' At this, they burst out laughing, and I knew I was on my way at least, to winning them over. I silently thanked my late poet-friend, Dike Omeje, who had first penned the 'the more you drink...' line I'd just used. *I stole your line, Dike, please forgive me; it was a necessary theft. I like to think you would have approved, given my situation*. I handed out cups, let the whiskey circulate among them, and concluded. 'Yes, my father held this village in deep affection; he considered it the making of him – his North Star – his fixed point in a universe that rapidly changed throughout his life. He lived a life of trials and odyssey, of success and upsets, and it is only fitting that now, at the end of his story, at the end of his stay on this earth, that he has returned to the place he loved most dearly. Igbere. Let us raise our glasses to Igbere!'

We drank. There were murmurs of support, general noises of approval. Plastic cups were emptied and refilled. They rose from their chairs slowly, and one by one came towards me, to shake hands – with me and with the family around me. My half-sister, Ogechi nodded to me. 'I think you have won them round,' she said. 'Well done.' A whiskey bottle had circled back to me and there was a dram left. I drank it.

In the morning, I learned that the elders had finally consented to my father's burial in Igbere.

Three scent memories

Cocoa butter

Me and Macy are lingering at the bus stop after school as cars zip past blasting Abba's 'Waterloo' and the Manhattan's 'Let's Just Kiss and Say Goodbye'. Darkness creeps as close as our thighs, which finally press together, talking about everything except desire. Afterwards, I dream of kisses and underskirts and lips tinged with the cocoa butter that gave Macy's skin its sheen. Cocoa butter is still a thing with me. Its meadowy, petticoats aroma always spins me like a Diana Ross high note. One scent of it at parties and I lose the power of speech –

there's someone in front of me talking but I don't hear anything, I'm with Macy again at the bus stop as she playfully parts the hairs of my forearm and turns into me. This time we kiss.

New Car spray

I get a pound shop can of New Car spray and blast it around my fifteen-year-old Ford Focus. Suddenly the Ford's new, and I'm back in love with the ex, who's in the passenger seat, and the stroppy teenager has become a cute three-year-old dozing in the child seat in the rear. Rihanna is singing on a cassette about how *Ella, Ella* can come under her umbrella anytime. The sun is blazing, and the car's air conditioning is on full blast, so we are simultaneously sunned and chilled – the good times are truly rolling. The trick works for the first three sprays. Then the scent begins to lose its hypnotic power, it starts to rain, and not Ella's, nor all the umbrellas in the world can hold off the downpour.

Lagos airport

The heat, on going down the mobile steps onto the Murtala Muhammad forecourt, brings with it a smell I've only ever encountered in Nigeria: aviation fuel and, under that, some unknown vegetation, then the dry, tongue-coating, riverbed-and-metal tang of concrete dust that rolls around the airport runway aprons in soft swirls of warm air. At this, my father's body smell comes to me; yet I wonder now how much of this last smell is my invention – something I want to be true, and so my brain complies and constructs the olfactory bridge. Or maybe my father carried that airport's scent on him when he stopped at the family home. He was always on the move. After the journey by road to Abia and the sombre reception, the agreement on provisional funeral arrangements, I looked inside the wardrobe of his final room in the compound, and saw his favourite shirt, the blue, short-sleeved one that looked like an airline pilot's. I took it into my face and breathed in. It was the same scent.

All hail human zoo, Prince Peter Lobengula

Let us raise our Edwardian glasses to circus equestrian & impresario extraordinaire, Prince Peter Lobengula. This is chutzpah. This is Showbiz. This is Imperialism dressed in spangled leotards. This is a story, Sparkling and Splendid and True. Plain Lobengula arrived from South Africa in 1910 as a handsome, Matabeleland equestrian artiste. He became star of the 'Savage South Africa' human zoo show, held *by Royal Appointment* at Earls Court, London, 1900.

The Exhibition featured an astonishing re-enactment of Matebeland battles in which the great Lobengula and other shimmering, semi-clad African males appeared in full war paint. It was a sensation. Lobengula drank champagne with the Prince of Wales. Sadly, the show was too successful. Especially with the ladies. There was dark talk of banning the spectacle, or restricting it to menfolk, as so many white women were arriving to admire the African male physique. How fragile is the white male Imperialist ego! The scandal grew into a furore, that became Savagery v Civilization! The hyena press finally dragged their prey down. The exhibition closed in ignominy. No matter. Circuses are mobile. The show went on the road. Empire and exoticism rode out to the North of England. It pulled in the crowds in smoky Salford, in abject Ancoats, in miserable Middlesborough.

Yet again it was bedevilled. Yet again there were

rumours of White Women Attending the Tents After Hours! – Save Them! The press panned the degenerate travelling show. History repeated itself. No matter. Somewhere among all this, Lobengula, doubling down, had the temerity to get engaged to a white woman! Her name was Miss Florence Kate Jewell, Kitty for short. She was, the press was careful to mention, 'of Jewish extraction', and the daughter of a Cornwall mining magnate. A hue and cry went up over this tawdry joining together of the fragile white bride to the Black savage. The baying mob ran the two lovebirds out of town. The marriage turned sour. Kitty testified in court that Lobengula beat her. The judge dissolved the marriage and expressed deep sympathy with Kitty. Kitty disappeared. A bundle of her clothes and a note were found by the banks of the Irwell canal. How forlorn. How miserable. How theatrical. Lobengula was publicly shamed. Yet the show must go on.

Lobengula, re-emerging now as Prince Lobengula, asserted that, as *Royalty of a colonial outpost,* namely Rhodesia a.k.a. Matabeleland, he was entitled to vote. He went to a Salford court to get this royal prerogative. To general astonishment, he won his case. Lobengula becomes a *cause celebre*; a circus of journalists followed him around. Again, ever the recidivist, he froo froo'd with English aristocracy. Then married the excellently named Lily Magowan, daughter of Belfast; they reside in Salford and are blessed with children. This time, happily, if undramatically, there is no bundle of clothes left with a note on the banks of the Irwell canal.

Once again, ever the recidivist, Prince Lobengula enters showbiz. God loves a trier. Salford needs theatre! Behold my Spectacular Theatrical Show and Be Amazed! It doesn't work out. The beholders stay away. No matter.

Even royalty can fall on hard times. Ever resourceful, Prince Lobengula went down the mines of Salford. He died a coal miner, of a coal miner's disease – pulmonary tuberculosis. The people of Salford lined the streets of Salford for his funeral. He was Salford royalty.

So, drink with me. Let us hail Prince Peter Lobengula. This is how to live. This is true royalty. Compare his magnificence with the nonentity that is Prince Peter Kalu. Prince Peter Kalu has never learned to ride two horses at once while doing a handstand, blindfolded. Nor has Prince Peter Kalu ever had the honour of drinking tea with English royalty, little finger cocked. Prince Peter Kalu never scandalised English society by romancing a rich magnate's daughter! Yet royalty respects royalty. Let the record show that on this day in August 2025, Prince Peter II raised his glass to Prince Peter I. Let us all drink to Prince Peter Lobengula!

Notes from a bathtub

I was steepling my fingers, pondering something idle when my near vision sent a note, and it dawned on me that I was looking at the hands of an old person. How did old age creep up on me? I looked further along the water and saw my legs – my thighs and my calves. They are moderately youthful. Continuing this impromptu inspection, I notice that the greying of my body hair begins at the chest with a sepulchral grey and this colour continues hesitantly down my torso, before becoming salt and pepper at that locus of faded delights, my groin; then colour revives itself, my body hair becoming glisteningly, luxuriantly black along my thighs and shins. I conclude I have aged unevenly. I have the feet of an 18-year-old and the chest of an octogenarian.

Holiday snap – a roll of film

In the photo, I'm on a beach somewhere in North Wales, half turned to the camera, and I'm holding something high into the sunlight – a long roll of negative film. My right trouser leg is turned up at the ankle. I'm wearing shoes, partially buried in spiral wrack at the slope of a small boardwalk. Behind me is a yawning expanse of water – the Irish Sea. I think the photo is posed because my curiosity has always been a frowning one – I frown when I look at things – yet here I smile, perhaps for my mother who holds the camera – perhaps also at the absurdity of such a photo: boy examining trash. The shirt, even in the black and white of the photo, is vivid, floral – I imagine orange –and the scruffy trousers are deep blue and a favourite pair. I always loved trousers with pockets and here the pockets are huge and at the front, possibly sewn on by my mother. Despite the fake smile, I *am* curious. Nothing is always something. Whose holiday snaps did this roll of negative turn into? Did they, too, wear their best shirt to go on holiday, squint their eyes at the sun, smile brightly so that their mum could be pleased, even if she said beforehand, *You don't need to smile for the camera*? I stand there, seaweed tangled around my feet, squinting into the celluloid, attempting to work out the positives from the negatives.

Floaters

I have floaters in my eyes. Debris. From childhood teasing. Hopes that soured. Friendships that crumbled. Shrapnel lodged in there from lost battles with bureaucrats. Clumps of scattered pride from scams I fell for. Races lost. Ladders I never got to climb up. Hills I never got to roll down. So much debris.

The swimmer

'I don't know what to do, Pete. That's why I'm in this pool, doing these laps up and down. Because I can't take any more of the arguments. And I know, once I drag myself out of this water, the arguments will start up again. They always do.' My instinct was to give him advice. Something like, 'Maybe try talking to her before you smoke any more of that shit' or 'Try buying her something' or 'Just say sorry, even if you don't feel it.' I resisted the urge. Instead, I sat with him by the pool side, my feet dangling in the water. And for a long moment, we were silent, vibing his situation without trying to fix it. Finally, he looked at me. 'Well, say something, you bastard. I was expecting advice!' We laughed then, and I slid into the pool with him, and we fooled around doing weak butterfly strokes and submarining. Pretty soon she joined us in the water, and it was all fine.

Ghosting grandparents

In the dream it was summer, and I found myself in the garden of my dead grandparents' many-roomed Victorian house. I went straight to the swing on the side lawn and swung up into the sky. My two friends were on the swing with me, one at my shoulders and the other sitting in my lap. We got bored with the swing and jumped off. We crossed over to the croquet lawn in front of the conservatory and played football, with our t-shirts as the goal. Then we wandered inside the house. My friends went down into the laundry room cellar because it was cool there, while I went up into the kitchen. I was eating a bacon sandwich at the kitchen table when the light became darker, the atmosphere stormier, inside as well as out. Suddenly, I was crying into my child hands. Someone came down the stairs. I saw only their lower legs and feet: the legs hairy, the feet in crocs. I was crying because my grandparents had died long ago, though I was only a child. The voice owning the hairy legs said, 'It's OK, your grandparents told us this would happen, that you would return, and we switched off the alarm system so you can wander around the house and the garden whenever you like. You can play here forever, you and all your friends. Don't cry.' I woke and wiped the tears off my face.

I never met any of my grandparents; none of them ever lived in England.

Death goes dancing

The ceremony is taking too long, my father is bored and climbs out of his coffin. The pallbearers throw their hands around his shoulders and a brief knee-drop dance breaks out between them all, shoulder to shoulder, my father's face glowing, the pallbearers sweating. The dance spreads as the villagers join in – thigh slaps, shoulder rolls, stagger dances, the pastor spraying water from water bags to drench one and all. Deftly, amidst the chaos, the chief pallbearer asks Dad for more money for services rendered. The pallbearers gather round him and press the matter. Dad relents, consents, sprays them naira, then dollars, and they high-step with delight. Dad breaks free of them, moves around, shaking the hands of villagers, wiping tears from the faces of family. He stops by the gravediggers, and they swig whiskey together, then his brothers encircle him, and his sister, and they unfurl a map of the compound and surrounding lands.

Dad points, asks questions, and they agree which land should be kept, which sold. *It is well.* Horns. Fanfare. The drummers pick up a new beat. There is some commotion. It's my mother, arriving for the first time at the Igbere village, striding up the dirt road in an orange, traditional Igbo dress, including head tie. The second wife is to her left, the third wife to her right. Assorted young children scurry behind and between them. Mum finally breaks into a smile and starts to sway her hips. Dad catches those hips, and they dance dance dance. Shrieks. Laughter. Whoops. We all sit. The villagers are eating now. The sauce is rich, the rice steaming, the gari just fine-o. Speeches are being made and during these my father disappears. He comes back as the speeches wrap up with a handheld super 8 cine camera and begins filming everything: the open grave, the elders laughing and talking talking talking under the parasols and gazebos, the children running under his feet, the wives swaying, the tree leaves fluttering, the dusty, red road. He looks across to me, one last smile. A tear falls from his face through the smile. 'I am tired now,' he says; 'it is well.' Unnoticed, except by myself, my father climbs back into his coffin. He eases the lid low until it is three-quarters closed, then through the gap, beckons me closer. 'Here,' he says. 'Catch this.' He throws his super 8 cine camera. 'Go now; film something for me. Bring it back when you join me.'

A dream as filmscript: Die now, England motherfucker

Assailant: Die now, motherfucker.
Me: OK, I get that, but could you say something else? I mean, on the very remote off-chance they make a film out of my life, that would be the last line wouldn't it, and it sounds so American. I'm more like, based in England, you know?

Assailant: OK. Die, you England dog!

Me: Sorry, again, not quite. It would be English dog, not England dog. Even that doesn't quite work. I don't really identify as England or English, my identity is more nuanced than just the one nationality.

Assailant: What if I say nothing and just kick you to death?

Me: Yeah, good, good, I can see that working. What footwear though? Because obviously that will be in the close-up end shot?

Assailant: I'll do it barefoot.

Me: Umm. Would that be believable – here in the West? We are in the West, right? People have such soft feet here. And also, bare feet might have an erotic overtone. What genre of film is this?

Assailant: Erm…

[At this point I wake up.]

ACKNOWLEDGEMENTS

In dialogue with:
Blaise Pascal. Montesquieu. Mikhail Bakhtin. Adriana
Cavarero. Jean Genet. Yukio Mishima. Hannah Arendt.
Wayne C. Booth. Roland Barthes. Chester Himes. Stuart
Hall. Nina Simone. Audre Lorde. Wolfgang Iser. James
Baldwin. Oliver Sacks. Mike Phillips. Graham Mort.
Charles Fernyhough. Anais Nin. Nawal al Saadawi.
Eddie Chambers. Colin Grant. Kadija Sesay. Gabriel
Gbadamosi. Irenosen Okojie. Thomas Glave. Lynne
Pearce. James Wood. Leone Ross. Jaqueline Roy. Biyi
Bandele. Helen Oyeyemi. Kei Miller. Roger Robinson.
Akala. Roxane Gay. Reni Eddo-Lodge. Desiree Reynolds.
Fereshteh Vannani. Charles Bukowski. Corinne Fowler.
Florence Okoye. Martin Glynn.

Sounding boards:
Muli Amaye. Tariq Mehmood. Melvin Burgess. Julia
Davis. Clare Ramsaran. John Siddique. Amy Lai.
Graham Mort. Marcia Hutchinson. David Yeates. Tony
Flynn. Saima Mir. Ishy Din. Katy Massey. Clementine
E. Burnley. Amanda Vilanova. Martin De Mello.

Angels:
Royal Literary Fund. Writers Mosaic. Society of Authors.
Cultureword. Hawthornden Foundation.

They Fed Me (not a metaphor):
Fereshteh Vannani. Tariq Mehmood. Melvin Burgess.
John Siddique.

Dedication:
To Dike Omeje (1972 – 2007). Thanks for all the good
times, brother. You revived my soul.

INDEX OF TITLES

Author photo © Fereshteh Mozafarri

Pete Kalu is a 2024 winner of the Society of Authors Travelling Scholarship Award. He has previously won the BBC/Contact Dangerous Comedy Award and The Voice / Marcus Garvey Essay Award. He received his PhD in Creative Writing from Lancaster University in 2019. His essays can be found scattered in publications including *Encounters with James Baldwin* 2024 and academic journals. His most recent short stories have been published by Peepal Tree Press. He is a Writers Mosaic alumnus and was writer in residence at University of West Indies, Trinidad Campus. He is a Reading Fellow of Royal Literary Fund. More info here: https://writersmosaic.org.uk/people/peter-kalu-2/